# FINCH
*Kindred Book Six*

# SCARLETT FINN

Copyright © 2016, 2024 Scarlett Finn
Published by Moriona Press 2016, 2024

All rights reserved.

The moral right of the author has been asserted.

First published in 2016

No part of this book may be reproduced in any form or by an electronic or mechanical means, including information storage and retrieval systems, without permission in writing from the publisher, except by a reviewer who may quote brief passages in a review. It may not be used to train AI software or for the creation of AI works.

All characters in this publication are fictitious and any resemblance to real persons, living or dead, is purely coincidental.

ISBN: 9781914517358

www.scarlettfinn.com

# **Also by Scarlett Finn**

## **NOTHING TO...**
NOTHING TO HIDE
NOTHING TO LOSE
NOTHING IN BETWEEN: ONE
NOTHING TO DECLARE
NOTHING TO US
NOTHING IN BETWEEN: TWO
NOTHING TO SAY
NOTHING TO GAIN
NOTHING IN BETWEEN: THREE
NOTHING TO YOU
NOTHING TO THIS PREQUEL: ONE WILD NIGHT
NOTHING TO THIS
NOTHING IN BETWEEN: FOUR
NOTHING TO DO
NOTHING TO FEAR
NOTHING IN BETWEEN: FIVE
NOTHING TO DENY

## **GO NOVELS**
GO WITH IT
GO IT ALONE
GO ALL OUT
GO ALL IN
GO FULL CIRCLE

## **EXILE**
HIDE & SEEK
KISS CHASE

## **WRECK & RUIN**
RUIN ME
RUIN HIM

## **THE BRANDED SERIES**
BRANDED
SCARRED
MARKED

## **FORBIDDEN PREQUEL DUET**
ALL. ONLY.
ONLY YOURS

## **THE FORBIDDEN NOVELS**
FORBIDDEN DESIRE
FORBIDDEN WANT
FORBIDDEN WISH
FORBIDDEN NEED
FORBIDDEN BOND

## **TO DIE FOR...**
TO DIE FOR TRUTH
TO DIE FOR HONOR
TO DIE FOR VIRTUE
TO DIE FOR DUTY
TO DIE FOR LOVE

## **LOVE AGAINST THE ODDS STANDALONE COLLECTION**
SWEET SEAS
HEIR'S AFFAIR
RESCUED
MAESTRO'S MUSE
GETTING TRICKY
THIRTEEN
REMEMBER WHEN...
RELUCTANT SUSPICION
XY FACTOR

## **KINDRED SERIES**
RAVEN
SWALLOW
CUCKOO
SWIFT
FALCON
FINCH

## **THE EXPLICIT SERIES**
EXPLICIT INSTRUCTION
EXPLICIT DETAIL
EXPLICIT MEMORY

## **MISTAKE DUET**
MISTAKE ME NOT
SLEIGHT MISTAKE

## **RISQUÉ & HARROW INTERTWINED**
TAKE A RISK
FIGHTING FATE
RISK IT ALL
FIGHTING BACK
GAME OF RISK

## **LOST & FOUND**
LOST
FOUND

# ONE

CLAMBERING INTO HER seat, Devon gripped the edges of the upholstery beneath her thighs and tried not to panic. "Why are you doing this?"

"I'm sorry, Devon, really, I am sorry," Thad said, concentrating his frown on the desert. It was etched so deep that Devon hoped it was a sign of him regretting his choice as opposed to it being an indicator of how determined he was to get to where he was going.

If she could just convince him of the former, maybe he would turn around, and they could go back. "Why would you sabotage the Kindred? You're one of them. They're your family."

His sneer didn't suggest remorse. "You don't know anything about my family. You don't know half of what's really going on. You think Zave's your savior. You think this is straightforward that we go in and take down the bad guys. What you haven't seen is that most of the time, we *are* the fucking bad guys."

"You just left them out there! Abandoned them, how will they—"

"They'll call Kadie or jack one of the cars at the motel," he said. "Think I don't know my cousins? I run around with medicine and bandages and patch the Kindred up to send them back out. They don't give a fuck about me, not really. They use me because they need me."

Devon had never seen him so resolute. "You can't believe that," she said.

He didn't flinch. "You don't know anything."

Trying to seek out the gun, she was pissed to discover it was in the door well on the other side of him. If she wanted to get to it before he did, she'd have to lunge over, somehow getting past both his arms and the steering wheel. Unlikely.

They hit a divot and bounced up, and then the tires began to purr as they settled into the rhythm of the streak of tarmac now stretched out before them. This was a road. But not the same one the motel had been situated on.

With every second, they were getting farther from safety. Panic began to thud in her throat. "Where are we going? Did you know you were going to do this?"

He must have planned his escape from the Kindred if he'd sabotaged Game Time last night. Hell, he must have known before that. In all the time they were talking about poison gas and viruses, Thad knew he was going to fill those canisters with nothing.

"My contacts need those devices."

If that was an explanation she should agree with, it was lost on her. "You've spent years trying to take down the cartels that hurt Bronwyn, and you just gave up your best chance—"

Slamming both of his hands on the wheel, he silenced her. "Don't talk to me about Wynn, Devon! Don't fucking do it!"

Had she ever heard the doctor swear before today? She couldn't remember. But the tension in his shoulders made her reassess everything she'd thought about him. Even though he'd stolen her away from safety, she hadn't believed he was capable of causing her harm. Until now. "Why did you save my life if you were just going to kill me? Why did you save me?"

Breathing out an ironic laugh, his scrunched expression got tighter when he pursed his lips. "They wanted you to die. You won't believe what the fuck they said when they found out I saved your fucking life."

He was making up for all those missed opportunities to curse that he'd had in the past. But he had just destroyed his whole life in the space of a few seconds, so his aggravation was justified. Though she still couldn't figure out what his motivation was for making such a dramatic choice.

"Are you in trouble?" she asked because that had been Zara's impulse. "Was Zara right?"

"What have you been told about using real names outside the fold?"

Did he still care about the Kindred, or was it just Zara he wanted to protect? But his impulse to correct her inspired hope. "You are still Kindred. You can't help yourself. You want to protect them."

"Conditioning," he mumbled, dismissing her plea. "And Zara... I don't want her to get hurt."

So the man wasn't made of stone. "I think she's hurt right now," Devon said, and he flashed her a snide look. "You just destroyed a friendship she valued."

"She doesn't know you that well," he grumbled.

"I'm not talking about me," she said, touching his forearm. "I'm talking about you."

Shaking her hand off his arm, his knuckles went white when he returned them to the wheel. "In the glovebox," he said. "There are cable ties. Take out one, put it round your wrists."

Exhaling, her head tilted and she sagged. "Don't tie me. I'll be good, I promise you."

He glanced at her again. "Sorry, Von, I have instructions. My contacts don't trust you." With quivering fingers, she opened the glovebox and took out one of the black ties. "Do it."

Looping it around, she made a circle and put her hands inside to pull it around her wrists. Thad either didn't trust her or thought he was helping her out, but he reached over and tugged it tight, forcing her palms together.

She didn't want to hear what he might say, but she had to know. Bowing her head, she licked her lips with a dry tongue. "Are you taking me back to them?" she whispered because the cartel was her greatest fear, and he could be about to deliver her to them gift wrapped. "They'll kill me, you know. They'll rape me. They'll torture me and they'll kill me."

After being rescued, it hadn't occurred to her that she might ever be back in that metal box. Marrying Zave gave her a whole new level of confidence that made her sure about coming to this place with the Kindred to fight back. Zave loved her and he would keep her safe, it might take him some time to find her, but he would get to her. She knew enough of his tenacity not to doubt that. But if she had any chance of convincing Thad that this was a bad idea, to get him to turn around, then she had to take advantage of it

Deep down, she knew that he would never have stood up against the Kindred unless he was sure about the steps he was taking because once those ties were severed, they wouldn't be restored.

The Kindred held a grudge.

In spite of that, she had to feel that she was doing something to help herself, anything.

"No," he said and was shaking his head. "That's not what this is about. You won't be hurt. You'll be let go. They need you to deliver a message... that's all."

He had to abduct her from people she could trust to take her to an unknown place, just so she could deliver a message? A shot of annoyance made her snap, "Haven't they heard of email?"

"I needed cover," he said, and she got a real sense of the adrenaline that was keeping him amped. "I had to get out of there."

But there were other options. It hurt her that she'd been seen as the weakest link, the easiest one to take advantage of, or maybe she was just annoyed that she'd let it happen. Although, there was little she could've done to fight off the twitchy guy with the gun to her head.

Thad and his contacts had come up with a plan that made her the victim. "You could've stayed at the motel with Kadie," she said. "You could've taken her."

"No, they need her," Thad said, making her think that

this scenario had been considered.

"Need her? For what?"

"Not her exactly, they need her cousin... Turning Swift would've been impossible. The next best thing is the guy who trained under him for years. Kadie's cousin, Dempsey Harris, doesn't even realize what he can do with the shit he knows. We'll teach him. But if we hurt Kadie... he'd never join us."

Devon didn't like the sound of what he was spouting. This was more than an impulse to screw over the Kindred; there was more than one objective. Whoever these people were who Thad had allied himself with had a terrifying agenda. "They're putting together their own team?"

"Synonymous," Thad said. "They're calling themselves Synonymous."

Something in his voice was distracted, like he was trying to think a thousand thoughts at once. Devon wasn't sure he knew that he was answering her. He just kept his eyes on the road and spewed his responses. "Synonymous with what? The Kindred... I don't understand."

"You will," he said. "We'll be on the road a while. Give your mouth a rest."

Devon didn't know Swift well. But she'd have thought if anyone was impossible to turn, it would've been the good doctor, the man actually related by blood to the original Kindred. His reasons for doing this were alien to her, and without understanding them, it was difficult to change his mind.

But she had to keep trying. "You can still go back. We can turn around right now—"

His head was twisting side to side again. "No," he said. "There's no going back... Zave... he doesn't know how to forgive."

Having firsthand experience of his inability to forgive himself, she doubted he'd be any more likely to forgive his cousin for this betrayal. "I can talk to him. He'll listen to me."

"How the fuck did you get him to fall in love with you?" he asked, narrowing one eye and tilting his head. "How the fuck did you do that?"

Devon didn't know what he wanted to hear, but her relationship with Zave didn't seem to be part of the plan. "I... I don't know."

"The guy has been a wall for years. Hard as stone and as thickheaded too. He listens to no one. Always thinks he knows best. But you... you got through... how the fuck do you suck the self-loathing out of a guy in less than a year?" She didn't know such a thing had time constraints. "Your blowjobs must be epic."

Thad would never find out, and his comment gave her a chance to garner her anger. "Is that what this is about? You're pissed at your cousin? Why? Because he didn't listen to you?"

"Bet you must be wondering what the fuck is wrong with this family, huh?" Thad asked, leaning over the wheel. "We've got brothers who can't stand each other, cousins who stab each other in the back and parents who murder each other."

Devon didn't know about the brothers or the parents, but she knew the cousins. "I envied what you all had," she said. "When I saw the way the Kindred stood up for each other... I thought it was amazing."

How wrong she had been. Maybe Thad was right regarding how little she knew about what was really going on. But Zave wouldn't have hidden information that could endanger her life. There was no way Thad's betrayal had been anticipated.

"Yeah well, you're wrong. It's not like that on the inside. Not unless you're willing to idolize Brodie or Zave. Those of us not willing to do that, those of us who question them... we're ignored, pushed aside. I can't live like that anymore. I need to make a difference, and I can't just wipe noses anymore."

This family had pathology, all right. Devon didn't have the qualifications to begin to analyze it though. "You were making a difference to the Kindred. Zave, Brodie, they're your blood... And your mom, oh my God, Thad—"

"Don't you mention her," he snapped.

His glare returned and she sank back in her seat to

think about Bess. The woman would be devastated when she found out about this. "You can't do this to her, Thad, please."

He opened his mouth and then clamped it shut again. She wanted to prompt him into saying whatever had gotten stuck in his throat. Devon had used his real name and perhaps he was going to chastise her, except… if he wasn't Kindred anymore, did that mean he wasn't Wren anymore? Had he cast off that identity? Maybe that truth was just hitting him now.

"My mother doesn't understand," he said after a while.

Focused on her joined hands, she twisted them to look at the diamond Zave had put on her finger. "I can't let you do this to Bess, she's a good woman," she said. "What will you do if these people hurt you? What if you want out?"

"I'll figure it out."

"Swift will be watching your bank accounts," she said. "If he doesn't empty them. You can't be down here on your own with no exit strategy."

"Sounds like something Swallow would say," he said.

Curling her fingers, she managed to pull her engagement ring from her hand, and she reached over to slip it into his hip pocket. He jerked and grabbed for her, but she held open her hands as best she could to show she was no threat and sat back.

"That's your way out, it's worth a fortune," she said, though she didn't have a clue how much Zave had paid for the stone. It was large enough that she knew it would've been expensive. "Sell it if you need money."

Gritting his teeth, he set his eyes on the road again. "I won't."

"Humor me," she said. "This way I'll be able to look your mother in the eye… because she won't believe this is your choice, you know. She'll be sure you're acting in the Kindred's best interest. She won't believe you'd be this selfish… this cruel."

"Give it a rest, Von," he said, and the name made her think of her brother. What the hell would Rigor do when he found out she'd gone and gotten herself kidnapped again and right from under the nose of the new husband he didn't know she had.

"I—"

"Wait," he said, leaning back and digging in his pocket to pull out the ring. "Where the fuck did you get this? Did he give it to you?"

Who else would've given her an engagement ring except her fiancé? But he didn't wait for a response. His act of putting the window down made her twist to brace herself against the door. "No, please don't!"

Tossing the diamond out the window, he grabbed her wrists to pull her nearer. "What else did he give you? What other jewelry are you wearing?"

"Just my wedding ring," she said, and he began to try to wrestle it off her finger. "No, please! It's just a ring!"

She didn't want to lose the gift her husband had given her the day before. Losing the diamond was bad because it contained the GPS tech, but the wedding ring was a symbol that meant so much more to her.

"You think I believe that?" he yelled. "You don't know him!"

When he threw her ring from the window of their moving vehicle, she leaped forward and punched at him, screaming and fighting to hurt the man who'd broken her heart and deceived the man she loved. "You fucker! You bastard! You—"

Thrusting her away, he held her tethered wrists down. "You better calm the fuck down, Von! Don't make me give you a shot!"

And he could. Thad was a doctor and would know what drugs to give her, and he'd have contingencies for this. When they brought women back from the auctions, they were drugged by the cartels.

But Devon had woken up on the island, no single drug would keep her out for that long, Thad had to have administered something to keep their rescuees out until they were secure in the custom-built suite.

Devon didn't want to be drugged; she needed her wits about her. Thad had said they were going to be driving for a while, so there might be more chances to talk to him later. For now, she let her head fall back so she could look into the sky out her side window… God knew when she might next see it after Thad delivered her to her destination.

# TWO

SHE HOPED FOR a long drive, maybe one that would take days or take them back over the border into the States. Devon got neither wish. Being spoiled by Zave recently meant she'd gotten used to getting what she wanted and being treated like a princess. Another fantasy shattered.

It was dark by the time Thad pulled off the main road. They were in a city, she didn't know which one, as she'd been drifting in and out of reality throughout the trip. The heat was tough to bear, and the air conditioning could only do so much when she wasn't hydrated.

Driving through the streets, she tried to pinpoint landmarks but had never been to Mexico before… Well, not out in the open while conscious. Thinking that they were going to stop somewhere for food or maybe to rest, she tried to think about how to approach breaking through to him when they pulled into the parking lot of a decent-looking hotel.

"This place is nice," she said and stretched. "Can we afford it?" Given that he'd thrown their only source of income out of the window a few hundred miles ago.

"We're not paying for it," he said, retrieving his gun, and horror made her eyes grow when she saw the silencer he pulled from the same door well. He screwed it onto the front of his weapon, then snagged her wrists. "Come out this side."

Bruised by the brake and steering wheel, she couldn't say no when he dragged her across the front of the vehicle and out onto the asphalt at the driver's side. "Wait," she begged, trying to pull away when he started toward a side door. "Are you saying your contact is in there? That this is it?"

The hotel was a nice spot to spend some time if, while she was here, she would spend the night trying to get through to the doctor. It wasn't such a great prospect if this was where she was going to be handed over to his contacts. The caliber of this hotel was high enough that it could hold a buyer, the sort of buyer who would've taken her home if Zave hadn't been at the auction to purchase her.

"Please," she said.

The side door had been propped open an inch, and when they got to it, he yanked her in front of him and stuck the gun into her ribs. "You're not going to make a fucking sound when we go up these stairs or in the service elevator. If you do, I'll put a bullet in you… and this gun is registered to Brodie McCormack, so you don't want me to do that."

Devon didn't think Brodie would be dumb enough to leave a weapon at a crime scene or that he would register a murder weapon in his own name and address. But that didn't stop someone else from doing it for him. Pushing her forward, he kept her going up a set of metal stairs and then to a huge service elevator door.

Nudging her forward, she took the hint and pressed the button to call it. "Why him and not Zave?"

"Murdering the new wife, if we set it up that way, we'd make it look a helluva lot more kinky than a corpse in an elevator. And your new cousin-in-law has left a trail of dead bodies across the globe. That kind of attention would take down the great Raven… you don't want to be responsible for that, do you?"

The elevator doors opened and he pushed her inside, stabbing a button with the barrel of his gun before sticking it into her kidney. "You hate them so much, but they taught you a lot," she hissed over her shoulder.

His medical degree might be useful to the Kindred, but Thad had failed to see just how much the Kindred had given him. "It's because of what they taught me that Synonymous want me."

"That and the medical degree," she said. If he was being used by one group, it made no sense why he'd switch allegiance to another who planned to use him too.

The elevator opened and they went through another door, this time coming out in a sleek, carpeted corridor. "I know you hate me, Von, and I don't care. But take this as a warning from a friend," he said, shoving her up to a white door. After knocking, he turned to paste his back against the wall beside it. "Don't piss these people off."

The door opened, and she was examined by the tall, lean guy in its space. Drawing back, she wanted to flee because she'd never been so consumed by such a sinister scowl. The narrow icicle-blue eyes pierced through her skin to squeeze her organs like he had the power to freeze her from the inside out.

"Well, shit, quack, you actually fucking did it," the guy said, and when he smiled, she didn't know what to think.

Glimpsing the scar on his neck and the angle of his nose, this guy had seen some kind of war, professional or… personal. Thad moved to her back and pushed her again. "Out the way."

The guy did as told and held the door to sweep an arm in a gesture indicating they should enter. This was a suite because the large living space had couches around a table, a TV area, and a separate dining room. It was larger than any hotel room she'd ever been in.

"Damn, I wish I'd been there," the guy said, closing the door and passing them after Thad stopped them on the edge of the living room. "What was his face like? Bet he was shocked. Ha! That fucker!" Going to the TV area to the right of the space, he dropped onto a couch and grabbed a beer bottle to take a slug of liquid. "The amazing fucking Raven McCormack pissed on by one of his own. Wish I'd been there to piss on him too… How'd Zara look? Did you hurt her?"

His glee left when he queried Swallow. "Didn't touch

her. I wouldn't," Thad said.

So this guy was a Zara fan, too, maybe. Devon couldn't tell. Maybe he wanted to hurt her himself. His frozen eyes dragged over her figure, and he put down his beer to rub his hands together. " 'Bout time you brought me something to do, I'm bored up here." Leaning back, he opened his lap to her. "Come sit over here, little girl… You're Rigor's sister, right? God…" He grinned. "I love keeping it in the family."

"Cool your jets, Caine," a dark voice rumbled from an open door through the space and she froze, her eyes fixed on that void, waiting for the speaker to make himself known. "Devon… welcome."

"She's tired and hungry," Thad said, but she noticed he didn't take the gun from her back, so he couldn't be that worried about her well-being.

"I got you, little sister," Caine said, grabbing his crotch to give it a shake. "I'll fill her up."

"She's a married woman," Thad said. Again, he didn't seem to be defending her. He seemed pissed by the confidence of the letch in the corner.

That was when someone came through the door, just when she wasn't expecting to see anyone. The older man had gray hair and lines on his face, but his body was tall and toned. He might be older, but he was no slouch.

"He married her?" the man said, looking past her to the doctor behind. Thad must have nodded or something, she didn't see it, but a smile split the older man's face. "The fucking idiot!"

He laughed, and she didn't know what was so funny. Neither did Caine, but he was happy watching, saying nothing and not reacting. Thad didn't laugh either, and she didn't like having him behind her. It wasn't just the weapon that made her uneasy, it was the barrier between her and the only exit she knew of.

"Who are you?" she asked. The situation might be terrifying, but she didn't appreciate this man having a laugh at Zave's expense and she couldn't stop that irritation from making it into her tone.

"I wish you'd brought Zar," Caine said, bending

forward to grab the remote for the TV to turn it off. "This would blow her mind."

Thad gave her another nudge forward and around to an armchair, pushing her into it. He looked at the gun in his hand like he didn't know what to do with it now. Letting it fall to his side, he went toward the older man. "This is Frank Mitchell," Thad said. "My father."

Maybe if Zara had been here, this would've meant something to her. Glancing at Caine, she saw his grin falter like he was disappointed that she didn't have more of a reaction. "He's the guy that ran CI when old man McCormack kicked it," Caine said. "Mitchell mentored young Grant McCormack, Brodie's big brother." Brothers who couldn't stand each other was what Thad had said to her in the Jeep. "Oh yeah, and he died nearly three years ago… looks good for a dead man, huh?" Caine sat back, satisfied he'd filled in some blanks, and he pulled a pack of cigarettes from his pocket. "He's not the only corpse we've got around here."

Devon fixated on the healthy, definitely alive man. "You… you died?" she asked.

"It was necessary to fake my death," Mitchell said. "My ward and I needed to leave our former selves behind to put her plan into action"

If she was here to take a message back to the Kindred, as Thad had said she was, then Devon assumed she was here to get details. "What is your plan?"

"We have had to alter it several times," Frank said, going to the armchair at the head of the table, opposite hers. "The Kindred were more… persistent than we'd thought they would be."

"Have you known about this all along?" she asked, focusing her rage on Thad because he was the only one in the room that she had a past with, a relationship.

"I didn't know he was my father, but I confirmed it all, it's true."

"His mother and I made an arrangement years ago," Mitchell said, disregarding her anger. "I didn't want a family. My career was the most important thing to me back then. His mother and I met and had our liaison after an event celebrating the birth of Grant Junior. The infant was born before Brodie or Xavier."

The infant was standing there beside his chair and at almost six feet, he wasn't anyone's baby now. "So that's how he got you?" Devon asked Thad who wasn't looking at her. "He came and announced himself as your father and you dropped everyone else?"

"Thad was tired of watching the Kindred work in half-measures," Mitchell interjected on his behalf. "He won't have to worry about that with Synonymous."

Her fears of being put back in that metal box dwindled as she got to grips with this new agenda. "So you're building some kind of anti-Kindred group?"

"Their work is their own and as long as they leave us alone, we will leave them alone," Mitchell said. "My colleagues have retrieved the Game Time devices planted by the Kindred last night. We will need those, and they won't be returned."

"Is that the message you want me to deliver?" she asked, hoping they might cut her loose.

Mitchell took his elbows to his knees. "Your brother helped to put us in a tough spot," he said. "I guess you don't know much about what he does." She shook her head. "He and his men joined forces with the Kindred to clear out a compound... one he still inhabits... That was meant to be Synonymous property. The arms and the land."

"That was a good show too," Caine said, sitting back to fold his arms. He liked to inject his little comments but was so intent on watching events that she felt a bit like a performer, there for his entertainment. "Better than this one."

"You were there?" she asked him.

His head bobbed in assent. "Watched Grant McCormack Junior face plant. Sure did. Watched Zara and her lapdogs hightail it out of there like terrified rats, too," he snarled, and again she heard his hatred for the male Kindred leader.

"How did you get out?" she asked.

"Leatt told me to split or eat a bullet, not a tough choice," he said, putting his foot up on the table as he folded his arms. "Who'd have known we'd all end up here?"

Devon hadn't known any of these people existed while all that was going on. But there had to be a culmination of events that drove these people to join forces. "How did you end up here?"

"Caine was the easiest to recruit," Mitchell said, and Thad scoffed.

"Offer him a bottle of Scotch and a hooker, he'll belong to anyone," Thad muttered.

"Least I got payment," Caine said. "What are you doing here, quack? Pissed off that your cousins kept making all the money and getting all the girls while you handed out scripts to pensioners who couldn't get it up?" Thad took a step toward him, but when Caine surged onto his feet, Thad stopped. Caine laughed. "Yeah, that's what I thought… Not so clever without your cousins around, are you? Why don't you give me that gun? You might hurt yourself with it, quack, and who'd be around to patch you up?"

"Caine is our sniper," Mitchell said.

"Our resident murderer," Thad said, putting his hand over the gun as he sneered at Caine. "Which is why you're not allowed to touch weapons until we can trust you."

Caine laughed and stubbed out his cigarette. "There's only one person in the world who can trust me not to put a bullet in them… least not until I fuck her hard and dirty in front of her husband… preferably while he's chained up, after I've cut off his eyelids, so all he can do is watch."

Devon's initial impression of Caine was that he was creepy. Every impression after that got worse. His fantasies weren't typical, they involved torture, rape, and murder… and he was sitting twenty feet away making eyes at her.

"We're going to order room service," Mitchell said, ignoring the men. "You'll need some rest, you'll be our guest for a while, Devon."

"But you said…" Thad still wouldn't look at her, though he returned to his father's side. Giving up hope that he would stand up for her or that he'd been telling the truth when he said that she was going to be set free, she gripped the arms of her chair. "Why did you bring up my brother, Mr. Mitchell?"

"Because they set you up, sister," Caine called. "They arranged for you to be taken to teach your brother a lesson… Can I be there when you tell Rigor that? I missed seeing Rave get shafted… I should get some reward for this bullshit."

She was taken because of Rigor. His mistakes usually bit him on the ass, but now it was her turn to take the heat. "You had me kidnapped to teach my brother a lesson about getting involved with the Kindred?"

"I didn't know," Thad said.

"Not at the get-go," Caine said. "But you're no innocent. They set Devvy up to be top of the bill 'cause it's the real sick fucks who buy those girls… And, right now, you've got a plant in your cousin's own house… staying with your mommy… No one here feels sorry for you, quack."

Jennifer. She was the last girl Zave had bought at auction, and she was staying on the island with Bess right now. "She's a plant?" Devon's panic made her bounce to the edge of her chair.

"Bess won't be hurt," Mitchell said. "Jennifer has done her job. She had to make contact with Thad… and she'll keep you and your husband in line for us."

"My husband?" Devon asked. "What do you mean?"

Mitchell's smile made her sick, especially when he shared it with Caine. "Wouldn't look good if the media got wind of the prodigious Xavier Knight going to Mexican slave auctions and coming back with a prize… who knows what he and Jennifer have done together on his isolated island where he's been keeping her prisoner," Mitchell drawled.

"They haven't even met," she said.

"That's not what Jennifer will say if you come for us," Mitchell said, stretching out his legs and leaning back.

Jennifer was their fail-safe guarantee because if she made accusations of something perverted going on at Zave's manor, it would be difficult to prove otherwise. These men didn't look like they'd be squeamish about beating the crap out of a woman if it had to be made to look good.

Her attention rose to settle on Thad. "I can't believe you're part of this. He only goes there because of you, because of Bronwyn."

"Don't say her name!" Thad snapped. For a man who'd always appeared easy going, he'd been harboring rage, because this kind of anger didn't come from nowhere.

Devon couldn't reply. She didn't want to get into a physical altercation, Thad still had a gun, and the other two wouldn't help her. Mitchell spoke again, "Go to the washroom and splash some water on your face, Devon. We'll order food and we'll talk more when everyone is back here."

Mitchell got up to go back into the room that he'd come from. Devon didn't like the men that were here, and she didn't want to meet any others. But Thad hadn't been honest with her, so she'd have to do as she was told and hope that, like last time, if she behaved herself, Zave would find a way to save her ass again.

# THREE

DEVON REFUSED TO eat, and when Thad said that Zave would tell her to eat because she didn't know when her next chance would be, she almost spat at him. Asserting herself had never been her forte, and the longer she sat in this room with these domineering men, the deeper she sank into the cushion of her chair.

Caine had no decorum because he didn't care what anyone thought and made no excuses for his bad manners. Mitchell didn't say much, but she got the impression that he was reflecting and planning, that his mind was always working, not that he was reserved or modest. There were times that Thad seemed to forget what he'd done. He would eat, relax, smile, and then he would catch a glimpse of her glare and he would tense again. But she couldn't believe he felt guilt or remorse, he didn't look apologetic.

When his eyes landed on her, he regarded her like she was a disgusting reminder of a part of his past that he wanted to forget. The Kindred couldn't have been that bad, he counted himself as part of their ranks for years. He'd let his mother live in Zave's house most of the time, so he couldn't believe that his cousin was evil.

But then, she could be missing the point. Maybe Thad

was as psychopathic as she believed his father to be, and deep down he just didn't care whether his mother was hurt or not.

When they figured out that she wasn't kidding around about not eating, they put her in one of the bedrooms, of which there were apparently three. Devon didn't care about being segregated, not until she sat on the bed and spotted the crumpled cigarette packet on the nightstand. This had to be Caine's bedroom. The curtains were drawn over the window, the lamps were built into the walls, and she couldn't find any kind of weapon.

This was a decent hotel, but it wasn't a fancy five-star chain that would boast elite clientele. The furniture was subtly bolted down beneath the carpet. Management wanted people to enjoy their pricey stay, but they didn't trust their clientele to be of good enough breeding not to try to swipe the nightstand if given half the chance.

Devon took being put in Caine's bedroom as a subtle threat. Of all the men out there, he was the most dangerous by far. Thad disgusted her because of what he'd done to the Kindred, but she couldn't believe he'd take any pleasure in hurting her. Maybe he would if necessity arose, but he wouldn't do it for the thrill. Caine might.

Mitchell's tanned skin was clear, his nails were neatly trimmed, and there wasn't a hair out of place on his head. She couldn't see him as the type to get his hands dirty if he had an animal like Caine around to do the grunt work.

They'd said she would be their guest for a while. She didn't want to bunk in with Caine while she was here. Except, there was nothing she could do about it.

Devon elected to sit in the chair next to the door as opposed to on the bed. This was more reminiscent of her initial days on the island than of her time in the cartel's shackles. But that didn't make the unknown any easier to accept.

Sitting, waiting, she counted the hours that passed by monitoring the noise level in the street. It grew when people began to get together to socialize, at restaurants and clubs, then dwindled once the restaurants and bars began to close.

She thought about trying to bang on the window to

draw attention to herself, except after discovering that the windows didn't open and that her view consisted of a brick wall ten feet away from the glass, she gave up hope of rousing anyone. Devon could kick and scream, but that meant risking a confrontation with Mitchell or Caine.

When she was nearly asleep in the chair, more voices joined the ones on the other side of the door. Although she couldn't make out exactly what was being said, there were definitely more people in there than there had been before.

Devon wanted the rest of Synonymous to arrive because then she would learn what she was dealing with. There was always a chance, as Thad had said, they'd called in some entertainment for the night. Maybe some women to dance or screw with. As much as she didn't want to listen to those men partying, getting drunk or high, she would rather they got their kicks with willing women they paid than use her to satisfy their depravity.

The bedroom door unlocked, and she leaped from her chair to dart over to the opposite wall. Cowering behind the edge of the drape, she waited to see who would come to join her. Caine had been drinking beer earlier and may have been drinking all day. He'd be drunk by now for sure.

But it wasn't him who entered, it was Mitchell. He came in alone, turned on the light, and scanned the room to land his gaze on her.

"After Grant Senior died," he said without any greeting. "The media frenzy was insane. Law enforcement had everyone under a magnifying glass, and I lost my nerve." He clasped his hands behind his back and came a few paces closer. "I buried myself in business and caring for the boy, Grant Junior, his son, who wanted it all to go away. It took me years to realize that sometimes murder is necessary."

Well, this was quite an opening. "Necessary? How can murder ever be necessary?" she asked.

The point of the story was lost on her, though it could simply be a prelude to his explanation of why he was about to kill her.

"Because eleven years later, I was confronted by Owen Knight, Xavier's father. He and Grant Senior had been close, in a professional sense. They leaned on each other for advice, respected each other. What I didn't know was he'd been snooping around in old CI R&D files."

"Why would he be doing that?" she asked.

"Who knows? Inventors often take inspiration from each other… or maybe he just needed some piece of tech to complement something KC was working on and he thought he might find it in CI inventory. The point is, he started asking questions about a device that was created under the title of Game Time, file number zero-zero-seven-nine-three. The reminder of it scared me because that's what Grant Senior died for. I shut Owen down and scared him away.

"But then I started to think… I started to remember the potential I'd seen in that device that Grant Senior had been too small-minded to see. I thought about all the things I could do with it and devices like it. One thought led to another, as it so often does, and Synonymous was born."

"Thirteen years ago?" she asked after doing the math.

"I didn't call it that then, of course, but the concept was planted by Owen Knight's questioning. I wasn't content with living my days in a boardroom crunching numbers, reading forecasts, worrying about the bottom line. It was all so… boring."

Releasing the curtain, she was agape that entertainment was his dominant thought at that time. "Boring?"

"It didn't help that I had Arthur Poole in my ear, raving about how proud he was of Brodie and how they were changing the world. The Kindred was around then, in the earliest stages of its newest form."

The detached business style might be a good way to convey information, but she couldn't understand how a privileged man could make a decision to play with people's lives without being more passionate about it.

"So you wanted to be like Art and Brodie? You thought it was going to be fun?"

Finally some emotion came when his lip curled in loathing. "It sickened me that they thought so small. Maybe my days in the boardroom had made me arrogant. But I wasn't happy with nickel and dime. I wanted to deal in platinum bars and diamonds."

The metaphor made sense coming from a man exuding wealth, as Mitchell did. "And it's taken you thirteen years to get here?"

"I faced obstacles," he said, like it was some sort of excuse for dragging his ass. "I tried to get Owen Knight on board, and for a while I think he was tempted. He understood my vision… until his wife, Philippa, the damn woman, stubborn and righteous like her siblings, Melinda, Art, and Bess. The four of them were all the same. Philippa put her foot down, told him no, and demanded that they focused on their great Xavier and shelter him. It was funny because she was the one who foresaw the fracture in the family."

"A fracture?"

"The brothers, Brodie and Grant Junior, cemented that fracture with a falling out when they were teenagers, and the family never recovered." He ran a hand down the seam of the drapes. "The Kindred was there, and I didn't want to be subordinate to them. I had grand ideas and wasn't interested in their miniscule ones."

"But Philippa, Zave's mom, she knew that if you tried to take on your own causes, you wouldn't be able to do it alone."

He nodded. "And by recruiting Owen," he said, rubbing his thumb over the tips of his first two fingers as if he was checking for dust. "Then I would be recruiting her son and all that Knight Corp was capable of. Yes, in a lot of ways, she had more vision than her husband did, I have to give her credit for that.

"Owen Knight was brilliant in business. Thorough. Single-minded. Focused. All excellent attributes in the boardroom. But what I needed was a doer, someone who would take risks and get things done. A big thinker. A problem solver."

"Zave," she said. "You wanted to recruit Zave."

"When Philippa said it wouldn't happen, I tried to circumvent her. I spent a year trying everything I knew from flattery to bribery to blackmail. I tried to break the couple up, too, but that didn't work. I tried to ruin the company after I'd tried everything I could to get them onside, and when that didn't happen, I spent the rest of the year trying to shut them up, trying to make sure that Owen and his banshee of a wife wouldn't go to authorities to tell them my plans."

Something told her it wasn't just the law he was worried about. "Wouldn't go to Art," she said. "Or Brodie."

"It is true the Kindred were stronger in combat than I was."

That was an understatement. If Art or Brodie had heard of his plans back then, they would have shut him down. "Weren't you lucky when Owen and Philippa died," she said. As soon as the words came out, suspicion sprang up.

The pleasure in his eyes and the twist of his lips betrayed his complicity. "I leave nothing to luck, Mrs. Knight."

After believing he wasn't a man who would get his hands dirty, she was shocked and questioned her own ability to judge character. "You killed them," she whispered.

"I'd seen how easy it was when Grant Senior and Melinda had gone down twelve years before. The media and the police busied themselves trying to make a show of solving the crime, but they had no clue. Their interest faded, and everyone forgot about the tragic accident. The Knights were easier because they visited the island so regularly, and Philippa loved to sail despite the loss of her sister at sea. I thought there was something poetic about losing the Knights in the same way."

This man was capable of anything if it served his own ends. He'd killed two innocent people to silence them and set in motion a chain of events that had brought them to this moment. The man Devon loved had suffered every second since that day, and whether it had been Mitchell's intention or not, he changed the essence of who Zave was by snatching his parents away in that cruel way.

"Why are you telling me this story?" she asked.

"It took another three years for the frenzy to die down enough for me to think about taking action. I wanted to make sure there was never a hint of suspicion. It had to be seen as one of those sad coincidences, like the Kennedy Curse. People speculated with conspiracies but quickly dismissed them when they found no evidence. What Grant Junior didn't know, was how I was grooming him to be at my side, not in CI, but in Synonymous. See, we had to work hard in CI to split up ventures over as many bases as possible. I taught him the value of spreading out operations and limiting information, of divvying up finances and resources in a way that made them easy to siphon from."

"Siphon?" This hotel was not the type of place a dead man could afford unless he had funds at his back. "You stole from CI?"

"I spent the five years after their deaths gathering what I needed, money and supplies. I had to stash different things in different places, we would need a base, but nothing could link back to me. We couldn't have paperwork with our names on it because if it did, Synonymous would lose our edge, and we needed to be unknown. If the world thought we were dead, we could do whatever we wanted without ever worrying about suspicion falling on us.

"See, Brodie McCormack never died. He disappeared. Everyone speculated on who he was, where he was. Now he's married, CEO of CI, and that damn cowbell can't be silenced. He can hide in his manor and sign everything over to Zave and never set foot in the CI building again. But all it takes is a bullet from a gun, registered to his name…"

This had to be the same speech that Mitchell had given Thad, because Thad had made that threat already. "But you're dead," she said. "So you can commit any crime, and who would ever look for a dead man?"

"Now you understand. I brought Grant around to the idea gradually. In the end, he was the only one who knew, and as my next of kin, he was called upon to identify my body."

Except he hadn't, Devon thought, he'd identified a stranger as Frank Mitchell, his mentor, because the real one stood in front of her now. "And you went into hiding," she said. "What kind of an existence is that?"

"Look around you," he said. "It's luxurious. It's freeing. I've never been so exhilarated in my life. I can do anything I want. Be anyone I want to be. I answer to no one and have no responsibilities. I make my own rules."

He spoke like a God and opened his arms to breathe in deep, like he savored every word he uttered.

Witnessing a man so swept up in his own majesty, she wondered if he had any grip on reality at all. "I can't believe this," she whispered.

But he didn't hear her astonishment. "I had to go ahead," he said. "To set up the next stage of our plan."

"What was the next stage?"

"After I was dead, Grant put resources into developing Game Time. Selling it gave us the opportunity to do reconnaissance on possible allies… or possible marks. We identified Albert Sutcliffe. He'd amassed a stockpile of weaponry and land, resources that would be useful to us. And he had little protection, with no organized crime group backing him. It was our plan to take from him what he had. The Kindred got in the way. Your brother got in the way."

So Rig hadn't just allied himself with the Kindred, he'd made an enemy of a group he hadn't known existed. "And that's why I was taken," she said. "Because my brother upset your plan?"

"One thing I will make sure Synonymous become known for is getting even. Your brother had no place there. He lives in a house now that doesn't belong to him, and the only reason we let him live is because he has men and that place was only of use to us when it came with Sutcliffe's arsenal. But the Kindred cleared that out making it useless."

Mitchell had already voiced dislike for the Kindred, by ruining Mitchell's plans, they only intensified that hatred. "No wonder you're bitter."

He didn't grace her comment with a response. "By that time I had built us a temporary base and had started gathering supplies that I believed we would transfer to the compound we would take from Sutcliffe."

"You couldn't get involved," she said. "You were dead. Too many people there would've recognized you. Brodie knew who you were."

"Yes, he did. As did his now wife, Zara Bandini, who

Grant believed would be loyal to him and join us in our venture. I tried to get him to be subtle in his persuasion and to do it over time, but he didn't listen and Brodie got to her first."

"But Caine said he saw Grant die in the same compound you lost. So all of your plans went to shit that day, didn't they? Because you were alone with nowhere to go and no weapons."

He smiled again. "Failures make us stronger," he said. "Thad wasn't difficult to turn. He'd been marginalized by his cousins for too long and made to feel insignificant. I'm his father. I promised him that we would avenge the death of the woman he loved, not by sneaking in and stealing the occasional woman away from these people or hacking their bank accounts. We will declare war and take all of these guys out without tiptoeing or apologizing."

That could lead to the death of the captive women, too, and she worried that a high-handed approach like that would have repercussions beyond one ambush. "How are you going to do that?"

"We've been waiting for my people to come back from a mission that will disrupt the cartel operations and will bring us the Game Time devices that were stolen from us. We needed those devices intact."

"What mission?" she asked. "Is this something to do with the meet?"

"We paid a man in that room to start a fight. Not long after you left, the guns would've started firing, and of the twenty men there, only three came out alive. The Kindred were too busy trying to track you to care. They didn't even notice my people going in to remove the devices that Thad directed us to. But my men are back now, and we have everything we need. So it's time," he said, reversing in short, quick strides. "For you to get to know everyone."

He opened the door, and Thad came in first. "I don't want to know everyone," she said, glaring at Thad. "I don't think there is one redeemable man amongst you."

"You know my son."

Her doctor. Mitchell moved behind him and put his

hands on his shoulders. The new Synonymous doctor, who'd been the Kindred doctor, who was so angry about Bronwyn's death, he didn't seem to have a shred of integrity left.

Caine came in next, but he didn't line up neatly beside the doctor in the way Mitchell probably wanted him to. He went over and flopped onto the bed on his back.

Kicking off his boots, he linked his hands behind his head. "If you want to send a message to the Kindred, send me," Caine said, continuing a conversation he'd been having before he came in here or one he'd been having in his own head. "What's our little sister gonna do when Raven kicks off? No. Nothing. Nothing. She's not gonna do nothing." He winked at her. "You can come over here and do something if you want."

"What a team," she said. "The Kindred will take you apart."

"He's not finished," Thad said.

But if she was supposed to know the next man who wandered in, she failed, because she didn't recognize him. Yet she was surprised by him because with brown hair, blue eyes, and dimples, he didn't look like the type who would fit in with this trio. He was tall, attractive, and his smile was warm.

"Benedict Leatt," he said. Coming over to hold out a hand, she lifted hers and let him shake it. "How is Zara doing?"

Exasperated, it seemed that everyone and their brother knew who Zara Bandini was. But his gentle handshake and affable demeanor suggested he was referring to a common acquaintance rather than someone he had a vested interest in checking up on or threatening.

"How are you connected?" she asked.

His brows went up as he backed away to lean against the end of the bed behind where Thad stood. But it wasn't Leatt who answered the question, it was Caine. "He's the guy who killed Grant McCormack Junior," Caine said. "I was standing right there when it happened."

"Killing Grant was a one-time job," Mitchell said. "He didn't get my attention until I saw how he got himself involved with Kahlil Samara and Nykiel Sikorski. I called and made him a better offer."

"On the morning of the Game Time exchange," Leatt said. "In hindsight, I'm glad I missed that meeting."

He drew his eyes to Caine, who nodded. "Yep, Samara was my kill… If what I heard is right, Raven took down Sikorski later."

All these deaths and no one was bothered. "I got a call to meet these guys," Leatt said. "And I've been a part of the team ever since."

"You stole Game Time today?" Devon asked.

Leatt nodded. "Didn't do it alone."

He cast his eyes toward the door and even Caine lifted his head. Thad turned, Mitchell did, too. Devon held her breath, expecting the devil himself to walk through the door. It took too long. She was sure either nobody was coming at all or this was a man who liked to make an entrance.

Whatever the case, someone did saunter in. Wearing jeans and a tee shirt, his hair was finger combed, but his eyes were keen. He took two strides in, examined everyone, fixated on her, and smiled a deliberate, conniving kind of smile that absorbed her features and seemed to read her thoughts.

"Who…?" she asked in a small voice. "Who are you?"

"Devon," the stranger said. "Your pictures don't do you justice." He came closer. She retreated until her back hit the wall, but he appeared to enjoy startling her. "I'm Grant McCormack. Welcome to the family."

"He's my cousin," Thad said. "Zave's cousin too."

Caine had to speak as well. "Raven's brother."

"The man I killed," Leatt said after.

Mitchell laughed. "Something to everybody. He's my boy."

"You don't have to be afraid," Grant said without responding to anyone's stated connection to him. "You're valuable to us as you are now."

"Apparently, I was supposed to die as some sort of sick message to my brother."

"And now you're some sort of sick message to your husband. By the way," he asked. "How's Zara?"

Caine laughed. "That bitch must have some ego," he said. "Next time, snatch her, quack."

"Zara wouldn't come easy," Thad said. "And Brodie wouldn't have let her go."

With admiration in his voice, Caine agreed, "That's the truth. Zara would've bit you in the balls, clawed out your eyes, grabbed the wheel and flipped the car, and she'd still have walked away with attitude."

Devon wasn't quite at Zara's standard yet. But Zara had been doing this for almost two years. "So this is Synonymous?" Devon asked, backed into a corner in a bedroom filled with formidable men.

"Not completely and we'll be going by Syn. It's easier on the tongue," Grant said. "Soon, we'll be going to pick up our last member."

This was quite a troupe already, and the Kindred couldn't afford to be outnumbered. "Who's that?" she asked.

If the others planned to keep the secret, they hadn't told Caine to do the same. "They don't have a Swift," he said. "And plan to pick up his bitch's cousin."

"They?" Leatt said and leaned over the end of the bed to smack Caine's foot. "You're coming with us, you prick."

Caine relaxed with a muttering sigh. "What do you need me for? I'm not going to shoot him. Do you want me to shoot him? I can shoot him. I haven't shot anyone for a while… Yeah, okay, I'll come. If he doesn't play nice, I'll shoot him."

Caine closed his eyes after having that conversation with himself, and she was flabbergasted. No one else was affected by how glib Caine was about taking life.

"You'll spend the night here, Devon," Mitchell said. "In the morning, you leave."

Maybe Thad hadn't been full of shit after all. "You're going to let me go?" she asked.

"No sense in keeping you," Grant said. "You'll get in our way… I've learned my lesson about keeping pretty women around who I can't trust."

"We might have killed you," Mitchell said. "If you hadn't married him. Now you're exactly the distraction we need."

She didn't like the implication of that statement. "We don't need him and his resources tearing this country apart looking for you," Grant said.

"Or more importantly, looking for us," Leatt said.

"You're going back to the Kindred to tell them Game Time belongs to us now. They should concentrate on marrying their women, playing house, and running those big-ass businesses they left hanging around our necks," Grant said. "You tell them we'll take over saving the world... and we're going to do a better job than they ever did."

"We won't be playing by Art's rules. We'll make up our own," Mitchell said.

Leatt was the first to walk out. "I'm gonna get a drink," he said before he disappeared.

Grant looked her up and down again before sauntering out. He and Mitchell were already talking before they crossed the threshold into the other room. Thad was holding back, but Caine wasn't going anywhere, he was happy lying on the bed.

"You'll sleep in here tonight," Thad said.

"Just what I was thinking," Caine grumbled and patted the vacant side of the bed. "Plenty of room. I'll even share you with the quack if he wants a piece, long as he keeps his hands off my junk."

"Caine, you're out front," Thad said. "You're supposed to be the guy with the gun, protecting us all. Look at you lying there drunk."

"My aim drunk is better than your aim sober," Caine said and forced himself to sit up with a groan. "Have you ever shot a gun, quack? Ever thrown a punch? Ever fucked a pussy? Just what is it we need you for anyway, quack?"

Drunk or not, Caine wasn't coming off as honorable, but she appreciated hearing him put Thad in his place because she wasn't much of a fan of the doctor herself. Thad had no witty answer. "Fuck you, Caine."

But Caine didn't care about the pathetic insult. He lifted his head to blink smoldering, drunk eyes at her. "You change your mind, don't ask permission," Caine said, rising to unfasten his belt before he began to make for the door. "You just come right on out and suck me dry. I always repay the favor… unless I'm paying for it."

He winked again and disappeared, leaving her alone with Thad. "I'll take you to the airport in the morning," he said. "I swiped your passport with mine at the motel. I'll put you on a plane to Seattle and give you enough money to get a cab to KC."

"Don't pretend you're a good guy," she hissed. "I trusted you. We all trusted you, now you've thrown in with them. Mitchell is deluded, and he has access to God knows what, money and machines that could change the world."

"That's the point," Thad snapped. "He thinks big. The Kindred are so caught up in being subtle and mysterious that they don't make enough of a difference."

Leaving her corner, she stretched her arm toward the living area. "Mitchell and McCormack faked their own deaths so no one would be looking for them. Isn't that mysterious or do you think it's cowardice? Who do you think will be left holding the bag if *Syn* do get caught?" she asked, saying the moniker in a mocking voice. "It will be you, Caine, Leatt, the three who are still alive."

"No," he said. "My father wouldn't do that to me and I work in the background, I—"

"Didn't you screw over the Kindred because you were tired of being insignificant and living in your cousins' shadows? McCormack is your cousin. Mitchell is your father, and now you're telling me that you're going to exist in their shadows? So what was the point? They want me to go back and tell the Kindred to back off, to shut up and let them be, and what happens if the Kindred don't? What are Syn going to do? Set Brodie up for murder? Have Jennifer accuse Zave of rape and torture? Where does that leave your mother or don't you care?"

"I asked you not to talk about her."

"You told me not to talk about Bronwyn, either," she said, walking up to him. "But I can tell you, I might not have known her, but as a woman, I'd be disgusted with the man you are."

He pushed hard and she stumbled but managed to balance herself before she fell. "Do not. Say. Her. Name," he snarled.

Devon wasn't afraid of him. "Why? Because you know I'm right. If I say her name again, what will you do? Hit me? Yeah. Your mother would be real proud."

Walking away from the lost cause, she sat on the end of the bed. At least if Caine wasn't coming back here, she didn't have to worry about being violated. Once Thad had gone, she had every intention of using the chair to block the door to stop anyone from getting in.

"You'll have enough money to get to KC," he mumbled without bothering to look at her. "Call your brother from there, he knows how to contact Raven."

"Do you think I couldn't figure that out by myself? Don't use me to make yourself feel better. I won't forgive you for what you did today. I won't. And if that's how I feel, I don't blame Falcon and Raven for bringing war to your doorstep. I don't want to see them ruined. But they'll find a way to bring you and your people down. I guarantee it."

Now he did look over his shoulder at her, but he didn't say anything else, just stormed from the room and slammed the door. Devon would take their message back to the Kindred and hope that her guarantee to Thad stood up because Syn didn't deserve to get away with this.

The Kindred were proud and had made sacrifices before, but would Zave and Brodie have to go to jail for the rest of their lives to stop Syn from taking over the world?

As she lay down, it scared her that she considered they might. She and Zara were going to be the only thing that might be able to temper their men's' reactions to this. Devon wasn't confident about her ability, but she stroked her naked ring finger and thought of her husband somewhere out there, worrying about her, and resolved to do anything she could to support him, even if that meant standing by him while he served twenty-five to life.

# FOUR

IF CEDRIC MOORE hadn't been walking through the KC lobby while she was arguing with the receptionist, Devon might have been tossed out on her ass. He came over and saved the day by asking her what was going on and where Zave was.

The older man had been friends with Owen Knight, and to this day made all the decisions for KC that Zave didn't. He left the suits he was escorting out of the building and took her to the express elevator that went directly to the top floor.

"I'm surprised to see you here without Zave," he said.

Devon had felt him side-eyeing her throughout the ascent but was too busy trying to figure out what to say to her brother, Rig, about what had happened. She couldn't think about being social or explaining herself to this man whom she'd only met once.

"Would it be possible for me to use a phone?" she asked.

That was all she'd wanted at reception too. She'd only been in this building with Zave and although he'd told her she had security clearance, she didn't feel right about traipsing around the building, picking up random phones, as if she belonged here.

Zave would argue that she did, and she might get used to this building in time. For now, the only thing she needed was a phone, and she'd used every cent Thad had given her to pay for the cab from the airport. It hadn't even brought her all the way here; she'd had to stop him a few blocks down and hurry the rest of the way on foot because her money had run out.

Upon entering into reception, she'd asked to use a phone and stressed that her need was urgent. Devon had expected hospitality not hostility. The blonde at the main desk argued that this wasn't a library or a coffee shop. KC phones were used for KC business and weren't available to people who walked in off the street.

This was a valid policy and one that Devon couldn't argue against. It would've been petulant of her to stamp her foot and demand respect simply because she'd said, "I do" to the man who owned the building.

"You can use a phone," Cedric said. "Zave's office had been shut up for years. But after your visit here the other day, we cleaned it up and aired it out. It's ready for him. He said that you were a permanent feature, so his office is yours."

As long as the phone worked, she didn't need to know anything else. "Thank you for this," she said. The elevator door whooshed open, and she rushed out only to realize that she didn't know where she was going.

The only floor she'd spent any time on was the one beneath this where the conference suites were located. "Straight ahead," he said. "The double doors."

The curved space had other doors around it, but she rushed straight forward to the grand double doors and came up short when she saw the illuminated security pad awaiting a fingerprint. She might embarrass herself by trying, but she didn't want to ask permission, she needed to get onto the phone. So, just as she did on the island, she pushed her fingerprint into the circle. It flashed once and she opened the door.

Yes, this was all she needed. Access.

Devon didn't even take the time to look around. She hurried across the room, bounded up the two stairs to the elevated desk, and darted around it to drop into the massive, black leather chair to grab up the phone.

"Dial nine."

Her gaze shot up to land on Cedric, who was in the doorway, wearing a smile. "There's a television behind the panel on the far wall. Use your fingerprint to reveal it, and the bar is secreted there too. It will slide out if you use your fingerprint twice." He pointed to one corner. "And if you go through that door, you'll find the washroom."

"Thank you," she said.

Cedric backed out and closed the door.

Dialing nine, she punched in Rig's number and listened to it ring. The office was beautiful. With a ceilings twenty feet above, the wall behind her was glazed to showcase the city streets below. This platform elevating the desk allowed her to inspect the room from a decent vantage point. To her right was a conference table with eight chairs around it. Opposite that, by the internal wall, were couches arranged around a narrow table. It was on the wall behind that where the television was, according to Cedric.

There weren't any knickknacks in the room, but if it had been locked up for so long, there wouldn't be. The carpets were pale gray, the furniture was black and the walls were white. She'd never paid much attention to the décor in the rest of the KC building, but none seemed quite as drab as this.

Had Zave selected these colors after his parents' death, or had it been decorated for him without his input? It didn't fit with the image of the fun-loving, frivolous Zave he was before the loss of his parents. But maybe this was where Owen spent his time. Had it actually been his father's office?

"Who the fuck is this?"

Startled by the abrupt voice in her ear, she stopped scanning and slapped a hand onto the desk. "Rig! Oh, thank God you answered!"

"Von? What the fuck number is this? Where are you?"

"I can't explain. Something happened. I need you to call Raven. I need you to tell him to call me here."

"What? Am I your fucking answering service now?"

God, her brother knew how to say the wrong thing at the wrong time. "Rig! You don't understand, this is serious. Stop fucking around. Something happened during the last Kindred op. I was taken and I have information—"

"You were taken? Where are you? Tell me where you are, what can you see?"

Under other circumstances, she might appreciate her brother's concern. But it was too little, too late. She needed him to get his finger out of his ass and stop wasting time. "No, I'm safe now," she said. "Can you please just get him to call me?"

"Not until you tell me what's going on. You're my sister, I've got a fucking right to know before he does."

So he was worried that he would be kept out of the loop? "Listen," she said. "I was taken. They gave me a message, and they released me. They put me on a plane, and I am right now sitting in the CEO's office on the top floor of the Knight Corp building in Seattle. I am safe. Safer than I've ever been in my life."

She understood that the Kindred liked to keep their true identities secret, and she didn't know what Rig did or didn't know about who the members really were. But she'd gone and married the KC CEO, so either way, her brother was going to learn about her association with this building. Though now wasn't the time to share the happy news.

"You're where?" he asked.

"I'm safe. But people I care about are not safe, and they're worried about me. I have to tell them what I know. Lives could be at stake and as far as I know, they're in Mexico scrambling to find me and I'm nowhere near where they are. So, please, get him to call me. I need to tell him what's going on. Until I do, they're in danger and they saved my life, Rig, please, we owe them this."

Silence met her statement. She was quite proud of how concise and honest she'd been, and yet he had no response. Concerned that the line might have disconnected, she was about to say his name when he spoke. "I'm writing down the number," he said. "I'll get him to call you back."

"The number doesn't matter, just tell him I'm in the

KC building. Please."

He had no patience, but her brother had always been easily riled. "I'm doing it, and then I'm getting on a fucking plane and coming to get you."

"To get me?" she said. "I don't need you to get me. I just told you I was safe, didn't you hear me?"

"Yeah, I thought you were safe before this phone call, now I find out you've been in fucking Mexico on Kindred operations, getting kidnapped! Ha!" He laughed. "I don't fucking think so. You're coming back with me."

She exhaled in disgust at his attitude. "Whatever, Rig. I don't care. Just get him to call me."

Rig's fight was one she would save for another day because every second she spent arguing with her brother was a second more that the Kindred didn't know what was going on. "Just call them. Now." She slammed down the handset before he could say anything else.

Crossing her legs, she then uncrossed them. She sat back, folded her arms, and then sat up straight. What was she going to do until that phone rang? All she could do was sit here. Did this phone even ring? Did Zave have an assistant who might intercept the call? If the number Rigor had written down went through some sort of switchboard, she was screwed. That little blonde sitting on reception in the lobby would never dream of putting a phone call through that was directed to her.

Devon could just imagine how that one would play out:

*"Good afternoon, thank you for calling Knight Corp, how may I direct your call?"*

*"I'd like to speak to Devon Knight."*

*"Devon Knight? There's no one here by that name and I only help the rich and privileged, not those in desperate need. Goodbye."*

It would be worse for Brodie if he tried to give a physical description because the blonde would recognize her as the wild-eyed, panting female who'd harassed her earlier in the day, which would probably just make her snootier.

The bar seemed like a good idea. Except, she'd been on an early flight, so although she didn't know exactly what time it was now, it had to be around lunchtime, not the time of day to start drinking, especially alone. Though she wasn't sure there ever was a good time to drink alone.

Although, if there was ever a situation that called for her getting blind drunk—the ring of the phone interrupted her thoughts. She snatched it up.

"Raven?" she asked, desperate, hopeful, terrified, and exhilarated all at the same time.

"Fuck," was the breathed word she heard first, but it wasn't Raven's voice.

Devon shot to her feet. "Zave!"

"You're really there? You're in my office at KC?"

"Yes!" she said. "Yes, I'm safe."

"Stay there," he ordered. "I'm coming to get you."

Her heart had never worked so hard, and tears flooded her eyes. All of her senses were tingling at once. She wanted to fall into his arms because that was the only place she could feel safe. "I have so much to tell you. So much you need to know."

"I don't give a fuck," he said. "You stay in that room and you do not leave, do you hear me? Do not leave that room. Security will be there within sixty seconds, and they will not leave that door, I promise. You will be safe."

"They're not coming for me again. They took me for a reason, I'll explain everything, but... there's something you have to know. Something you have to tell Swift."

"Swift?" he snapped. "What does he have to—"

"They're going for Dove's cousin. They want to recruit him. I don't want to explain everything over the phone, but they'll be on their way there now. If someone doesn't get there quick..."

"I understand. I'll pass that along. But I'm coming back to you."

"They threatened you. And they threatened Raven. They said if either of you got in their way, they'd set you up."

"Set us up for what?"

Aggravated, her forehead fell to her palm. "I don't know what the right thing is to do," she said. "I want you to stop them and I want you to help the man they're going after, but if you do that, if Raven does that… they're going to hurt you."

"Raven won't care. Swift is like his brother. He'd never leave him swinging in the wind."

Devon was caught in a tough spot. She didn't want to explain everything on the phone, but she needed them to be prepared. "But it is his brother," she said and wasn't surprised to be met by silence. "Grant McCormack Junior isn't dead and neither is his mentor, Frank Mitchell. They've started their own group, and their message to the Kindred is to stay out of their way."

While Rigor's silence had been infuriating, this one broke her heart. One tear slid down her cheek, and more escaped into the nothingness that followed until they dripped from her jaw onto his desk.

"I'm sorry," she said. "I'm sorry for all of this."

"None of it is your fault, shy. Thank you for letting me know. I'll be there as soon as I can."

The line went dead, and she assumed he'd gone to talk to the others about what she'd revealed. She didn't know what kind of plan they'd come up with, there was still so much that she hadn't revealed. But if she'd let them travel back here and then told them it all… Syn would've gotten to Kadie's cousin and it could all be over.

Devon didn't know Kadie's cousin, but he didn't deserve to be ambushed or drawn into something more sinister than he realized. The only way to prevent that from happening was to send Swift to intercept them. At the least, he could warn Kadie's cousin about who these people really were. Except, as of right now, they didn't know everything. She didn't know, and she'd spent the whole night with Syn.

Given a choice, Devon would choose this office over any place she'd been in the last twenty-four hours. Zave promised her security, but that wasn't what made her feel safe. This space belonged to her husband, and although he wasn't here, he was providing her a secure shelter.

Adrenaline would keep her amped for a while, but she knew the crash was coming. Devon had done everything she could, but that didn't mean she could sit and watch bullshit

TV as Cedric had suggested. After sitting for a while, her shoulders began to loosen and her eyes grew heavy.

Sleeping soundly in Caine's bed had been impossible. But there was space for her to sleep here, so she went over to the couch in the corner, took off her shoes and lay on her side to close her eyes. There was nothing she could do now except wait. Zave had told her to stay here, and that was exactly what she was going to do until he reached her.

# FIVE

SHE HADN'T REALIZED how tired she was. Waking up with a start when the door opened, she sat up in an instant and took some time to orient herself in the unfamiliar surroundings. Devon was still in her daze when someone crouched in front of her. Absorbing his features, she brought his face into focus, and everything else faded away.

"Lord," she whispered, sinking forward onto her knees in the space between his thighs to capture his mouth with hers.

Even if this was a dream, she didn't care, it felt real, he felt real. Clambering to hold him tight, she tried to crawl into his lap, but he took her waist to lift her back onto the couch. She hoped this dream was about to get more intimate, except he didn't lay her down, he sat beside her and stroked her face as he broke their kiss.

"Did they hurt you?" he asked. "Did they touch you?"

"No. No," she said, shaking her head as she stroked his chest and grasped at his tee shirt. Letting go to skim her hands up to his shoulder and then to his face, she tried to kiss him again. "I thought I'd never see you again."

The tears heated her face. "Can you guys do the emotional reunion later? I need to get to Swift."

Devon hadn't thought to look for anyone else. Her ordeal was fresh in her mind, but when she twisted and saw Raven standing a few feet from the couch with Zara just behind him, looking pale and smaller than Devon had ever seen her, empathy welled within her.

"Zara," Devon said. Something about the meek look on her face made Devon rise and go to her.

Grabbing her shoulders, Devon pulled Zara forward, squeezing her in a tight hug. Zara returned the embrace and didn't hurry Devon out of it, as Zave had done, or pester her for information, as Brodie had. Before this, she and Zara had still, to an extent, been circling each other, trying to figure out what the other was all about.

"You saw him?" Zara whispered.

Devon didn't release the hug but did lean back to look into her face. "Everyone I saw asked for you," she said. "All of them."

"She means Grant," Zave said, and it was funny that Raven hadn't mentioned his brother at all.

"We buried him," Zara said, and her voice cracked at the end when she inhaled and as if to hide that second of weakness, she pulled Devon back into her arms.

"The fucker," Brodie grumbled, offering his first substantive contribution to the conversation. "I swear to fucking God, if a guy wants something done right, he's got to do it his fucking self. I should've killed him. I shouldn't have trusted that fucking Leatt had done it. I should've put a couple of bullets into him myself—one in the chest, one in the head. Make sure he had been blasted off this Earth."

Devon's initial thought that these men were brothers, meaning Raven's comments should be shocking, wasn't backed up by her own emotion. She certainly didn't feel any affinity with Grant McCormack.

But it was Zara's reaction she was more concerned with. "Did you care for him?" Devon asked when Zara backed away from the hug to take both of her hands.

"It's a long—"

"Complicated story," Devon said, cutting Zara off. "I understand."

"But Mitchell," Zara said, narrowing her eyes and shaking her head once. "I went to the man's funeral. I stood outside the room when Grant identified his body. I was there. I don't know how—"

"Neither do I," Devon said. "Thad took me to a hotel. I don't know where it was. Far away from where we were, we drove for hours. I was put in a room and Mitchell came to see me last night and explained." She let go of one of Zara's hands to turn and face the men. "He's a bad man, the things he did… he knew about your parents, Raven. He was your father's best friend, but he—"

"I know," Brodie said. "I know what he did to my parents. I don't need you to tell me that."

When her eyes flicked to Zave, her heart swelled again. "And yours. He's responsible for everything," Devon whispered, wishing that she could have this conversation with her husband in private.

Zave was a private man who wouldn't want his business aired. He'd admitted to being reluctant in speaking to Zara, although bridges had been built during their work with the merger.

"What about my parents?" Zave asked.

"We need to sit down," Zara said. Keeping Devon's hand, she crossed toward the couches and grabbed her love as they went. But instead of sitting with him, Zara pushed Brodie onto the couch next to Zave and guided Devon to the one opposite. Linking their arms, Zara twined their fingers together. "I was there when Rave found out about his parents. I fought with him about learning the truth. Whatever you have to say, Devon, none of this was your fault. You're Kindred. So you have to tell us everything, leave nothing out. Don't worry about sparing anyone's feelings. We're family."

But it was Zave that Devon looked at for permission. "I don't have to tell you what he said, if you don't want to hear it in front of other people."

"Like Zara said," Zave said, intent on her. "Tell us everything."

She'd seen the way Zave and Brodie spoke to each other, and from everything she knew, they were honest with each other. Zave had opened up to Brodie after losing his parents, and Brodie had helped him through that trauma.

Zave kept Zara at a distance because he didn't want a repeat of the Bronwyn situation, but Zara must have proved herself to the Kindred, and she'd married Brodie. They weren't sitting in a room of strangers. They were sitting in a room with trusted friends.

"Okay," Devon said. "But no one can leave this room until I'm finished."

"Agreed," Zara said and nudged her. "Good rule." Pointing a finger at each of the men, Zara swung it between them. "That means you two keep each other in line, as well. You're too big for either of us to stop on our own. So if either takes a hissy fit, the other has to put him on his ass."

Devon appreciated Zara's candid attempt to break some of the tension because they were all nervous, and this was about to get worse.

"Okay," Devon said. "I'll start with what he told me in the hotel room."

Recounting the story of Zave's parents to him was difficult. But it taught them all about what they were dealing with. Devon started with Game Time and a lot of it she thought the others already knew. But there was some information they had been ignorant to.

She spoke for nearly an hour, and at various points everyone except her was on their feet, storming away, or turning their back. The bar had been opened for Brodie, her, and Zara, but Zave wasn't drinking. She'd never seen him with alcohol.

"I can't believe Thad would do this to us," Zara said. "I can't believe it."

Devon had gotten to the point in the story where Mitchell had said he was going to introduce his team to her. "Fuck him," Brodie muttered.

"Why would he do this to us?" Zara asked.

Devon had neglected to tell them one fact, one that she was desperate to hold onto. Except, she didn't want them to be blindsided with it. "There's one more thing," Devon said.

Brodie was at the bar, staring into his empty glass. Zave was seated on the couch, elbows on his knees and his hand over his mouth. Zara was on her feet, at the end of the coffee table. Devon was seated exactly where she'd been when she started talking. "What?" Brodie snapped.

Squirming, she was hesitant. "I didn't want to tell you."

"It can't be any worse than what you've already told us," Zara said, going over to give Zave's shoulder a squeeze before she joined her man at the bar. "And I thought we were telling each other everything."

"It's about Thad?" Zave asked, and she made eye contact.

"Yes. But… it's about Bess too. I don't know how we're going to do it. I don't know how we're going to go to that poor woman and tell her what's happened."

The pressure of heat in her sinuses pissed her off because she didn't want to get upset. But when she thought about returning to the island, somewhere she wanted to be, and walking into the manor, the first image that came to mind was Bess and how she was going to react when she noticed that Thad wasn't with them.

She may panic that something had happened to her son, that he'd been hurt, or worse. But when they told her that he had betrayed the Kindred, she wasn't sure Bess would recover.

"We're family," Brodie said. "We protect Bess same as we always did. What that fucker of a kid did isn't on her."

Zara stroked his upper arm, but he ignored the comfort.

Devon couldn't look at any of them as she made the confession. "Frank Mitchell," she said. "Is his father."

Zave sat back, his hands sliding from his knees, up his thighs. Brodie swept an arm around to push Zara away as he moved a step toward the couch. "How the fuck did—"

"They hooked up at a party after Grant was born," Devon said. "I don't know, his christening or naming ceremony, whatever he had. She got pregnant. All he told me was they came to an arrangement. Money for silence, I guess,

I don't know for sure.

Zara was aghast. "Thad knew?"

"No. Not until recently, I don't know when, but I think that's how they got him. They played on the father thing."

Devon wished that she had more answers and could make sense of this revelation for the men who had to be shocked by it. All their lives they'd been oblivious to who had sired their cousin, and it hadn't mattered to them. But they could never have known that the man responsible for Bess' pregnancy would wield power with his offspring decades later or that he would even want to.

"His father," Zave said, twisting to look over the back of the couch at Brodie. "His fucking father."

The cousins weren't as audibly shocked as Zara was, but their amazement was unmistakable. "You're telling me," Brodie said.

Still trying to get a grip on what this meant, Zara was both alarmed and astonished. "You had no clue?" Zara asked. "Didn't anyone ever think to ask Bess?"

"You don't ask shit like that," Brodie grumbled. "She never told and we never asked."

Taking some time to process, no one said anything for a minute. "Do you think Art knew?" Zara asked, reigniting the men's fixation on each other.

"Probably," Zave said.

Brodie reached for the liquor bottle. "I'd kick his fucking ass if he did. How could he know that and not tell me?"

"Because he was protecting his sister," Zara said, walking around Brodie to come back to the couch. "Puts into perspective why Art and Mitchell never saw eye-to-eye. Mitchell knocked up his sister and abandoned her."

"If he'd told me, I'd have taken him out," Brodie said.

Zara scowled at her husband. "It doesn't matter what happened then. What matters is that we know now. And you had to tell us, Devon, because at some point we're all going to be in a room together. Anything we don't know can be used against us."

Devon appreciated Zara's support. On the flight north, she'd made the decision not to tell anyone about Thad until she'd spoken to Bess. But as Zara said if any of them were faced with Mitchell, Grant, or Thad in the meantime, she didn't want them to be surprised with this information. Syn may take that omission as a sign of weakness that the Kindred weren't being honest with each other.

"So we've got Old Man Mitchell, wiener Grant, and fraidy-cat Thad to take on?" Brodie asked and tipped more Scotch into his glass. "I'm quaking in my boots." He picked up the measure and raised it toward his lips.

Zara stormed over and clamped a hand over the top of his glass before it could reach his mouth and forced it back down onto the bar with a bang. "You're not drinking anymore," she said. "Swift is going to need us, and we've got Maverick in a truck down the stairs, he's sober, so it's all on you."

"My aim drunk—"

"Is better than your aim sober," Devon whispered, remembering what Caine had said. She hadn't meant to say it aloud, and it got Brodie's attention.

He abandoned his wife and his liquor to storm over. "Where the fuck did you hear that?" Brodie demanded.

Devon bypassed Zave in favor of concentrating on the scowling man looming above her. "There's more than just the three of them. Thad, Grant, and Mitchell are the only three that are blood, as far as I can make out. They want to recruit this Dempsey because he trained under Swift, and they knew they could never turn Tuck. But they have two other men on their team already." Switching her focus to Zara, Devon rose to her feet. Brodie backed off. "Both men asked about you."

"Me?" Zara asked, going to stand behind Zave on the couch. "Who else do I know?"

Zara peered at Brodie, who answered, "You know fucking everyone."

"But who else is…"

"Enemies of the Kindred?" Brodie asked, and he wasn't as incredulous as his wife. "We've got plenty of those."

Zara probed for specifics. "They were both male?"

She nodded. "One of them didn't fit in at all," Devon said. "He was… normal." It took her a second to pick the right benign word. "He was warm, friendly even, and had the cutest dimples—"

"Leatt," Brodie spat. "Another fucker who felt you up. This your ex convention?"

Devon was learning that Brodie didn't make a lot of friends. Maybe that was why so many people asked after Zara because Zara made a positive impression while Brodie just rubbed people the wrong way.

"Benedict Leatt," Zara said, her brows high on her forehead. "Ben is in league with Grant?"

Brodie wasn't surprised. "Makes sense. He's the one who killed him."

"That was a one-time job," Devon explained, trying to remember exactly what had been said. "He said that was a one-time job and he didn't join Syn until after…"

"After what?" Brodie asked, dropping down onto the end of the couch she was on.

"Something about getting a call on the morning of a Game Time exchange, something about a Kahlil and a Sikorski. He joined Syn after that." Taking her eyes from the table, she searched everyone else. "Does that make sense?"

Zara didn't answer directly, but the words she said to her husband betrayed that she understood. "Kahlil told us that Leatt was watching from close by." Zara smiled. "The lying little shit, God rest his soul." She took a breath. "Money. Money and power," Zara said. "That was what Leatt wanted, remember? I guess he thinks he'll get it with Syn."

"Good," Brodie said. "Because he won't get it with the Kindred. He won't be getting a sniff of your pussy, either. All he'll get is a meeting with Maverick, soon as I line up the shot."

Leatt wasn't the last man on the team. Devon had to make them aware of the other member because she was still sure he was the most lethal. "You won't be alone, they have a sniper."

This piqued Brodie's interest, not in concern, but amusement. "Who the fuck they got?" Brodie asked. "I know everyone in the game."

"Tell us what you remember about him," Zara said. "Anything will help."

Her frown was slow, as she recalled the details of Syn's sniper. "He was... I don't know. He wasn't like the others. He was crude and terrifying, and he kept asking me for sex."

Zave sat up straight. "Did he touch you?"

"No," she said. Having had time to reflect, Caine was one of the things that wouldn't leave her thoughts. "I think he wanted to scare me because he wanted to see how I'd react to the shocking things he said. But the whole time all he did was... watch."

Again, she looked to the others for some sign that they understood. But it was the color draining from Zara's face as her folded arms fell to her sides that intrigued Devon. "No," Zara said.

"I told you," Brodie said, slapping his hands on his thighs before he stood up. "I fucking told you, baby!"

"No," Zara said again.

"You know him?" Devon asked. It wasn't a leap that they did; Caine had asked about Zara. But she would like to know more about their shared history.

Zara swallowed and moistened her lips, before her glare became almost vicious. "Slick-looking motherfucker with a scar right here." She drew a line on her neck with a fingertip, and Devon nodded. "That's exactly how Art described him to me."

Brodie went to put an arm around her shoulders. But Zara pushed away from him with both hands. "Come on, baby, don't sweat it," Brodie said, still trying to pull her to him.

"He doesn't seem to like you, Raven," Devon said. "Did you piss him off?"

"That's an understatement," Zave muttered.

Zara shoved away from Brodie. "No," she exclaimed, shaking her head. "No! I won't let him! That bastard!"

Storming across the room, Zara was on a mission. "Whoa!" Brodie said. Going after her to grab her arm, he pulled her hard against him. "What the fuck are you gonna do? Grab his ear and drag him back? If Caine wants to shoot for them, let him. You've got nothing to worry about. You know I'm sharper than him."

She hit her hands on Brodie's chest. "That's not why I'm annoyed," she said. "I'm annoyed because we saved his fucking life—"

"You saved his life. I didn't, wouldn't either," he said, as if he was insulted by the idea that he might.

"I saved his life. I found out that woman was playing him. I looked after him! I brought him into the fold."

"And he told you that you were even," Brodie said. "It's how the game is played, baby. That's the way it goes. He's right. You saved his life. He saved yours. He doesn't owe you a damn thing." Zara's mouth opened, she kind of croaked and then shut it again. "You want him to be good. Just like you want Grant to be good." Brodie opened his arms. "And look where the fuck we are!"

# SIX

DEVON FELT RUDE staring at the married couple. So instead of focusing on them, she left her seat and went to sit next to her husband. When she rubbed his thigh, he sat back, shifting into the corner of the couch so he could scrutinize her. Although he didn't take her hands away from his leg, he put distance between them and that was enough to upset her.

"Raven and Swallow will go help Swift. I'm taking you back to the island," he said.

"I haven't finished. Jennifer. She's a plant. You were meant to buy her. They wanted her on the island so she could talk to Thad, but that's not all." Devon twisted to see that Brodie and Zara were still hissing at each other. "You guys have to listen to this."

Brodie didn't immediately shut up, but Zara took his arm and dragged him to the couch. "What?"

Devon only wanted to say this once, and maybe announcing it to the group as opposed to one-on-one would dilute the impact of the news. "They put the girl on the island. They set it up. I don't know how. They're already in with the cartels because... well, because I know they are," Devon said, having not explained about how she'd ended up being taken in the first place.

"You don't get away that easy," Zara said. "Tell us everything."

Devon went on to tell the rest about how she'd ended up in her metal box and everything she'd been told about setting up the men who were here. The couple seated on the couch opposite her and Zave listened to every word, and although they didn't converse, Devon could sense they were each making plans.

"We'll get her off the island tonight," Brodie said. "Swift can handle things for a while. You shouldn't be alone with the girl."

"It won't matter if you're there, beau," Zara said. "You could hardly stand up in the witness box and claim his innocence, could you? You're family. You're business partners. And they're going to put a gun in your hand. So what's to stop this Jennifer girl of accusing Zave of rape, and then right in the middle of the trial, they put a bullet in her from a weapon registered to you."

"So you're saying they have us by the balls and we should sit here doing fuck all?" Brodie asked.

"No," Zara said. "But you should be smart. Zave, you have access to security guys. You could have someone remove her, or you could just put her on a boat and set her out to sea, who cares what happens to her? As for accusing you of rape, unless they have a sperm sample, they don't have any proof. Nobody in this room is going to stand up and say they laid eyes on her."

"They could put Thad on the stand," Brodie said. "He could testify to seeing his cousin rape her. He could testify to treating injuries under duress."

Devon hadn't thought about that. But Brodie's point was valid. With Thad traveling back and forth to the island so frequently, Zave could've been torturing and raping women throughout the years of his seclusion and simply forced his doctor cousin to patch up the worst of the injuries to prevent the women from dying.

All the equipment and drugs that had been provided over the years, and the sedatives, oh God! If Thad testified those were to satisfy Zave's sick urges, there would be no way to refute it.

"You guys didn't have sex anywhere she might get her hands on… you know," Zara said, eyeing Zave's groin.

"Your jizz," Brodie said.

Curling her fingers into Zave's knee, Devon didn't want to share their intimate secrets. "No," Zave answered, not as modest as she. "We kept it in the lab."

The sex, they kept the sex in the lab, not Zave's sperm. Devon was just pleased that no one asked him to clarify that. Except, Zara wasn't done with the questions. "Condoms go out with the trash?" she asked.

"No condoms," Zave said.

Mortified, Devon's face flamed, but Zara smiled. "Good… I mean not good, but, yeah… no condoms is good. It means no evidence, and Devon would've noticed someone sneaking in to swab." Brodie laughed and Zara elbowed him. "You're not helping."

"You're babbling shit and making the girl uncomfortable. Not all women are as wanton as you, baby, some have reserve."

"Wanton?" Zara asked. Twisting all the way around to glare at him, she dug her elbow into his knee. "Did you just call me wanton? Damn you and your private education, McCormack."

Brodie opened a hand to the couple opposite. "You're talking about my cousin's spunk, and I'm sitting saying nothing about it. I love that you're loose and easy, baby. It's always worked out for me."

He gripped the back of her neck and turned her away to pull her back onto his chest. Zara moved on from their sniping and got back to the point. "You could get the women," Zara said. "The ones you saved. Have them testify on your behalf."

That was an excellent idea. They'd been saved by this man, standing up for him was the least they could do to return the favor. Devon was one of those women and wouldn't see her savior flounder. Except, he wasn't of the same mind. "I wouldn't put them through that," Zave said.

"And most of them were taken home by Thad,"

Brodie offered. "So would we even know where to find them?"

Zave shrugged. "I don't care about that."

"I do," Devon said, twisting to focus on her lord. "You don't care because you're intent on punishing yourself and you'd be quite happy to spend the rest of your life in jail, because for some reason, you still think you deserve to be punished. If you go to jail, what the hell am I gonna do? Are you really gonna let them win?"

"They've won anyway," Zave said. "What are we going to do? If they want to go out there and save the world, then fucking let them. As long as they're not hurting innocent people, what do we care?"

"We care that they have Game Time," Zara said and took her husband's hand. "There are Kindred who have lost their lives to prevent that device from falling into the wrong hands. Are you telling me you don't give a fuck about that?"

"I do. You want to get Game Time back, I'm on board. But I'm not going on any crusade. Not after what happened to Devon."

Taken aback, she couldn't let him put up barriers between himself and the Kindred. "Don't use me as an excuse to retreat and put yourself back into isolation," Devon said. "I'm supposed to give you hope, not torture you, and if looking at me will only make you think of Thad, then I'll walk away right now."

The phone rang, startling her as it had before. Devon was still on edge, expecting something to happen, something to go wrong at any moment. It rang again, and she wondered why Zave wasn't getting up. But in some sort of Pavlovian response, Zara was the one to rise, cross the room, and pick up the phone.

In the sleekest, most professional voice that Devon had ever heard, Zara chirped, "This is the office of Knight Corp's CEO, Xavier Knight. I am Zara Bandini, how may I be of assistance?"

Brodie scoffed. "She's way too fucking good at that," he murmured and lifted his hips to adjust his jeans.

"That's no problem, send him right up," she said and

set the phone back into its cradle. "Well, fuck a duck, the gang's all here." Zara planted her hands on the desk to swing her ass up onto it.

From professional to potty mouth at breakneck speed. Devon was impressed. "Who was that?"

"Security. We have a visitor."

Brodie cracked his knuckles. "Am I getting to have some fun?" he asked. "Tell me my brother rocked up, and I swear I'll get you pregnant by sundown."

Zara laughed. "No fun for you, but there might be a fight."

Devon didn't know what that meant, but Zara enjoyed holding onto her secrets. She and Brodie continued to make eyes at each other, but Devon was worried about her own man and his vacant stare, fixated on the table. He was switching off, pulling away, she'd just gotten him to open up, to relax enough to let her show him affection. And all of this was going to put him right back where he'd been.

Someone rattled the door, but it was locked, so they began to pound on it. Zara went over and opened it with a flourish as though she was welcoming a professional colleague whom she was happy to see.

But when Rig came barreling in, Devon leaped up. "I forgot about you," she said, holding up her hands while she rushed over to her brother. "Calm down! Okay? Calm down. You don't need to be here. I don't need to…"

He stopped fuming long enough to snap his gaze to Brodie, and just to make sure there was no uncertainty, Rig pointed at him and asked, "You armed?"

Brodie held up his hands and slid his ass to the front of the couch in a slouch. "Like I'd need a gun to take you down, Rigor," he said, tipping up his chin in a nod. "But you have your fight. I've got no beef with you today."

"Good," Rigor said and grabbed Devon's arm. "We're leaving."

Her brother was much stronger than her and when he began to tug her along, she stumbled to keep up. When she glanced back, she saw the Kindred men on their feet. "Whoa, now, wait a second," Zara said, slamming the door and pressing her back to it. "Devon's been taken from us once this week. We won't let it happen again."

Rigor was determined. "You're welcome to come with me, sexy thing, or if you don't get the fuck out my way, I'll go through you."

Brodie groaned. "Now we have beef," he said on a sigh as if this was just inconvenient.

Devon didn't like the menace in the fixed expression he wore when sauntering to them. "He didn't mean to insult her," Devon said. "He wouldn't hurt Zara, not really."

But Brodie didn't listen, he walked over, grabbed Rigor's shoulder, and picked him up to shove him. Rigor let go of her and pushed the sniper in kind. "Fancy digs for a no-forfeit fight, but I'm up for it. If you think you can take my sister—"

"Nobody's taking me," Devon said, trying to get between the men. "I'm here because I want to be here, Rig. You don't need to save me."

"I thought you were safe," he said, glaring at Brodie and then at Zave. "I'm a dick. I told her the Kindred would keep her safe, that no matter where the fuck she was, the Kindred would have her in the safest place on Earth. Then she calls me and says she's been kidnapped in Mexico… again! You're not staying here, with these fuckers, Von. You're going back to your boring, bullshit life."

Typical that he would think he could just storm in and take over without knowing the full story. "Where nothing bad happens to me?" she asked. "It was that boring life I was snatched from, remember?"

"And wait until you find out why," Zara said, coming up behind her, although Devon wasn't sure that this was the best time to tell her brother the complete truth.

"We shouldn't," Devon said, shaking her head. "It won't change anything."

"It will," Zara disagreed, folding her arms. "We're going to need all the help we can get on this one, which means, beau, you've got to holster your pistol because I can't call Caine if we need muscle. Rigor's helped us out before."

"Yeah, and I lost half my men," Rigor said.

Zara didn't hesitate to stand up to him. "And look what you got in return. I think once you hear what Devon found out, you'll want to help us again."

Getting everyone sitting down was no easy feat. But, somehow, they managed to do it. Devon was saved from telling the story, Zara was regaining her equilibrium and was in a pragmatic mood. She was right, too, Devon would never have thought on her feet the way that Zara had. But by bringing the men onto the same side, the aggression dwindled, camaraderie grew, and it was nice to see her brother communicating with Raven and Swallow.

Yet Devon hadn't seen Zave react at all. She was in the chair at the end of the table, with her brother perched on the arm. Zave's lack of reaction to anything that was said made her nervous.

"You tell me what you've got planned and I'm there," Rig said. "Do you have a plan?"

"We're just learning this now," Zara said, "but we'll get there. We're waiting on word from Swift, and as soon as we have it, we'll move out."

Distracted, Devon was only half listening. "You guys plan," she said, because she couldn't take her eyes from Zave who hadn't looked at her, or anyone, for the longest time. Getting up to go to him, she took his hand and gave him a pull. "Will you talk to me a minute?" He didn't move. "Please. Just for a minute. Don't make me beg in front of an audience."

He didn't respond to her honest quip except to stand up and skirt the couch, leading her with him. Taking the twining of their fingers as a positive sign, she was happy to follow him into the washroom in the corner, which was larger than some group offices she'd worked in.

Closing the door, she turned to see him propped against the vanity. "Do you want me to leave?" she asked. His arms were folded and his legs were straight, his face tipped down. His body language screamed that he was closed off. "If you want me to leave, I'll go." Opening her left hand, she examined it. "It's funny. It feels bare, but I only wore your rings for a day. I'm sorry that I lost them. I should've—"

Lifting his hips from the counter, he reached into his

back pocket and pulled something out. Moving closer when he presented his palm, Devon gasped when she saw the glint of her diamond and her modest wedding band.

"How did you find them?" she asked.

"GPS, I told you," he said, taking her left hand to pull her closer so he could slide both rings back to their rightful place.

"But the wedding ring?"

"That has a tracker in it too, I just never told you."

Devon threw her arms around his neck, so grateful that he was thorough and grateful that they were together again. "I really thought I'd lost you. When I was in that car with Thad, I thought…"

"You don't have to worry about that ever again," he said, stroking her back. "Together or not, I'm going to have security on you twenty-four seven, shy. I'm already thinking about how I can make a subcutaneous tracker that can't be tossed from a window or traced by any scanner."

Turning her face into his body, she opened her mouth to breathe him in. "I want to be together," she whispered. "But if it's too difficult for you…"

Shunting her back, he held her face. "I can't lie, there's a part of me that wants you as far away from me as you can get," he said.

The words were like acid chewing through her organs. Losing him, after only just possessing him, was too much pain for her to process. "You don't love me anymore?" she murmured, hoping he didn't believe she was tainted by what Syn had, or had not, done to her. "I swear they didn't touch me. I swear you're the only man—"

He silenced her by putting a finger to her lips. "I love you. But look at what I've done to you. You were in my house, and I made that man treat you."

More guilt. Zave had so many talents but blaming himself for everything was one she wished he'd lose. "If you hadn't, I'd have died. Thad is still your cousin. As much as Brodie and Grant. He is still your blood."

"Don't remind me," he said. "Everyone around me gets poisoned. I told you that, and you didn't listen." He seemed angry, and as usual, he turned his hatred inward. It wasn't her that caused his rage, it was himself. "Look at what's happened. Look at it. Thad was in my house all the time, and somehow, he became so bitter, and grew to hate me so much, that he threatened the first woman I've ever loved. And what will this do to Bess? I have to walk in and tell that woman I didn't bring her son back, and then I have to tell her why. His hatred for me can only lead to hers. She won't be able to look at me… and I won't blame her."

He'd already been tortured so much, and this was another burden he didn't deserve to bear. His years of excess had convinced him that he deserved all the negative things that happened to him. Hearing him so troubled tore at her heart. "Bess won't hate you; this wasn't your fault. Thad has his own problems; he was messed up by Bronwyn."

"Another person hurt by me," he said, and his arms fell away from her.

She was forced to move aside when he walked away to put his back to her. "You didn't hurt Bronwyn. You couldn't know she'd left the house. You couldn't know she'd been kidnapped. You couldn't know—"

"Couldn't I?" he asked. Scrubbing a hand over his mouth, he turned. "She made a move on me."

Devon didn't know how to react to that admission, and her shock must have been apparent to him because he nodded. "What?"

"We were in my house, on the island, alone. She tried it on. I rejected her. Humiliated her. Told her she was making a fool of herself. I might not have seen the boat leave. But I never should've walked away from her that night, not the way I did."

Thad's great love had made a pass at his cousin. Some of Zave's guilt became clearer. "Oh, Zave," she said, going over to stroke his face.

But he grabbed her hand and wouldn't let her offer comfort. "You think if I'd fucked her, we'd still be here now? Do you think she'd still be alive? You know how many nights I've tortured myself with that? If I had just let her suck my cock, sure, Thad would've hated me, but she'd be alive."

"You don't know that," Devon said. "They came for me on purpose. Maybe she was a deliberate mark as well."

"Or she was a random grab, in the wrong place at the wrong time," he said. "She was upset, but I didn't care. I was just pissed off that she'd... you know..."

"And you think that's why Thad hated you?"

"You want to know the ironic thing," he said, his expression growing dark. "I never fucking told him. I've never told anyone. If he hates me now when he thinks all I'm guilty of is not paying enough attention, how much will he fucking hate me when he finds out I've been sitting on this fucking secret for years? Will he believe me? What do you want to bet he'll think Bronwyn and I went at it after he hears that truth? The girl he loved, the girl he's spent the last five years of his life avenging, wanted to fuck me."

"She didn't love him," Devon said. While she absorbed this news, she moved back to lean on the vanity where Zave had been. "No wonder you felt guilty. You've been carrying this secret alone for years. But it wasn't your fault, you did the right thing. Another man's woman propositioned you and you walked away, that's what you're supposed to do."

But that didn't seem to comfort him. "What I was supposed to do was take her to her room and bar the damn door. Instead, I went to the lab and stayed there for days. It infuriates me that I still don't know when she walked out that door. Was it thirty seconds later? Was it as soon as I tossed her aside? Did she go out there in the night? Then I think, she couldn't have, because she'd never have made land in the dark... but she knew how to sail, so maybe... When did she leave? Why? What really happened?"

She didn't have any answers for him. "We'll never know," Devon said. "Because she's gone."

His frustration was coming out as more anger. "And I know why Thad rips himself apart about that, because the not knowing kills me," he said, smacking his palm on his chest. "Imagine how it tortures him."

Devon was amazed that Zave could feel any sort of connection or sympathy with the cousin who'd just betrayed the Kindred. But it was a testament to the humanity he claimed not to have that he could experience a complex range of feeling about one person.

Zave had to hate Thad for betraying the Kindred and he was probably angry at his cousin for taking Devon. He would be upset that he'd lost a close relative he trusted, a friend, someone he'd had in his life all the time.

And then there were the emotions he'd harbored for years. Guilt over withholding information that Bronwyn wasn't an angel on a pedestal as Thad thought she was. The embarrassment that another man's woman had tried to get into his bed. The shame of not knowing, of walking away and leaving Bronwyn alone. Frustration must eat up such a logical, pragmatic guy who was used to being in the know. And although it was unknown to him, that decision had delivered Bronwyn to a grave fate.

To top all that off, he had to think about Bess, a woman who had cared for and nurtured him, who he'd have to devastate because Thad was too chicken to tell her the truth himself.

Devon couldn't judge him if he chose to shut down and lock himself away from the world because those were only the emotions related to one man involved in this scenario. There were so many other factors to consider. Brodie, Zara, his wife, his company, his parents, the other Kindred members, and his officially deceased apparently-alive cousin who was on a mission to take over the world and that same man was threatening to ruin Zave's life and take his liberty.

Zave wouldn't focus on himself and what he needed. Devon needed to ask him to act in her best interests, and without being explicit, she'd make sure all of her requests would alleviate some of his trouble. "I want to go back to the island," she said, standing up straight. "I want to go back as soon as possible."

"We'll have to talk to Bess," he said, thinking again of someone else's needs before his own.

But just because the conversation was going to be difficult didn't mean they should avoid it. "She deserves to know. As Zara said, we're going to get your employees, security guys, someone who can fly, to get Jennifer off that island before you go back. I don't want you spending another second with her."

"She could cause trouble," he said. "I won't let you or Bess go near her."

"We would never believe anything she said about you."

"I don't give a fuck if she tells you I touched her," Zave said. It would be a tough sell for Jennifer because Devon knew how long it had taken her to wheedle her way into the lord's bed. "The only reason I trust that Mitchell was telling you the truth about Jennifer not being there to hurt Bess is because I have a team of guys on the island doing work who would notice if Bess went missing."

Others on the island? Devon would like to know when there were going to be strangers on land she was beginning to consider hers. "That's good to know," she said, because she had been concerned for Bess' well-being.

Zave blinked. "You were all I thought about and now that you're safe…"

"You're worried about Bess." For a man who had once claimed to be a monster, he held an ocean of compassion inside of him that he didn't acknowledge. "We can take an army and scare that bitch away for good," she said. "I wish we could take the jet to the island. It would be quicker to—"

"We can. There's been an airstrip on the island since the house was built. It hasn't been maintained since we lost the last plane. But as soon as I knew the jet was ready, I hired a team to get it back in shape."

"Those are the guys there?"

He nodded. "They would've been in touch with me if anything had happened to Bess." So, they could take the plane to the island. That was a relief. "I've ordered a full check of all the jet's systems. It came from the manufacturers to the airstrip and we needed it in a hurry, so I'm confident that it hasn't been tampered with. But we will need to get security to check it out because Thad knows his way around a plane."

It was still difficult for her to think of Thad as an enemy when for so long he'd been an ally. But the good doctor had made his choice, and she wouldn't be trusting him again. "What about Bess? Will she stay on the island with us? We should make her stay. If she comes back to the mainland upset…"

Zave was growing calm. "The island is her home, she knows that. But we'll support her in whatever she wants to do."

"What if she wants to talk to Thad? I wouldn't know how to get in touch with him, but even if we could, I don't think he'll speak to her." Talking to his mother would mean acknowledging what he'd done and explaining his actions. Devon wasn't sure he could or would do that.

"Did he talk about her?" Zave asked.

"He got angry with me when I brought her up. But the last thing he said to me at the airport was… was to tell her he was sorry."

His glare got intense. "Did he apologize to you?" Zave asked, and she shook her head. "Then fuck him. We tell Bess the truth, and we won't stand in her way if she wants to go and join them."

Devon couldn't envision Bess hanging around with men like Caine or Mitchell, her ex. She was too bubbly and open. Except Thad was a joker, too, and he was right at home with evil.

"You said that only part of you wished that I was far away, but what about the other part?"

"The other part wants to tether you to the island to make sure you never leave my sight again. There won't be any more auctions or any more women."

She'd had so much of her own to tell that she'd forgotten to ask about what happened after Thad had dragged her away. "Mitchell said there was a fight at the meet, that the cartel started shooting."

Zave nodded. "It will take them a while to arrange their ranks. There will still be auctions, but I won't be a part of them."

Women were going to die. There was no doubt about it. Because of Thad's selfishness, innocent women were going to be sold to sick, perverted men. That had always happened, but at least Zave had saved a few. But he was right, they couldn't take the risk anymore, not with Syn out there, threatening to drop a dime on him at any second.

In spite of the looming threat, she had to help him keep a clear head. "I want you to listen to me," she said, going over to press both hands to his chest. "I know it took a lot of effort for you to let me in and to come back here to KC. I don't want you to let what's happened over the last couple of days undo all of that."

"You deserve better," he said.

No, she wasn't going to let him question himself. "You told me that if I slept with you, I would be your responsibility for the rest of my life." Devon showed him the rings on her fingers. "And I said, 'I do' because that's what I want, to be your responsibility and have you as mine. Every time you want to slam a door, you can do it. If you want to say nothing for a month then say nothing. But don't think I'm gonna get squeamish and bolt. I'm gonna keep chipping away at you, just like I did before, and eventually you'll let me back in."

He didn't understand, it was clear from how he peered into her. "Do you like being treated worse than you deserve?" he asked.

She smiled. "I like you… If the Kindred want to come up with a plan, then let them, and we'll do everything we can to help. But for a while we're going to focus on being married. We're gonna focus on you."

He put his left hand over hers and a spark of possession fired her with courage when she saw his wedding band, there on his finger and proud. "I'm not important, shy."

But he was. "You're important to me," she said, taking her free hand to his jaw. "You're the man I love. The man I'm going to spend the rest of my life with. The father of my future babies."

His moment of ease snapped into instant tension. "You want kids?"

"Dozens of them," she whispered, leaning forward to rest her body on his. "It's not like we don't have the space for them."

Bristling, he tried to back away, but there wasn't enough space behind for him to get too far. "I don't know what kind of a father I'd be. I don't know if I'm comfortable—"

"I'm kidding," she said. "We'll make all those decisions when the time is right, and that time isn't now. We'll decide together. My point was that if I do ever carry children, they will be yours. Because I'm not going anywhere. I married you on the promise there would be no divorce. No division of assets." Her smile crept higher as she recounted to him what he'd said in her bedroom.

Zave was more pragmatic. "We can't ignore what's happened, and we can't abandon Raven."

"We won't," she said, but she believed they had time to regroup. "Syn are still trying to get their shit together."

"They have Game Time. You don't know how dangerous that is. My uncle, Art, died to stop Game Time from getting into the world."

If there was anyone who understood how dangerous these people could be it was her. She'd seen them together in a group and felt the power of their collective ability. "Mitchell promised Thad they'd go after the cartels."

"If they use Game Time around those guys, they could hurt the women they're keeping prisoner."

Which was exactly the reason the Kindred had decided not to use anything contagious in the Game Time canisters. But they'd failed to see the bigger picture. "I've been one of those women," she said. "And I'm telling you, every single one of them would rather die than be sold as slaves."

His hand pressed harder into hers. "You condone what they're doing?"

She couldn't tell if it was surprise or suspicion in his voice. "No," she said, not feeling any sympathy or affinity for Syn. "We will go after Game Time. But you're my priority."

Zave's view wasn't as clear-cut. "Kindred priority one is to watch each other's backs. Raven and Swallow will come up with a plan, and I'll be there to execute it with them. No matter the cost."

She hadn't expected to be so expendable to him.

"You'd sacrifice me?"

"Our marriage, not your life," he said, stroking a hand through her hair. "If you want to leave me because I stand by them—"

"No, I would never leave you. We'll do whatever they need us to."

"No 'we', me."

He'd found his center. Focusing on the mission kept him calm, but it detached her from him and she didn't want to be held away like a precious jewel. She wanted to be in the embrace of what mattered to him. "So I'm not Kindred anymore? I'm not 'Finch'? I get abducted on my first mission and that gets me the boot?"

Her distress didn't inspire any in him. "We call Bess Kindred, but she doesn't come into the field. I won't play with your life. You've been through enough."

Devon had to assert herself. "I'll make those decisions. You and Raven can whisper as much as you like. But if I'm needed, I can't promise you that I won't step up." She couldn't promise that she would either, although it would depend what they wanted her to do. She wasn't skilled like the others, and she didn't only have to worry about her husband's reaction to her taking risks, she had to worry about her brother's too.

"Rig," she said.

Reminded that he was there, she curled her fingers between Zave's to pull him to the exit, filled with worry that her brother and Raven may have started another fight. But they didn't seem to be arguing when she and Zave emerged. At the exact moment they did, Rig leaped to his feet to begin a march in their direction.

"You're fucking married?" he asked.

Zara held up a hand. "That was my bad; I thought he knew."

Rig pinned a glare on her. "Yeah, why would she think that, Von?" he asked. "What the fuck? I thought you were safe and being looked after. The whole time you were being fucked by him!" Rig transferred his anger to the man behind her. "You were supposed to go in and save her. If you wanted some kind of fucking payment, you should've come to me instead of bullying my baby sister into—"

"He didn't bully me! In fact, I seduced him and it was hard fucking work!"

It wasn't until Zara barked out a laugh that Devon realized she may have shared too much. "Who's wanton now, beau?"

Sheepish, Devon glanced at her lord and tucked herself beneath his arm. "I'm sorry," she said.

Zave rested a hand on her crown. "I married your sister because I love her," Zave said. "You're entitled to have a problem with that. But if you're going to shout, shout at me."

The last thing she wanted was a row, especially one that was just for performance sake. "He's not going to shout at anyone," Devon said. "He's taking the clichéd big brother position because it's a good act, it's what righteous big brothers do. If he stopped to think about it for half a minute, he'd put his ego aside and realize I couldn't do any better than you."

"She has a point there," Zara said. "Zave's a stand-up guy. He's solvent. Sane—"

"For the most part," Raven murmured.

Zara continued, "And he's not a rapist or a serial killer. He's a decent guy with a house ten times bigger than yours, and he can protect her better than you can."

"She was kidnapped on his watch!" Rigor exclaimed.

"And do you think he'll ever let that happen again?" Zara asked, getting up to join them. "This guy builds all the Kindred tech, and I guarantee he's already cooking up ways to make sure she can never go missing again. He'll find a way to keep track of her even if she's naked."

Zara wasn't wrong. Zave had just told her in the washroom that he was going to implant something in her for that reason. Something chimed and Raven stood up to pull a device from his pocket.

He read it and then tucked the phone away. "Swift needs us."

Zara didn't hesitate. "Rigor, you're with us… Unless

you want to stay here to keep fighting with your brother-in-law," she said. "But he has a chopper, I'm not sure you'd be able to keep up."

That Rigor had been closer to her and arrived after the Kindred was a testament to flying commercial and it proved Zara's point.

"Is he in trouble?" Devon asked Zave. "They said they were going for Kadie's cousin. They didn't say they would hurt anyone. Why would they change their plans?"

"They probably didn't," Brodie said, showing remarkably good hearing. "They wouldn't have gone in hot. They'd have been watching to learn his routine and probably saw Swift there."

"And that's when the trouble would start," Zara said.

So, Swift's arrival was provoking a Syn reaction and forcing them to take action before they were fully prepared. That might make them sloppy, either giving the Kindred a chance to get in and out without hindrance or putting them in more danger because Syn were frantic and less organized.

"What kind of trouble?" Devon asked.

"He didn't specify," Brodie said but wasn't intimidated by the unknown. "We just have to get there."

Brodie headed for the door with Rigor in his wake. Zara stopped to address them. "You two stay here."

"Stay?" Devon asked, and Zave gave her shoulders a squeeze.

"You're back-up," Zara said. "You guys have to get to Bess to explain to her what happened. You have to get Jennifer out of your house. And Zave, you have to spend some time helping Devon get over what happened."

"I'm over it," Devon said, almost resenting being regarded as a burden.

Zara shook her head. "You took one for the team. You were kidnapped. Yeah, they let you go, but it's a psychological injury. So you're benched from the field until you've had some R&R."

Devon wasn't going to argue. She'd just told Zave that they had to focus on their marriage and on him. From how she understood Zave's role in the Kindred, he only acted as physical back-up when needed. His full-time role was to problem-solve and provide the gadgets that helped the group, not to be in the field taking action on every mission.

When they were needed, the Kindred would be in touch. But Zave needed some grounding in his lab, and with all that had gone on and this new development about Syn, he probably had all kinds of ideas about things he could build to aid the Kindred.

Zara wasn't done. "But your primary mission, both of you, is to uphold the façade. The business community is watching the progression of this merger like a hawk. If Syn is going to create trouble for us then we need you guys out there, showing everyone that this family is doing business as usual."

Kindred business would've just jumped up Zara's priority list, and she wouldn't be able to be as hands-on as she wanted to be. Zave wouldn't want to be dealing with the corporations either, but Kindred needed cover if Syn was going to be coming for them. There was no better way for Zave to build an alibi than by being in the office, working hard.

"Do the smiling, do the glad-handing. I know you hate it," Zara said, cutting Zave off before he could object. "You can have your assistants do most of the work. But you have to show up, you have to know what's going on."

Maybe working on the merger would help Devon keep Zave out of a funk. "We'll do what we can," Devon said when Zave said nothing, and she accepted a farewell hug from Zara.

Rig didn't even bother to say goodbye, which didn't surprise Devon because he wasn't big on emotions. His quick departure proved his outrage about her marriage was bullshit. Zara's points had been compelling and might have won him round, but she doubted it.

Rig enjoyed getting dirty and being in the thick of the action. Being next to Raven probably exhilarated him, just as it did Zara.

When the door closed, Devon wrapped her arms around Zave and let out a long breath. "I'm ready to go home," she said.

Talking to Bess wouldn't be easy, but they couldn't keep her in the dark any longer. The sooner she knew the truth, the sooner they could all begin to recover from the psychological injury Zara had mentioned.

Syn had a plan to execute, and the Kindred were playing catch-up. But if there was any group of people in the world equipped to take on this new threat, it was them.

# SEVEN

WITH A HAND on her hip, Zave ushered Devon out of the dining room and closed the door when they were both in the hallway. "I'm going to stay with her for a while," he said.

Devon had tried her best not to shed tears, but it was difficult when she saw the spirit drain out of Bess as she and Zave recounted what had happened on the mission. Zave had sent men ahead of them to come to the island to remove Jennifer, which meant by the time he and Devon got back, the threat was gone.

Bess was frantic. They hadn't given any information to her about what was going on, just given the men instructions to take Jennifer out and away. Bess would've led the men to the girl but wouldn't have known why she was being removed in such a way. But there were contingencies and passwords that made it go smoothly.

Just as Devon had thought, Bess was beside herself when she noticed that Thad wasn't with them. At first, maybe with wishful thinking, she asked if he'd stayed on the mainland in his own apartment.

Devon and Zave had taken her into the dining room to sit down with her, and for the past three hours, they'd watched her go through a spectrum of emotions from denial to anger, to upset. Guilt, confusion, and regret were in there too.

Devon clutched Bess' hand through all of them, trying her best to absorb some of the melancholy in hope she could lessen this good woman's trouble.

Bess had asked for a few moments by herself, and that's how they found themselves here, alone in the hallway.

"I wish we could make her feel better," Devon said, holding her hands together at her chest. "She doesn't deserve this."

"We'll get her through it. She'll always have a place here."

It was comments like that which boosted her love for this man. "I know."

Raising her arms, she kept her hands clasped, and he dipped to accept them over his head, and when he smoothed his thumb across her cheek, she felt the distance between them. "You should get some rest," he said.

He was acting like he was looking after her, but Devon got the sense he wanted his own alone time, just like Bess. "I slept all day in your office," she said.

But he wasn't confronting his need for solitude, he was hiding it from himself just like he was hiding his frustrated confusion from her. "Just the same, put your head down for a while. There's no one here but the three of us now. I know I promised you before that you were safe, but this time—"

"I feel safe here. I know I'm safe. Everyone keeps telling me that this wasn't my fault, but has anyone said that to you yet?"

He never liked to talk about himself and avoided the subject whenever he could, this time being no exception. Zave spoke again without responding to her question. "You should stay in your own room tonight. I doubt I'll make it to bed."

Dejected, she lowered from her tiptoes to let her heels touch the floor, and her hands drifted down as a result. When she'd thought he wanted solitude, she expected him to need a few minutes, not a whole night. "Oh. My room."

"Yeah, it just makes things easier."

Easier on who, she didn't know. They'd made

promises to each other, and she'd thought their days of separate bedrooms were in the past. Whether he made it to bed or not, she would still like to know she was welcome in his.

"I can sleep in your bed, in case you do—"

"Do we have to do this now?" he snapped, on the edge of losing his patience. Using her elbows to push her back a step, he strode away to turn his back on her.

"No," she said. "We don't."

He rubbed a hand over his mouth and turned, thrusting his arm to the side. "I have Bess to worry about. Thad. The Kindred. I have one cousin who's going to go to jail for life for doing what the rest of us couldn't. Brodie saved our asses, we all sanctioned those jobs, and he's going to pay for it. I have another cousin who wants to blow a hole in the Earth, just to prove he has bigger balls than the rest of us. I have KC merging with a company I don't even want, and there's no one overseeing it right now. And to top it off, I just sent away a woman whose first stop could be the first police department she finds, so she can accuse me of God knows what kind of depravity. Do I really have to worry about you pouting because I won't fuck you on demand?"

Devon was impressed, actually impressed. She'd learned throughout her time with him that he was great at bottling everything up. Zave was a genius when it came to being stoic and silent. Playing the dark, mysterious stranger in the corner, saying nothing and intimidating everyone was his forte. He was practiced at hearing new information and not letting any reaction show in his expression.

Indifference was his default. Apathy, his aura. And aloof was his natural state.

But when he did this with her, with no one else but her, she was allowed to see that things did get to him, that he did have the emotion, he just refused to show it.

"No, you don't," she said. "You don't have to worry about that. Fucking is the last thing I'm thinking about. I'm thinking that we said, 'I do.' I'm thinking that we lay in bed and promised each other we were gonna work on lowering these barriers. I'm not demanding that you get your dick out for my amusement. I'm demanding that if you lie down tonight, it be beside me. But you're right, there's far too much going on for us to be worried about arguing with each other as well."

From here, she knew the way to her room because it was almost directly above them. Devon left the covered hallway through the open, pointed arch. But before she got to the stairs, Zave grabbed her arm and spun her around.

"I'm sorry," he said.

Zave had never apologized to her before, and it was funny to hear such sincere words come in such a deadpan delivery. "You're worried about everyone else," she said. "You haven't figured out that it's your wife's job to worry about you. I'm worried about the Kindred, and I don't want Syn to get away with this thing they have. And I wish that Bess wasn't going through this shit. But these people only mean something to me because I love you."

Bess might be the exception, but they'd been forging a relationship since before Devon had even met Zave. But tonight, Devon wasn't injecting herself into that situation because this was a time for family, so she'd hung back to provide moral support as it was needed.

Zave knew how Bess worked. He was great at observing people and if Bess had a problem, he'd find a way to fix it, just as if she demanded to leave the island and never come back again, he'd find a way to talk her out of it.

Devon would be too emotional to be objective and make a reasoned argument. Zave's hand fell from her arm and rubbed his lips together. "I have to be with Bess."

Stepping backwards onto the bottom stair, Devon got enough height to cradle his face. "You know where I'll be if you need me." He accepted this and turned to go back to the dining room. But just before he went through the arch into the shadow, she called out. "Lord." He stopped. "Your emotions don't offend me."

They offended him, and that was why he got so worked up whenever they slipped out. Devon knew him well enough now that it would probably take him another day or two before he'd think about speaking to her again.

It hurt that he didn't want to share a bed with her, just as it hurt that he was pushing her away. The timing was unfortunate. She knew him well enough to understand that he'd have reacted this way whether they'd been married for six minutes or six years, because isolating himself, blaming himself, were the things he always did.

Zave took on the responsibility of the world. He'd done it after his parents died. When Bronwyn was lost. Now he was doing it again.

Devon would stick by him, and they'd come out the other side of this together and stronger.

\*\*\*

DESPITE CLAIMING THAT she didn't need rest because she'd slept in the office all day, Devon must have fallen asleep at some point. She woke up alone in the bed she'd spent most of her nights in over the past few months. Stretching her limbs until she pointed her toes, she rolled onto her back and wasn't even surprised, or offended, to see Bess standing at the end of the bed.

In fact, the view made Devon smile and sit up.

"There's something wrong," Bess said.

Oh, her smile fell. Devon pulled the sheet to her chest and crossed her legs as she sat up and began to panic. "What? Is it Zave? What time is it?"

"Somewhere around ten o'clock," Bess said, her eyes were bloodshot, the bags beneath them heavy. But it didn't surprise Devon that Bess had struggled to sleep given what she was dealing with.

"What's wrong?"

"Yes, it's Zave and it's you," Bess said, coming around to sit on the end of the bed. "What are you doing in here alone?"

Well if that was the only problem, they didn't have one. Devon stood her pillow up behind her back and rested on it while yawning. "Nothing's wrong," she said.

Bess' brow went up. "Don't you lie to me, dearie. You two spent all those hours talking to me and you didn't even tell me about the wedding."

It was unbelievable that Bess could be so selfless. Devon was so shocked that she almost laughed. This woman had been told that her only son had betrayed the people she cared about, and here Bess was worried and asking about Devon's wedding.

"It was quick. You know it was just at the courthouse," Devon said, leaning forward to show her the ring.

Bess smiled. "Oh, it's beautiful. Just what you deserve. How do you feel about being married?"

"Now?" Devon asked, gazing toward the window.

How could she answer that question? Zave had listed all of the things going on in his life, and she was worried about him. She couldn't understand Thad's motivation, and although Brodie was strong, it couldn't be easy learning that your brother had come back from the dead.

Then there was her brother trying to throw his weight around, telling her what to do, pissing her off. But he was out there too, possibly in a room right now with Syn, who wouldn't hesitate to hurt him. Rig was a pain, but he was the only family she had.

"You should be leaning on each other," Bess said. "Not moving into separate rooms."

"It's been a lot for him to take in," Devon said but was wary about putting too much onto Bess who was dealing with her own grief. "We'll be fine once he's processed everything. If he was planning to dump me, he'd have found an excuse to leave me in the city. He wouldn't have brought me back to the island."

"He loves you so much and I'm sorry that my son…"

Devon couldn't bear to see Bess broken like this. She shuffled down the bed. Hooking the sheet beneath her arms to keep her breasts covered, she took Bess' hand. "I wish there was something I could do. I said to Zave I wish we could take this pain away for you."

"I just don't understand," Bess exhaled. "I don't understand how he could've felt this way and never told me."

It was good that Bess was getting to a place that she could talk. "What about Frank?" Devon asked. "Did you know that Thad knew about his father?"

"I had no idea. He never came to me. I spoke to him every day. Why would he not have told me that he knew? Maybe if he'd trusted me and spoken to me about it, I'd have been able to talk him out of this."

Self-blame was prevalent in this family. "I'm not sure anybody would've been able to talk him out of it. He was so confused… sometimes he seemed to be sure that he was angry at the idea he might be hesitant. Other times he was quieter. I thought maybe he was reflecting, but…"

"But, what?" Bess asked, and it was the hope flaring in her eyes that really twisted the knife in Devon's gut.

"I don't think he regrets what he did. I could tell you otherwise and make you believe that he was being coerced, but I didn't get that sense. I'm sorry."

Bess sagged. "No," she sighed. "You've been through so many awful things, and I'm so ashamed that my boy put you through more trauma."

Being abducted hadn't been fun, and everyone was acting as if she should be traumatized. But Devon didn't feel that way this time. After being taken by the cartel and stuffed into a metal box to live in a hovel for months, it didn't feel like her time with Thad was a proper abduction. To be driven in a hot car for a few hours and then put up in a hotel, it just wasn't even close to the same thing.

On the plane on the way home, Syn had even paid for her to fly business class.

Devon hurt for the Kindred, but not really for her own ordeal. The most terrifying part had been Caine and now she got the sense, from the way Zara had reacted, that he was much more complex than just the brash thug he made himself out to be.

"It's all part of being Kindred," Devon said, hoping it would make Bess feel better to know that she hadn't been disturbed.

But Bess didn't perk up. "And that leaves me a bit lost," she said. "These boys needed me to look after them and to support them when they went to the auctions. Now Zave tells me that he won't go back."

"He can't. Syn have threatened to accuse him of—"

"Despicable things," Bess said, showing anger, which to Devon was healthier than being depressed. "Zave did everything he did because Thad asked him to. He used his money and his reputation to get them in. He risked his livelihood every time they went there. He would be disgraced if there was a suggestion he'd been party to what went on down there."

"Like I said, I don't want to give you false hope. But I get the feeling Thad's not the mastermind. Grant or Mitchell, someone knew what the Kindred were doing with the cartels. Maybe they found out after, I don't know, Mitchell's been away for a long time setting up a base for him and Grant. Maybe he was doing that in Mexico and that's how he got in with the cartel who took me. But it was because of what happened with my brother that I was taken in the first place, though I was never supposed to end up here. I was supposed to end up dead."

"That's probably when they found out what Zave was doing," Bess said. "Zave explained it to me last night, dearie. If Mitchell and his people paid the cartels to take you, they paid to make sure you were the headliner so that the most perverted of men would want you."

The most depraved buyers wanted what was seen as the best, they sought their prey at the top of the bill. "Yes," Devon said.

"They would never have done that if they'd known you were going to be bought by the Kindred, would they? They didn't bank on your brother going to the Kindred for help or the Kindred being able to find you. They thought you were going to be bought, tortured, and killed. And that Rigor would get the message. Zave was never supposed to buy you and never supposed to bring you here and fall in love with you. But he did."

Just like old times, Bess was reassuring her when it should be Devon's job to do that for her today. "What are you saying?" Devon asked.

There were tears in Bess' eyes when she closed her hands around Devon's cheeks to hold her face up, a couple of inches away from her own. "That even in the most dire, darkest, disgusting, and hopeless of scenarios, sometimes light finds a way through. When it does, it's our job to nurture and encourage that light, not to extinguish it."

Devon had no plans to extinguish her love for Zave and wouldn't walk away from him. She was astounded that Bess was taking the time to comfort her when her own world was falling down.

"Do you need a minute?"

Zave had managed to do it again. He had snuck up on her. He was standing just inside her bedroom, holding something in his palm. Being that he was fully dressed, Devon guessed he wasn't here to have fun with her. Although it was possible that he held a toy for her in his palm and that he'd come down here to sideline the drama for a while.

"No, I'm ready," Bess said and stood up.

Something was going on, Zave wasn't here to see her. Bess brushed her hands down her skirt and then bent over to kiss Devon right on the mouth. "Now you take care of him. I don't care what he says, keep poking and prodding until he lets you in again. Just like you did before."

"Wait!" Devon said. "What's going on?"

Zave gave her the answer, "Bess is going to stay at Thad's for a while. She stays in his apartment when she's on the mainland anyway, she has a key."

"He might have left a message for me," Bess said. "If he hasn't, well, someone has to pack up his things, don't they? If you're sure he doesn't regret his decision, then he's not coming back."

Devon couldn't let Bess go like this. She jumped out of bed, still holding the sheet to her chest but not really caring who she flashed. Throwing both arms around Bess, she squeezed her. "Please don't stay gone for long," Devon said. All the upset she'd locked inside seeped out in hot, wet droplets from her eyes. "Please come back to us soon."

"I will," Bess said, stroking her hair. "You've been good for us all, dearie." Bess pulled away and caught the sheet for Devon so that she wouldn't find herself naked.

Devon didn't want to let go, she didn't want to stop

hugging her. But Bess was using everything she had to hold back the tears that were weighing on her lashes. Zave widened the bedroom door, and Bess shuffled out. They both disappeared.

But Devon wasn't done yet. She wrapped the sheet around herself and tucked it in. Pulling it higher over her legs, she followed them out of the room and down into the foyer. Bess opened the front door and looked around the grand space. After smiling at Devon one more time, she went out.

Devon was only halfway across the lower floor. Zave paused to come back to her. "I'll be gone for most of the day," he said.

"If I'd known, I'd have come with you."

"You'll be safe here."

"It's not that I'm afraid. It's just… I've never been here alone."

His frown might be worry or it could be impatience. "I can send security if you need someone to stay with you. I'm taking the chopper, the guys who got Jennifer brought one of them back."

Taking the chopper just meant it would take longer to get there and longer to get back. "What should I do here?" Devon asked.

Being alone, the whole place was her responsibility, and suddenly she was afraid she might burn the building to the ground or something. "What you always do. This is your home, isn't it? Sometimes you're going to have to be here by yourself."

A small concession was still a concession. Zave touched her jaw and went to leave, but she caught his wrist. If she was going to stay here all day and not put up any protest at being left alone, she expected him to kiss her goodbye.

To his credit, he understood her pout and kissed her. "You will come back, won't you?"

"What do you think I'm going to do? Abandon you out here?" he asked.

Bess had told her there was food in the cold store, enough to last for months. So if that was his plan, Devon was more likely to go insane out here alone than die of starvation.

"If you do, I might have to go toy hunting." She didn't linger over the innuendo. "Is there anything you need me to do?"

"Yes," he said. She was surprised that he would entrust any task to her.

Concentrating, she was ready to memorize anything he said to her. Devon wanted to prove that she could follow his instructions, that she could be trusted. "What?"

"Eat, rest, draw, relax and take care of yourself. If you have any problems, go down into the basement, okay? Just keep going down." He kissed her again. "But only go if you're bleeding."

Okay, so that wasn't exactly what she'd expected and didn't give her much of a chance to impress him. She sighed. "Or aliens have landed?"

"Yeah. If one of those two things happens, get yourself downstairs. I have to get to Bess."

"Take care of her."

Devon stayed where she was and watched him leave. Wearing only a sheet, she wouldn't go outside to watch them take off and disappear over the horizon. But she did run upstairs to her room and open the window, though she would only see their flight for a few seconds. When the sound of the rotors faded to be taken over by the sound of the crashing ocean waves, Devon exhaled.

The island was hers.

She was alone.

Devon had the run of this whole place and could do anything she wanted. So why was it that all she could think about was Bess' well-being and Zave's sanity? And what might be in that basement.

# EIGHT

WHEN SHE FIRST heard the helicopter rotors approaching the island, Devon was excited. Being in the house alone wasn't as daunting as she might have thought it would be. Because she had plenty to keep her entertained, Devon distracted herself from reality with art supplies that were still in her room. When she relaxed, she enjoyed the down time.

Every time her mind wandered, Zave was the dominant feature in her thoughts. She wondered where he was, what he was doing, and when he might come back to her. Which was why when she heard the familiar sound of the aircraft, she pounced up to her feet and went to the window. Of course, she couldn't see it, the space created by her open bedroom window was too small.

So Devon left her room and ran up the stairs to the larger double window in the library that opened wide. She didn't want him worrying if she made a dramatic gesture of throwing open the window to wave at him. But she did open them enough to peek out, and that was when the excitement went away.

Yes, there was a helicopter on approach, but it was white, not like the one Zave flew. And there were boats in the water, far on the horizon, at least three that she could count from this distance. As she wondered what all these people might be doing in this area, another helicopter came into view on her left and then there was another approaching above the boats.

Slamming the windows, Devon locked the latch and held her breath. What was she supposed to do if Syn launched a full-scale attack on this island? Except, where would they get the resources to launch an invasion?

Going to her room, she dressed in the most sensible clothes she had. It was just lucky that Bess didn't have access to the lab, or she'd probably have moved all of Devon's things there while they were on their Mexican mission.

Tying her hair back, Devon wished she'd spent more time asking about weapons and security instead of busying herself with her art and expecting Zave to take care of everything. The Kindred went to the basement when they had their meetings, but she'd never gone to the lowest levels of the house and didn't even know if she had access, despite what Zave had said before he left.

Now was the time to find out.

Going to the spiral staircase that she knew well, she descended as far as she could and touched the security panel on the door at the bottom. It allowed her entry, and she thanked Zave for his forethought.

Except when she went through, Devon found herself in a long, black corridor that had doors and passages leading off of it. Where was she supposed to go? Which room should she go into? And then, as if someone had read her thoughts, a red light flashed along the top of one of the doorframes. Hurrying forward, she paused, wondering if she'd actually seen the light or imagined it, because she couldn't see anything up there that looked like a bulb.

Then, a wisp of red light, like a snake of smoke, flickered again from left to right along the top of the doorframe. There was a security panel on this door as well, and although she'd been granted entry to this floor, her heart was still hammering with doubt when she touched her thumb pad to the blue circle against it.

The door whooshed open. She didn't know where

she was going or even if this was where she was supposed to be. When she went in, surprise stopped her in her tracks. The dark room was lit by emergency lighting, and against the farthest wall was a bank of monitors displaying images of different locations.

In front of that was some kind of control station with three smaller monitors and three keyboards built into the desk. To the right was a circular conference table with swivel chairs around it. This was some sort of hub.

Moving forward, she explored the images and saw some that looked exactly like this house. Bess had said there were cameras dotted around, but Devon had never known where they were. One of the images changed and she saw a room that looked just like the foyer upstairs, but the décor wasn't the same and the carpet on the stairs was a different color.

She recalled what she'd been told about the twin houses and deduced that she was looking into Brodie's manor. Searching for clues in other pictures, she tried to figure out where the Kindred were monitoring. The KC building was familiar, but the images of other corporate offices were not.

"Shy?" The voice made her gasp and she whipped around, but there was no one in the room with her. "It's okay. Walk forward, I'm on the intercom."

"Zave?" He was talking to her. "Where are you?" she asked, rushing forward to the desk and that was when one of the monitors at the workstation flickered on to show his office at KC.

"I've sent someone to get you," he said, descending from a standing position to a seated one so she could see his face.

It was a relief just to look at him. "How did you know I was down here?"

"Motion sensors," he said.

It wasn't a secret that they were scattered across the island, but it hadn't occurred to her that the information they fed back would be accessible from anywhere other than his lab. "You can see them there?"

"The Kindred have to be able to access all of their

systems everywhere," he said. "I should've just given you a phone, I don't know what I was thinking." He was thinking that she would be safe here, and he had no reason not to believe that. She hadn't. "You did the right thing going down there."

Sinking into the first chair, she put a hand to the side of the monitor. "I'm not bleeding, but I didn't know where to go," she said, guessing that she didn't have to tell him about the choppers and boats. Zave had a habit of knowing more than she did at all times. "I don't know what to do. I can't defend the island on my own. The basement was my only shot and the light above the door…"

"Only certain doors have them. You were observant to notice it. Brodie's manor's rigged to show different lights when different fingerprints are used on different doors."

Information about the houses was fascinating, but it wasn't pressing and didn't explain why their island was being invaded. "What's going on?" she asked.

"This is Syn's opening gambit," he explained, and her worst fear was realized. They were literally invading the island. "I've sent a KC chopper to get you. Pack whatever you think you'll need; we won't be staying on the island for a while."

The Kindred were strong and they were proud, she didn't expect them to surrender without a fight. Devon might not be combat minded, but she would rather stay here and do what she could until reinforcements for her side could arrive.

"Where are we going?" she asked. "We can't give up this house to them."

Zave didn't seem as worried as she felt. Yes, there was concern in his expression, but not much more than his usual grim outlook. "Syn aren't the ones coming," he said. "What did you see?"

"Helicopters, boats."

"It's the media."

The media hadn't entered her thoughts. Maybe she was more battle-ready than she'd thought because she'd been prepared for a fight, not an interview. "Why?" she asked, panicking that Syn may have made their criminal accusations against him. Except if they had, he'd probably be in a police cell right now, not in his corporate offices.

"Syn weren't happy that the Kindred showed up. They didn't get Dempsey, but they snatched a kid who worked with him, a boy named Howie. They're pissed enough about not getting what they wanted that they want to stir things up for us."

Stir things up. Okay, so Devon would admit a preference for a media invasion than a Syn or police one, but how could they have gotten the media interested so quickly? Zave wasn't even on the island yet they were descending on it like they were expecting to find the story of the century. "So they send the media?" she asked. "Why would the media care about—"

"Our marriage," Zave said. "Did you tell Syn we were married?"

Thad had. Marrying the man she loved was important life news for her, and until now, she hadn't figured out that it may be of interest to the masses too. But, damn it, what a great distraction. Now Zave's hands were tied, he wouldn't be able to get involved with the Kindred side of things while the media held him under a microscope. The genius recluse who'd lost his parents in a tragic accident hadn't been seen for years, yet he'd somehow found himself a woman and got himself married to her.

Of course the world's media would be interested in one of the smartest businessmen of their generation marrying a woman no one even knew he was seeing. How did a hermit who lived on an island miles from civilization find himself a woman?

Maybe they thought she was mail-order or betrothed to him from birth. Whatever they thought, she was a target and so was he. They would want to know about her, why the relationship had been kept a secret, and what it meant for KC that its isolated leader was emerging to take the reins again.

Her concern became less for their safety and more for his reputation. "I thought Syn were coming."

"For now, you're safe," he said, "but you have to be quick. I only got a heads-up because PR called Cedric for comment. No one knew I was in the city today except you and

Bess. My guys are only maybe five minutes ahead of the press choppers. I want to make sure you're gone by the time they get there."

Garnering her determination, she began to think about getting out of here. "I'll be ready."

"Don't worry about stuff," he said. "No one will get into the house. It's illegal for them to set foot on the land and the building is secure. I can get you anything you need here."

The place that had been her sanctuary was under threat, and it felt wrong to abandon it. But she wouldn't argue with Zave's logic, it was superior to hers. There were practical concerns that left her at a loss. "Where will we stay?"

This was Zave's only home, as far as she knew, and Brodie's place was too far away. They couldn't risk dragging the media there anyway. So the only other place she knew was where Bess was staying and that made her uneasy.

"Don't worry about that," he said.

"I don't know how I feel about Thad's apartment," she said, making sure he knew about her misgivings upfront.

He bowed lower over his linked fingers to get closer to the screen. "Shy, we'll stay wherever you're going to be happy. You don't have to go near Thad's place. I'll get you a hotel or an apartment of your own. You want a house or a cabin in the woods? Anything you want. Just get upstairs and get into the chopper, you only have a few minutes."

He would take care of everything, she didn't have to ask questions or worry, she just had to follow his instructions. "Yes, sure," she said, leaping up.

"Petri will be the one to get you." It was nice that Zave had sent someone she was familiar with as opposed to a stranger, that was considerate. "He'll say, 'Are you ready to move, Mrs. K?' You say, yes. Then you leave. If there's a problem or you need to go back into the house, you tell him that you've forgotten your keys."

Devon hadn't had keys since she had an apartment before she was taken months ago. "I don't have keys," she said.

"It's code," he said, probably amused by her stupidity. "He won't actually think that you have keys or that you've forgotten them."

"Sure," she said, embarrassed by her idiocy, but her mind wasn't on common sense, it was on the hungry media desperate to descend on her and shatter what little peace she had.

With a quiet breath, he softened. "Shy, don't panic, sweetheart. I'll look after you. All you have to do is get on that chopper with Petri."

Devon had the time to gather what she would need in the city. Zave likely wouldn't be coming back. "Is there anything you need?" she asked. "I'll throw some things in a bag. If you need clothes or—"

"No luggage," he said. "You can bring one bag, don't go hunting for suitcases. We'll get you clothes, paper, pencils, whatever you need, Shy. We'll get it here. You bring only what can't be replaced."

There wasn't really anything like that, she'd learned not to get too attached to material things. Other than her rings. She was attached to those, but she was already wearing them. "Should I do anything? Turn anything off or—"

"I can access all the systems from here," he said. "They're going to bring you to me, so I'll see you in a couple of hours. Just keep your head down."

So much for her looking after him; he was doing all the heavy lifting again. "Okay. Are you sure there's nothing you need? Nothing you're working on in the lab that you need me to bring?"

Perhaps just to appease her, he gave her a task. "Under the bed," he said. "You'll find a black leather box. The combination is your birthday. Bring me what you find in there."

"Okay," she said, crowding closer to touch the image of his face with her fingertips. "I love you."

"Get moving," he said. "I'll see you soon."

The screen went black and instead of focusing on his lack of a response to her declaration, Devon jumped into action. Running upstairs, she grabbed the couple of pieces that she was working on and stuffed them into a tote she found in the closet. Shoving some underwear and toiletries in there, too, she brought her birth control pills, as well. Even if he said he was going to replace things, she would need enough to get her through the night.

Hurrying to the lab, knowing the helicopter must be close to landing, Devon snagged a few of Zave's things from the bathroom that she found on his curved, tower staircase, and then went up to his bedroom to retrieve what he'd asked for.

Pulling it out, she heard a chime overhead but looked around and saw nothing. Except the way this house was wired, the chime could mean just about anything. It could mean there was someone at the door waiting for her. Yanking the box out the rest of the way, she put in the combination and threw it open ready to scoop out whatever she discovered inside.

But her hand paused when she saw what was in there. The box that was lined with cushioned purple satin contained an intimate selection. "My toys," she whispered.

The chime came again, and there was no more time for her to waste on analyzing what it meant that the only thing Zave wanted from the house that they were abandoning were the toys he'd crafted for her pleasure. Bundling everything up, including a little black leather book from the bottom, she put the items in her bag and shoved the box back beneath the bed.

Rushing out, she went to his closet to grab a couple of items of the lingerie she'd bought, and then on hearing the chime again, Devon snatched one of his jackets and pulled it on over her clothes. Tossing the strap of the back over her shoulder, she ran to the front door.

It probably took her a good three minutes to get through the house, and by the time she got there and opened it, there was no doubt that there was somebody there. The chime had been insistent on her journey, and when she got within earshot, she heard a strong hand banging on the solid wood of the door. The blunt, thumping sound echoed through the cavern of the entryway, making her speed up.

Ashamed that she'd kept him waiting, Devon was also impressed that the house was so secure. Not even those who were allowed to get in could manage it.

She opened the door to Petri. "Sorry," she said.

"Are you ready to move, Mrs. K?"

And then she remembered what Zave had said. Devon had done everything she had to and she couldn't afford to delay anymore. "Yes."

Petri gathered her under his arm. Devon made sure the door was shut tight and was surprised that he kept her so close to his side as they walked away from the front door. She was about to comment that it was inappropriate for him to be holding her like this because it made her uncomfortable, and then a low flying helicopter whooshed past them.

Ducking her head into his chest, she figured out that he was protecting her, not only her physical being, but her privacy, as well. Devon followed him around the house to the side of the island where the helipad was, and she climbed onboard the KC emblazoned helicopter.

It probably wasn't smart that the vehicle she was getting into basically signposted who she was. But beggars couldn't be choosers, and she was happy to sit at the back of the craft with her eyes closed as they ascended.

Devon didn't want to see the choppers circling the island that she thought of as home. She didn't want to see the boats ripping through the ocean she'd come to love and drawn in awe. It felt wrong that these strangers were tarnishing the place that she thought of as pure. Even Jennifer hadn't been able to take that feeling away from Devon, and it sickened her that these people were trying to make her feel unsafe in a place she trusted.

Two hours was a long time when you were constantly bobbing and weaving through other aircraft who were trying to get pictures. All Devon wanted to do was be with Zave, that would be the only thing that could make her feel safe again.

Devon had to know how they were going to handle this and when they were going back to the island. She wanted everything to go back to the way it had been. So many things had changed, with Thad and Syn and Bess leaving the island, that maybe they would never be able to recreate those perfect days when she'd thought her future was bright.

Those doubts were why she needed to get to Zave,

because he'd help her see clearly when he showed her that he had everything under control. The last thing Devon felt right now was in control, and it wasn't pleasant to feel so messed up.

Each labored second was one closer to KC and her lord. So she'd sit tight and hope that when she got there, Zave would already have a plan.

# NINE

ON GETTING TO the KC building, Petri jumped out to retrieve her before the rotors had stopped. There were more restrictions in city airspace, but Devon was sure some of the media would be exempt or have permission to fly around here. So she was happy to run into the building, squashed into Petri's side, in the same way she had left the manor on the island.

The room that she'd had an intimate Kindred meeting in yesterday was teeming with people today. The office was artificially lit because there were screens over each of the windows, blacking them out, like there had never been glass there at all. It now looked like a fourth wall that hadn't been here yesterday, but it was preferable today. The shades were so large that she couldn't imagine maintenance having them lying around in storage, but the lack of windows wasn't important.

Devon had come rushing down here with Petri and her expectation had been that she'd find her lord, and she had. Zave was standing behind the desk, holding a bundle of papers. The surface of the desk was white with other sheets, and everyone in the room was talking at once.

Those crowded around the desk wanted Zave's

attention. Those standing beyond were talking to each other, and the ones around the conference table were quite animated about whatever they were trying to decide.

The din was reminiscent of her first nights in her metal box. Devon closed her palms over her ears, trying to block out the noise. Petri stood just behind her in the open office door. He pushed her forward a step, but she resisted.

"No," Devon gasped, and although she would say she hadn't been loud enough to be heard over the susurration, Zave's attention snapped around to fixate on her.

"Everybody out," he called.

No one hesitated to comply with his stern command. Petri put her just inside the door and used his body to shield her from the people funneling from inside to outside the office.

When everyone was gone, Petri glanced at the desk. "Sir."

"Thank you. You can go too." Petri didn't question Zave either. He just stepped outside and pulled the door closed. "I didn't know you still felt that way," Zave said, but the words were muffled and it took her a moment to realize that her hands were still pressed to her ears.

Self-conscious about her insecurity, Devon lowered them to smooth out her top and jeans, trying to be casual. "Sorry. It was just loud."

"And it brought back a memory?" he asked, putting down the papers to come round the desk toward her. "Of your first nights with the cartel?"

Devon felt silly and didn't want him coming over to soothe her like a child upset by an insignificant boo-boo. But he'd seen her do the same thing with her hands on her ears when she first recounted her abduction to him.

"What's going on?" she asked. "Why are the media scrambling around the island? Why did you call it Syn's opening gambit?"

Zave came all the way over, curled one hand around the side of her neck, and took her hand in the other. "We think they're trying to prove a point," he said, guiding her toward the couch they'd sat on together the previous day. "They didn't go straight for the jugular and get the law involved. They hyped up the story of our marriage, sent it out to the wires, and now the press thinks there's something to report."

"What? What do they want to report?" she asked. "We're married. Why is that a big deal?"

His head tilted because he knew she wasn't that naïve. "I've been locked away on the island for nearly ten years. If the press got wind of me coming back to the office, as I have been, they'd have made a story out of it. This is bigger. They want to know what brought the business world's most famous hermit out of his shell."

She sighed and collapsed against the back of the couch. "And now they found out that you have yourself a bride too. And as far as they're concerned, you didn't go on a lot of dates on your private island."

"Something like that," he said, propping an elbow on the back of the couch. He sort of curled around her as he stroked her outer thigh, opposite where he sat. "When else do you feel unsafe?"

"Let's not talk about that," she said, slipping her hands between his jacket and his shirt to rub his chest. He hadn't been this dressed up this morning when he left the house. Being a CEO of a multibillion-dollar company, it probably wasn't difficult to ask someone to get him a suit.

"You should talk to someone about it."

"I used to talk to Bess," she admitted, fingering his lapel. "Even this morning she was comforting me. When her whole world is imploding, she's still worried about me."

"She can't help it. Caring is what drives her."

"How was she when you left her at Thad's? Did she find any message there?"

He shook his head. "I went through every room first in case he'd booby trapped the place. It's not unusual for people who don't plan to return to their homes to do that."

"He would've known that Bess might go back there."

"Which is probably why he didn't set any traps," Zave said, tracing the back of his fingers from her cheekbone, over her ear, and into her hair. He did it again, and the soothing motion made her edge closer to him and turn her head to rest her opposite temple near his supporting arm.

"I feel like it hasn't been just us for weeks," she whispered, although it had only been a few days and they'd stolen a few seconds together last night and this morning.

"We haven't been alone since our wedding night," he murmured, and she wanted to remind him that that was his fault because he'd barred her from going to his bed last night.

But when Devon let her weighted eyelids peek open to see the drowsy desire in his, her motivation to chastise him fled. "We were planning to be part of a dangerous mission," she said. "But sharing that bed with you in the motel, I was content."

"What are you now?"

That was probably a dangerous thing to ask because she didn't know how alone they were. This room had been filled with people just a minute before. For all she knew, any one of those people could walk back in at any second.

But her hand carried on north until her fingers coiled their way to the back of his neck and then she pulled him down because kissing him would erase this panic. It would make her forget all the terrifying parts of their lives.

When he didn't resist or reject her mouth, Devon was content with him again. Kissing Zave, her husband, in this fully lit office was exactly what she was supposed to be doing right now, in this minute. His tongue wasn't insistent; it didn't seem to be pushing for more. But when his palm pressed to her breast to massage her through her clothes, she arched into the advance and whimpered.

She would let him take this as far as he wanted to. Being caught in an intimate clinch would embarrass her, but she'd told him that, as his wife, it was her job to fulfill his needs, and if this was what he needed, she wouldn't reject him.

For the first time probably since he'd known her, she was wearing jeans that limited his access to anything beneath her hips. Rubbing her hand up his thigh, Devon discovered how eager he was to take this further.

So, loosening his slacks, she liberated the hard urgency of his cock. Although his mouth was content to keep their oral joining slow, his hand was enjoying its quality time with her breasts. Devon wanted to seize this opportunity to be bold. He'd been closing down, shutting her out, and Devon feared that meant a return to an embargo on physical contact.

When she grabbed his dick, he didn't pull away. Maybe he'd learned that she could help him release his tension, even if it was just for a few carnal minutes with a superficial physical relief. Removing her top as she sank to her knees between his feet, she unhooked her bra and stayed high on her knees to take both of his hands to clasp one around each breast.

"Devon, a kiss is one thing," he said, rubbing his thumbs over her nipples.

The mischief in her smile was fooling no one. "That's all I want. A kiss."

After pumping her hand up and down his shaft a few times, she lowered and bent to kiss his head. It was a kiss. A long, slow, right down the back of her throat type of kiss and one that she'd been desperate to enjoy for a while.

He'd never let her do this, not all the way. Zave let her explore just enough of his dick with her mouth to let her believe he was being open with her and giving her what she needed. Devon knew that he held back, and for a man who believed punishment was all he deserved, it was a massive achievement for him to let her give him any pleasure.

His groan was enough to drive her on, and she sucked him deeper. His dick was long and wide, and she wasn't particularly practiced, so she used her hands to make sure all of him was stimulated. When her mouth needed a rest, she fondled his balls and pushed his head into her cheek and kept working him with her hand.

When Devon noticed that his eyes were closed and his head resting on the back of the couch, she pulled her mouth free. "Look at me," she whispered. "I want you to know who's with you."

He lifted his head and through his own arousal, she read curiosity. "Who else would be with me?" he asked, stroking her face. "Who else would be this generous?"

Zave underestimated his physical appeal. There were

many women who would love to be in her position right now. That wasn't even taking into account the money and the property. He was a good man, and an attractive one, who needed to be reminded that he was worth her attention.

Bowing forward again, she sucked the crown of his cock between her lips and flicked it with her tongue, circling and lapping until he groaned again. A pulse of certainty went through him from base to head, and she smiled to suck him down deep. But he grabbed her arms and pulled her onto her feet.

"What are you doing?" she asked. "I want to finish."

"You will," he said and opened the snap of her jeans to pull them down to her knees, taking her underwear too.

Separating her folds with his thumbs, he licked her clit until it was prominent enough for him to draw between his lips. "That's not what I meant," she gasped, dropping a hand to the top of his head.

"You wanted to be equal," he hummed against her and kept provoking her with his tongue, but he could only reach so far with his mouth while she was standing like this. "Take off your jeans."

Sliding the tip of his middle finger over her clit, down between her legs, he sank it into her. Circling the digit, he curled it to push its pad against the cushion within her. "Oh, lord," she moaned.

"You're wet. Wetter than I thought you would be."

"I guess sucking you off turns me on," she said.

"I'll remember that."

He pushed her jeans all the way down, pulled her boots from her feet, and stripped her bare. He stood up to whip off his own jacket and opened his cuffs. Then with his fingers on her cheek and the heel of his hand under her chin, he helped her regain some focus by uniting their eyes.

"This is going to be fast and filthy," he said, searching for her consent. "If you don't want me to—"

"I'll take fast and filthy," she said, so eager in her nodding that she made him smile before he tossed his tie over his shoulder.

He kissed her forehead. "Turn around, put your

hands on the back of the couch and a foot up on the seat."

Fast and filthy was right, he wasn't even going to give her a chance to go on top. He helped position her legs when she turned to do as he'd said. He hooked the thigh of the leg she had on the couch and held it higher. The angle wouldn't be great for him, he'd have to crouch, but that didn't stop him from plunging into her full force, making her cry out.

The people who'd been in here probably hadn't gone far. It was the middle of the day. This building was full of people. But he didn't scold or silence her. Zave did exactly what he'd said he would, he fucked her hard and fast.

Being this alive and spontaneous with him reminded her what it was they were fighting for. With the way he'd acted last night, she'd been sure it would take them weeks to get back to this point of intimacy. That he'd given in to her so quickly spoke either to his confidence in their relationship or the urgency of his need.

While he'd said it would be quick, he hadn't said it would be half-done. After delivering one orgasm, he slipped the hand he'd been using to steady her hip around to finger her clit, pushing her into a second.

"Zave!" she gasped.

Pushing forward in three final, stilted thrusts, Zave hissed so hard that spots of his saliva hit her back. Devon gasped again when he pulled out because the action was so abrupt. She imagined that he was cursing himself for giving in to his desire for her, especially in this public place. Maybe he thought it was disrespectful or showed a lack of the control that he valued.

Devon was still so high on the endorphins that she didn't want to turn around to see his shame. His hands met her hips and they slid up her waist to her ribs, reaching a ticklish spot, making her clamp them down.

"There's a shower in the washroom," he said. "I can get you something else to wear. What would you like?"

He didn't sound ashamed or guilty or angry or any of the other emotions she was used to him dealing with after they made love. So she had to turn and look at his face to try to get a read on him.

"Will you shower with me?" she asked but knew the answer would be negative, because he'd already pulled his pants back up and fastened them.

"I have to speak to Cedric," he said. "You go wash up. Take your time. I'll send something in for you to wear."

The physical release didn't last long enough, and the bubble of oblivion burst. "Are Syn trying to hurt us?" she asked, returning to their reality. "Does the attention embarrass you?"

"It pisses me off. But it always did. I never got why people cared what I, one guy, was doing. Why are my actions newsworthy?"

Except in this day and age, anyone rich and attractive was newsworthy. Understandable or not, that was the way celebrity culture had gone. "As far as they're concerned, you've been practically missing for ten years."

His impatience edged into frustration. "They've known where I was."

Maybe trying to make him see why he was so fascinating wasn't a good idea. But it was the reason the media were so insistent. "Yes. But what were you doing out there?"

Apparently, he saw curiosity as no excuse for their hounding. Devon speculated on how long this interest would last, probably until the next juicy story came along. It could be a day; it could be a month. "KC has had regular product launches," he said. "Most of them are predominantly my work."

She smiled and put her arms around him. Devon didn't need explanations. "I know that, silly. I'm not the one who's going to be asking. All those news people will."

"As far as I'm concerned, they can keep wondering," he said, picking up her chin to kiss her mouth. "Now grab your clothes and go into the washroom before someone comes in here and sees what's mine."

He'd managed to have sex with her without getting rid of his clothes, but she was standing here naked, which probably wouldn't look good if one of his little worker bees came in. His new wife was already newsworthy, to find her standing naked in front of her clothed husband would raise questions about the nature of their relationship.

Bending to gather up her things, she was pleased when he kissed her again when she stood back up. "I'll take my time, in case you change your mind," she purred.

But he vetoed the idea, though he was gentle about it. "I'll be in here when you're done."

"Alone?" she asked because she didn't relish the idea of walking back into the crowded place it had been when she got here.

"Cedric may be here, but no one else, I promise." He ran his finger down her jaw. "And we're going to talk about getting you the help you need too."

His genius mind wouldn't forget her embarrassing reaction to a bit of hubbub. His attention to detail was one of the things she loved about him… most of the time. "I don't need help. I was just overwhelmed and a bit surprised, I expected to find you here, not all those people."

"You don't have to explain to me," he said. "But don't ever hide when you're struggling. It's great that you trust Bess to help. But you have to let me know too."

That was somewhat rich that he demanded to be kept in the loop when he worked so hard to keep everyone out of his. But just like with the sex, she wasn't going to argue against any sign that he cared.

Devon hadn't been withholding. She just hadn't realized her reaction to a crowd would be so strong. The airport in Mexico had made her uncomfortable, but she'd assumed that was about her escort and not about lingering issues she might have from her captivity.

"I'll do my best," she said.

"Good, now go shower."

On his instruction, she took all of her clothes with her, leaving no signs of what they'd just done. Having a secret increased their intimacy, and this building was beginning to feel more like hers and less unfamiliar.

If they were leaving the island for a while and Zave planned to work here, she had a feeling that she was going to be spending a lot more time at KC, and if it was anything like the time she'd just shared with her husband, Devon was already looking forward to it.

# TEN

"IT NEVER OCCURRED to me to stop and think about how much money you actually have," Devon said, turning in a circle in the middle of the open-plan living space Zave had just brought her to.

The sleek lines, warm woods, and dark metal banister that curved to the upper floor were a testament to how much this apartment must have cost. But that was nothing to the wraparound balcony and the glazed walls of this penthouse space that had magnificent views across the city.

"Wait until you see the closets," he said, reading through some of the messages he'd been handed on his way out of the office.

For months she'd resided on his island in a beautiful stately home, more opulent than some tourist attractions. But it was like a retreat and her life there was abstract, like she'd stumbled down the rabbit hole and somehow the laws of normal life didn't apply.

Except after she'd come out of the washroom into his office, wearing the new clothes she'd found hanging on the back of the door, she was greeted by Cedric, the man who helped Zave run KC. Then she was handed a pile of apartment listings. Zave told her to pick one, and the men went back to work.

Devon, pleased at having something to do, had gone to the couch and spread out the documents. Apartment hunting in the past had been weighing lists of pros and cons. Deciding if she'd rather live with mold or with cockroaches, if she'd rather have graffiti on the walls or hookers across the hall. These listings were nothing like that.

She'd been so enamored with the first, she'd been ready to jump and declare it the winner, and then her eye caught the images on another sheet. So she went on to look at each one, and she couldn't find a single negative about any of them; everything was positive.

She didn't know if they were renting or buying, and there wasn't a hint of financial information on anything she read. All she had were dimensions and floor plans, descriptions and pictures, and it was like peeking into the lives of the rich and privileged.

Even after she'd picked this one, Zave hadn't looked at it or offered any input. He'd called a woman into the office, handed her the sheets, and carried on working with Cedric.

The light had begun to fade, and even though Zave had had a pile of files on his desk he stood up and declared that they were leaving after she yawned for the third time.

Usually that meant heading to the roof and jumping in a chopper. Not this time. This time they went to the private parking area of the KC building where a limo was waiting for them. Zave poured her a glass of champagne and began to read his messages. The man was still reading them after they arrived at the apartment.

She could only take his stoic silence for so long before her curiosity and need for his attention began to itch. "You're popular," she said when she stopped turning to notice him leaning against the kitchen island to the far left of the front door.

"Most of them are press requests," he said, flicking through one, two, three, and holding them up.

Maybe she shouldn't have asked. "What kind of press requests?" she asked, wondering if it had been wise to pick a place with a glazed wall.

Zave was still reading them. "Just the usual, requests for comments and interviews. Nothing you have to worry about."

Coming up with a plan with the Kindred to fight evil was less daunting than the idea of satisfying the media's hunger. "Do we want to give them an interview?"

He stopped reading to lift his eyes from the notes. "Do we?"

It was as if for a second she'd forgotten who she married, and she laughed. Devon didn't have to worry about being grilled by a journalist, Zave would sprout wings and fly before he'd open himself up to that kind of scrutiny. "I can't imagine you sitting on a couch next to Oprah, telling your life story."

"I haven't seen Oprah's name yet," he said, slipping another sheet from the front of the pile to the back and then another and another. "I'll let you know if she calls."

Marrying a guy who was in demand and alluring to the public was one thing, but there was another thought that was never far from her mind. "Is this meant to keep you busy?" she asked. "Do Syn just want you out of the game because you can't take action if the world is watching you?"

"You're driving yourself nuts," he said, putting the squares of paper onto the kitchen island. He took off his jacket and his tie. "Don't try to get into their heads. It's not a place you want to be. You can't anticipate insanity."

She didn't know where to focus her anxiety, with what had already happened with Syn or what was on the horizon. "I feel like I should've done something," she admitted. "Maybe I could've told Thad not to tell them about us."

As usual, he was unflustered. "He'd have told them anyway, or Mitchell would've found out another way. Our marriage is a matter of public record. It was only a matter of time before the press picked up on it themselves. Someone at the courthouse would've seen us coming or going, or they'd have leaked the paperwork. It doesn't really matter. It's done."

Frustrated, she inhaled. "But you hate that everyone's looking at us."

"I hate that this is your introduction to my reality."

But this wasn't his reality, not his reality immediately before her. His reality was living in his lab on the island, never talking to or seeing anyone until the Kindred needed him. "Are you going back to the office full-time?" she asked.

"Probably."

His whole life was different and she felt responsible for that, which was ridiculous because it was Thad's betrayal that had brought them to this point. If he hadn't run off with Syn, then dealing with their new adversary would be a lot easier. Now they had to wonder about what Thad might have done that they hadn't noticed or what secrets he might share.

"Because of me?"

It was amazing just how calm he was. "Because... it's about time. Come on, let's go look upstairs."

Devon was still clutching her tote over her shoulder when he took her arm to lead her up the stairs. Up here were two bedrooms. She'd read that there were three, so she guessed that there was another downstairs.

The master was obvious, as it took up half the footprint of the house. The large room had a pale carpet and white linen on the bed. The warm walls were a muted peach shade, and gauzy white curtains surrounded the three glazed walls that led to a balcony of their own.

Although the room was beautiful, she wanted to kick herself. "Well this was a stupid choice," she said. "They'll be able to see in here, won't they?"

Zave flicked a switch by the door and from the two ends of the solid wall, panels slid out on runners. They snaked all the way around the room to meet behind the head of the bed, encasing the whole room in a protective shell. As they closed to block the inside from intruding, warm light grew from under the bed, illuminating the space.

"Wow," she said and hurried to the nearest window panel. "These are like the ones I saw in your office." She tapped on them and found them solid.

"It's KC technology," he said. "They provide a hundred percent privacy, a hundred percent of the time. The panels are secreted in the partition walls during construction, they stack one on top of the other, and then they slide out and lock in place, ensuring there isn't any crack for light to get through."

Pointing at the bed, she began to move again. "Is this KC technology too?" she asked, and went over to peek under the bed, though she couldn't see where the light was coming from. "Can we get it for our bed at home?"

"Yes," he said.

Her exuberance must have been the cause of his smile. Suddenly, her appreciation for her role as the wife who eased her man's burdens bloomed. Just by showing him how he made her happy, she could help him to relax and see something good in himself.

"Can I ask you something?" she asked, sitting on the edge of the bed and dropping her tote onto the floor.

"Yes."

Taking the opportunity, since they were alone in their new marital bedroom, she turned his attention to their relationship. "Last night, why did you really send me to my room alone? Because today, in your office, you were open with me, and I didn't expect such a leap so quickly. Nothing I did caused it. I've barely seen you."

"Bess slapped me," he said.

It wasn't like her to get physical or to cause anyone harm. Devon gaped. "She hit you? Why?"

"For letting them win." He began to approach her. "She reminded me how many months we spent building trust, forming a bond, and how big a deal it was for me to sleep with you. I was so sure, I didn't hesitate to marry you. Everything was moving forward until Thad stole you from the Kindred."

Bobbing her head, she understood Bess' point. Syn wanted to cause fractures, they wanted to weaken and damage the Kindred and that meant attacking its members and their most treasured relationships. "Pushing me away was you giving into Syn," she muttered.

"I hate going backwards. Even if an idea doesn't work the first time, I change it and adapt and develop it into something that can work. You deserve nothing less than that same dedication. Destroying our marriage because of decisions made by others would be insane and illogical unless I was looking for an excuse to get out of it."

Worry hit her like a shot of adrenaline. "Is that what it was?" she asked. He came to a stop in front of her. "Do you want out?"

Crouching, he took her hands from her knees. "I thought about it. I left Bess when Cedric called about one of the outlets looking for comment, and I thought for a minute that I could spare you from it. That if we ended things before they really got started, you wouldn't have to deal with the media circus or the threat of Syn. And for one minute, it was the best idea I ever had."

She was pleased that he hadn't clung onto that notion. "Only a minute?"

"You know by now how my mind works. I don't think about a single step; I try to make a plan."

Like how he'd known before taking her to bed that he was going to marry her, he just hadn't clued her in. "And it was your plan to leave me?"

"When I thought about stage two and stage three of that plan, I realized they'd involve watching you walk away and when I thought about that, I got so angry."

Upset, frustrated, or distraught, she'd have understood. She'd even get how he could feel relieved, but anger? "Why were you angry?"

"Because I love you and when I tried to imagine my life with distance between us, I got so irrationally mad that you might need me and I wouldn't know it or that something might happen to you and I wouldn't be there."

"Rig would always call Raven if something bad happened to me."

"Not something bad," he said, touching her cheek. "I mean, what if I didn't know what you had for breakfast? Or I didn't know when you stubbed your toe? What if I didn't know if you'd pleasured yourself at night or worse… another man had touched you? Those are the thoughts that would torture me if you weren't near to me, shy. It's crazy, right?"

Warmed by his declaration, she was reassured. "Not so crazy," she said, putting a hand on his shoulder. "All those days when you would go away to your lab and I wouldn't see you, those are the kind of things I wondered. Is he awake? Is he thinking of me? Is he working? If I look out the window now, will I see him run by? Even when we're together, I think of you and wonder what's in your mind. You've never been at any risk of losing me, lord. Even if you tried to push me away, it would never have worked."

"It opened my eyes," he said. "Last night I wanted to put distance between us and maybe I would've kept doing that. Except just like Bess comforted you, she did the same thing for me."

Devon grinned. "She didn't hit me." She kissed his cheeks. "My poor baby, did she hurt you?"

"I think she saved this," he said, kissing the knuckles on both her hands.

"Then we'll definitely need to have a big reception when all of this is done to give her something to plan. Bess would love a chance to have a party for us."

"Speaking of which," he said. "The merger mixer is this weekend. With the media circling, the timing isn't the best, but they won't be allowed into the event."

A public place, media, crowds, it could be tough for her. "Cedric said it was important for you to show face," she said, recalling the first time she'd met Cedric, which was when she'd heard of this merger event. "How is the merger going? Did you get your reports?"

"They're still being worked on," he said. "It's been less than two weeks since we requested them, if you can believe that. We'll give them more time. Information is trickling through; I haven't had time to sit and analyze it all. I'll probably do that over the next couple of days."

So much had happened since the first day she'd been in the KC building that it felt like a million years ago. But he was right that not much time had passed. If only they'd known then what Thad was really up to and what the Mexican mission would bring.

The merger had been in the making since Grant McCormack had apparently died. Most of the hard work was done, but Zave had been relying on Zara's help and now her focus was elsewhere. "I'll be around to help if you need me," she said. "Zara has Kindred things to worry about," she said. "But if you need someone to do grunt work, that's what I've done for most of my adult life."

"Grunt work?" he said, sliding her further onto the bed. He picked her tote from the floor to move it aside. "You don't do grunt work."

Except she had never had an illustrious career. Filing, typing, making calls, they were all tasks she'd done during various jobs she'd held in her life. His action with the tote reminded her what was in there.

He probably figured that she had, but she said, "I got what you asked for."

"Good," he responded and slid a hand up her thigh under her skirt. "Do you want to play?"

Devon had more to thank Bess for than she could ever express. Having her husband offer intimacy was rare and not a suggestion she would snub. "I'm tired," she said. "But you know how to wake me up."

But he didn't flirt back, he seemed to be reflecting on something. "If the party's going to be too much for you, with the people and the noise…"

Devon had sidelined her misgivings because she couldn't worry about another thing today. After thinking about what the party would entail, she'd been confident that with Zave around, her anxieties wouldn't raise their heads. "I'll be okay. I can't be alone forever, and it's an odd thing. When you're around, when you're close enough to touch me, I never feel afraid."

His eyes narrowed. "At the party, there might be times I'll have to talk to people. I couldn't guarantee to be by your side all night. I want to be. But I wouldn't promise it because it might mean letting you down."

That did give her cause for concern. But if she was going to be married to KC's head man, she'd have to get used to corporate events. She swallowed. "If it gets too much, I can slip out," she said, and he shook his head.

"No. Not with the media sniffing around and Syn up to God knows what. If I put security around you, it might make a scene, but I'll do it if you want me to."

Putting this event to the back of her mind apparently wasn't an option. "No," she said. A scene would make her self-conscious, she didn't want half a dozen security men surrounding her at all times, blocking everyone off, and drawing all the eyes in the room. "If I'm too much of a problem, I can stay here and you can go alone."

"A problem?" he said, making eye contact again. "That word isn't in my vocabulary. I've risen to every challenge you've given me."

Already he was making her feel better enough that she could eke out a smile. "A challenge? The last time I challenged you, you started on what's in my tote."

A challenge for him tended to lead to orgasms for her. "And nobody ever said I was finished," he said and stood up to take off his shirt and slacks. "Now, Mrs. Knight, I think you should get your rest because in an hour or two we're going to make sure that trip didn't damage any of our fun."

Picking up her tote, he began to take out the toys, one at a time, to lay them on the bed. There were a couple she didn't recognize, those had to be the ones he'd said he was holding for a special occasion. The most intriguing was a gold box in the middle. He ran a finger over it in sequence with the others.

"Close your eyes, shy," he said and came around the bed to sit on the other side to begin removing her clothes. "We have a new home to settle into. A new bed to try out. As newlyweds, I think it's important that we take advantage of every second we have alone."

This might not be the manor, but he was still her lord, and when he began to massage her body, Devon exhaled her bliss. "Zave." She parted her thighs. "I think we should test those toys now."

"You're not tired?" he asked, the warmth of his breath heated her lips.

"Now that you've put the idea in my head that they might have been broken, I'll never sleep right until I know." It was a tease, but one he didn't discourage.

He laid on his side and reached over her to pick up

one of the toys, and when she tried to open her eyes, his hand rested over them to block her view. "Let me surprise you, shy." He kissed her again. "Let me show you what you mean to me and how little distance I want between us." Kissing her cheek, he licked her earlobe. "I love you."

He'd never said it without her saying it first or without prompting. With a smile on her lips, they drifted toward his. "Those words will get you just about anything with me."

"Big mistake," he murmured. "Now I have you right where I want you. Open those legs nice and wide for me, shy. We're going to test how much you can take tonight." He curled around her to whisper in her opposite ear. "And then we're going to make you take some more."

# ELEVEN

"WHAT DO YOU think?" Zave asked her from behind when he uncovered her eyes.

Her fingers loosened from his wrist when she saw the stunning blue satin gown hanging up in front of her. The walk-in closets in their new apartment were unremarkable, except that they were fully stocked with brand new everything.

Over the few days that she'd been living here with him, she'd explored the apparel and accessories inside, but she was still surprised and fascinated by hidden treasures.

This wasn't one of those exciting times and her grin slowly fell.

"It's beautiful," she said. The expensive garment was bejeweled and tailored to perfection. She couldn't deny that it was gorgeous. "But I won't be wearing it."

The merger mixer was tonight. Zave had retrieved her from their shower room, covered her eyes, and taken her to the walk-in closet while she was getting ready. He'd told her that she would have something perfect to wear and so she'd expected a dress. It was just a shame that he'd picked this one.

"You don't like it?" he asked.

Fingering the fabric of the skirt, she knew that sliding into this dress would be like wrapping herself in butter. The slick, soft material was inviting, but she let her hand drift away from it to fall at her side.

Honesty was the only way to explain her reaction. "I was wearing a blue dress when I was abducted," she said. "I wore that same dress all the months I lived in their metal box, and I made a promise to myself—"

"Say no more," he murmured and kissed the top of her head. "I have red and black options too."

Smiling at him over her shoulder, she was impressed that he was so prepared and that he didn't need her to go into great detail about why she didn't want to wear this color. "Thank you."

Zave took her hand to guide her out of the closet and into their bedroom. "You can pick which you prefer after."

"After what?" she asked.

Because he'd gone into KC today, he was still wearing his suit and didn't appear to feel any urgency about changing or preparing for the event.

Devon had been surprised that morning before he went into work when he woke her up and told her that a car was waiting for her. Without telling her what to expect, she was left wondering when she'd been whisked away and was delighted to find out that her destination was a spa. Her husband had arranged for her to be pampered for the day.

She'd thought that she was late back, but her lord hadn't been at the apartment when she returned, giving her time to shower. Devon had been drying her hair in the bathroom when he'd come in, covered her eyes, and told her he had another surprise—the dress.

As if those treats weren't enough, he took her to the bed and sat her down before retrieving a tiny gift box from the nightstand drawer.

"What's this?" she asked, adjusting the lapels of her bathrobe to let in a little more air. The bathroom had been humid, the hairdryer hadn't helped, and the whiff of Zave's cologne was making her overheat.

"We want you to feel safe and happy tonight. I don't want you to panic if you're by yourself or overwhelmed. To keep you calm and happy, I need to be able to touch you, to remind you I'm nearby even if I'm not at your side."

This was all getting rather cryptic, and she figured he was referring to the challenge they'd spoken about before. Devon's mind wasn't nearly as keen as Zave's, so she didn't even try to second guess him. "Okay," she said.

Taking her wrist, he put the box in the middle of her palm. "Where's the one place I touch you that no one else does?"

She blushed. "I don't think you can finger me on the dance floor."

"Think again," he said.

Mortified by the idea that he would think of making such a show, her chin dropped. "What will all your posh friends say if you toss up my skirt and bend me over right there in front of everyone?"

Squinting, he was confident. "Since when does my touching you have anything to do with physical contact?" he asked and nodded at the box. "Open it."

Dubious of his intentions, she had to acknowledge that he'd never embarrassed her before. Pulling the bow from the box, Devon made eye contact and thought of the time she opened the box that contained her vibrator. The first toy he'd made for her.

Zave urged her on and she took off the lid to lay it beside her. But when she unwrapped the tissue paper, she wasn't sure what they were looking at. On a square of metal were two transparent shapes with metallic lines inside them. One was curved, wider at the top than the bottom with a narrow strip leading off it. The other was long and straight.

"What are they?" she asked.

"Lie down and I'll show you," he said, taking the box from her.

They were supposed to be getting ready for a party, not starting a new game. Probably because she was anxious about being in a room with so many people, Devon didn't put up a fight. She slid back on the bed and lay down with her head on the pillow.

Zave kicked off his shoes, removed his jacket, his tie, and his shirt, and she was already salivating before he got onto the bed. Kneeling at the end, he parted her feet to move up between her knees.

"Should I take this off?" she asked when he reached over to pick up the box from the nightstand.

But he didn't answer, just put the box in front of his knees and loosened her robe for her. Opening it out, he ran his fingers from her throat, through her cleavage, to her core. Whimpering, she lifted her chest, and he lowered to suck each of her nipples into a peak. Except, it didn't seem like he was trying to arouse her, although he was doing just that. There was something clinical about the frown he had fixed on his face.

"Zave?" she asked, and he caressed her inner thighs.

"Open up real wide for me, shy." This wouldn't be the first time she'd been exposed for him, but she always enjoyed the power that ebbed inside her when she gave him her trust. "This is not the time for you to be aroused, shy," he said.

The texture of his hands as they rubbed the V of her hips made that command almost impossible to follow. "Zave," she said, but as her hips began to rise, he pushed them down again.

He'd had sex with her without hesitation earlier and being the guest at the party tonight gave them some leeway to be late. His thumbs rubbed down her outer labia against her thighs, and she sighed.

"I'm going to be with you tonight," he said. One of his hands left her body to open the lid of the gift box. "You're going to feel me with you, even when I'm not at your side."

One finger pushed down against her clit and straight toward her opening, but instead of going inside, it left her, and she whimpered. "Can I have you now?"

"Not now," he said. "All eyes will be on my beautiful wife. But you will know that you belong to me."

His hand came back, and she felt something cold circle the outer rim of her intimate threshold. Although she knew he'd put her newest toys in place, she got a surge of excitement when he bowed over her to kiss her lips. Except when she tried to extend her arms around him, he rose and pressed her legs back together as he retreated.

"Lord?"

They'd shared such a brief moment on this bed, and yet she wasn't sure she had the energy to rise from it. "Now you get to pick, red or black," he said. The back of her wrist landed on her head as she turned her narrow eyes toward him. "Don't look at me with that want, shy."

And she was pleased to see his own gaze grow in heat. "What are you going to do to me?" she asked because anticipation was half the game.

"I'm going to distract you," he said, standing at the side of their bed looking down at her. "I'm going to be with you every moment that I can, but if I have to slip away, I don't want you to feel alone."

"You plan for me to wear these while we're not alone… in public?"

Their games had always taken place in the privacy of their bedroom, until now.

"I plan to keep my promise," he said. "I will keep you safe and I will keep you satisfied. Do you trust me to do both?"

Devon didn't consider herself a prude, but the idea that he may arouse her while they were trying to charm elegant society members did make her blush. "I trust you in every way."

He held both hands toward her and although she would be happy to remain there, she rose onto her knees and put her palms on his. "Then you should pick your gown and we'll go to the event… and then we'll come home."

It was what he planned between now and then that intrigued her. "Will we make love tonight?"

He leaned in to murmur in her ear. "With what I plan to do to you, shy, I think sleep will be all you're thinking about when we come home." She wanted to argue with him because his toys always tantalized her. "Because there's not a chance in hell you'll be able to stay off my cock in the car on the way home."

Zave took her from the bed and led her into the closet. He didn't need toys. Her fluttering heart and boiling blood were ready to mount him now, and he hadn't even activated his latest gift. Zave liked to be in control and Devon liked to be in his power. Whatever he was going to do to her, Devon knew she was going to enjoy it.

***

THE FIZZING ANTICIPATION of arousal made it easy to forget where they were going. The whole time Devon was dressing, she felt naughty in the most wonderful way. As she slid on her panties, she could feel the toys he'd left on her.

Zave donned his suit and carried himself as the efficient businessman that he was. Hooking her hand into his elbow, he took her down to the car and helped her inside while he gave instructions to security as though he didn't carry their carnal secret.

Devon had worried that she might blush if he did anything to arouse her. But the truth was, the heat hadn't left her face since she'd left their bed. She waited for something to happen in the car, but nothing did. There was no chance for her to be anxious about the party or the crowd. She was too busy thinking about how it would feel when he touched her without being near to her and while they were in public, something he'd never done before.

They got all the way to the hotel, out of the car, and through the lobby before it hit her where they were actually headed. They hadn't taken four steps into the grand ballroom, that was brimming with people and littered with champagne, when she stopped.

Devon's hand nestled in his elbow, and it curled tighter. "If you want to leave, we can," he murmured when he turned toward her.

But she could already see the faces around them registering who they were. Some people smiled, others waved. Zave didn't reciprocate at all and when she tilted her head, she saw that his concern was on her. He hadn't even noticed that there was anyone else in the room.

"No," she said, touching his lapel.

Then she wondered if she was allowed to do that because she'd never been to a party where there was decorum and protocol to worry about. As usual, he read her mind, and when she faltered and tried to remove her hand, he caught it, and pressed it against his chest.

"I don't care what these people think, shy." He let go of her hand to elevate her chin. "Your happiness is all that matters to me."

Devon took that to mean that she couldn't go wrong in his eyes, that she could act in any way and do anything, and he wouldn't let himself be embarrassed by it. But that didn't mean she was comfortable with drawing negative attention.

She was his wife, a reflection of him, and a conundrum as far as these people were concerned. Xavier Knight marrying at all was headline-worthy news, but marrying a strange woman who had no breeding, no money, and no standing in the business world, they had to wonder how she'd come to be in this coveted position.

Devon knew that Zave was rich, successful, and brilliant, but when she thought about him, she remembered the man she'd seen on the shore, so intent and dedicated to his task that his focus was complete. He'd been aware of everything, of where the cliff met the shore, of the wind, of the device he held in his hand, and somehow, he'd been aware of her, peeking through the narrow space of the open window, staring down at him.

"Devon?"

The depth of his concern snapped her out of the memory, and she smiled. "I don't want to drink too much."

"You don't have to drink at all," he said.

Although they should probably be schmoozing by now, talking to him relaxed her, so she embraced this chance knowing that it may be the last one she had tonight. The faces around them were coming closer. Although they didn't speak yet, Devon could hear the questions, the sycophants and their compliments, fawning, pandering, all things that Zave would hate. So, for this moment, alone as husband and wife, she kept the conversation genuine.

"You never do."

"I don't," he said. "I gave it up like everything else."

"You think if you drink, you'll return to your partying

ways again?" she asked, and he lowered to kiss her hair.

"The only parties I'm interested in are the private ones I have with you."

Cedric came over before she could respond, and although Zave had told his colleague that they would be attending, Cedric seemed surprised that they'd actually come. He introduced them to a dozen people and then a dozen more. It was like being married to a rock star. Everybody wanted a moment of Zave's time, either to request a favor, or to tell him how wonderful he was.

Those from CI were a little more hostile, tenser, but no one was outright rude. What surprised her most was although Zave kept his responses to everyone brief, he was sympathetic and much more patient than she ever thought he could be.

Devon lost count of the number of times he mentioned his uncle who had started CI. He spoke of his great respect for Grant McCormack Senior and how he planned to keep the company great. Perhaps it was conspicuous to her, but he never once mentioned his cousin Grant McCormack Junior, the man everyone in this room considered dead, but whom she'd stood in front of and listened to as he recounted his plans for world domination.

The man in jeans with the unkempt hair hadn't struck her as a consummate professional businessman. But she'd also sensed something lacking in what he tried to project. He didn't carry himself as a hooligan, like Caine did. Caine pulled off the thug act without giving it a thought, with him it was effortless. He told the world he didn't give a fuck, and she believed that he meant it.

Leatt was genuine, which in itself was odd. He didn't try to be cool or to exude apathy. Leatt hadn't tried to make himself seem any more or less dangerous than he was. These were all things that Grant McCormack seemed to be trying to make himself out to be.

Grant wanted her to fear him, he wanted to seem dangerous, edgy, to seem like the world should get out of his way or risk his wrath. But Devon didn't get that sense from him.

"You don't mind, do you?"

Devon had again been lost in thought, as she had been frequently tonight. The group of men she'd been standing with were talking about projects she was unaware of and so she'd zoned out because the technical specification was too detailed for her to follow.

Cedric smiled, and then the men were moving away, Zave included.

This was it. The test.

Devon was near the edge of the room, but not in a corner, which made her vulnerable. Zave had held true to his word, she'd stuck to non-alcoholic drinks all night. There were so many people here, and she'd only met some of them. It was a wonder to watch them all conversing and smiling.

She had never been in a room full of so many perfect people. Every item of clothing was tailored and from high-end designers. Apparel was complemented by shoes that looked brand new and jewels that sparkled when they caught the light of the crystal chandeliers that hung high above.

The ballroom was immaculate, there weren't empty glasses lying around, used napkins, or cardboard beer mats. All of these things would be found at any of the bars she'd gone to on nights out before. Until now, that was what she considered a party—going and sitting in some dimly-lit corner bar, surrounded by sweating bodies and faded tee shirts. But not this.

These people were from different levels of Knight Corp and Cormack Industries. There wasn't an eyelash out of place. The men's hair was gelled, and handkerchiefs stuck from breast pockets. Devon couldn't imagine that any of these people could understand what she had been through. But the Kindred proved that not everything was as it seemed.

# TWELVE

MOST OF THE people here probably thought that Xavier Knight was eccentric or selfish. He'd shut himself away, hundreds of miles from the building where the hard work was done and conducted himself from a distance, like these people were somehow beneath him and he could do whatever he saw fit to do and they were expected just to put up with it.

But he wasn't like that. He was generous and risked his life completing missions to save others. Devon couldn't dislike or resent anyone here because as she looked at the beautiful women with their shining hair and flawless makeup, she found herself trying to identify the youngest, most vulnerable ones, considering that they may be candidates for one of the cartels metal boxes.

These unsuspecting women could find themselves just as she had. One day they could be going about their business, living their lives, and then boom, everything changes.

Devon wondered if any of the voices she'd heard on those nights she spent in her box belonged to anyone that these people might know. Could they have been a daughter to one of these people? A cousin? A friend?

Her belly grew tighter, and her breathing became

shallower as the voices around her seemed to get louder. She knew it was an illusion and that her anxiety was growing with each second that she stood here alone without a distraction or protection, without her husband.

"Uh," she yelped, and her hand flattened on her stomach when a zing of pleasure fired between her thighs.

Right there on her clit, it was warm and the stimulation began to grow. What had been nothing but a sea of faces a few seconds ago became a blur. When her gaze lifted to the right, it landed on her husband, who stood clear on the other side of the room. But his eyes were on her. This was it. The warm, tingling grew, and although he stood with others and his expression didn't change, Devon was sure the others were as blurred to him as they were to her.

Any thought of anxiety was gone, just like before they got here, because he could feel the way he caressed her. The pulsing on her clit seemed to circle counterclockwise in a slow, deliberate move that fired down toward her opening and return before reaching it. Zave was touching her, pleasing her, and she couldn't ignore the enlivening effect of what he was doing.

Retreating toward the wall, she came up against a square column and was pleased of the physical support at her back. While others sipped champagne and exchanged small talk, a whisper of contact tickled her opening, and she could feel herself growing more ready for the man controlling her emotions from the width of a room away.

It became more difficult to focus on his gaze when the sensations grew. A weight sank through her body into her core, pushing and contorting her hormones from within. This wasn't as intense as the vibrator or invasive as the egg; it was subtle but stimulating enough that it was like hearing the whisper of his words and the promise of what lay in her future.

Licking her lips, Devon took in a breath and saw a couple of people nearby peering at her. Did they know what her husband was doing to her? Did they recognize what the flush in her cheeks and the obvious pulse in her neck meant? Could they sense her arousal, or was she being paranoid? Partygoers had been examining her all night, just as she'd known they would.

Devon was the woman who'd stolen Xavier Knight. To them, she was enigmatic and mysterious, two things she'd never been before in her life. But she was a stranger intriguing those who were a part of Zave's circle or at least felt they were entitled to be.

She wasn't one of those people and never would've been if it wasn't for the Kindred and her brother. The vibration stopped, and her quiet inhale was almost a squeal. She took two steps forward when she saw a tray of champagne passing and snagged a flute.

Devon needed something cold and immediate to cool her. She'd just finished the glass when her husband appeared in front of her. "Did you enjoy that, shy?" he asked and took the empty flute from her fingers to discard it on the nearest table.

There was a light in his eyes that invigorated her. He was a serious man in a place he didn't want to be, and she didn't know if he was referring to the champagne or his previous act. "It was incredible," she whispered. As much as she'd tried all night to restrain herself from being too affectionate, Devon tucked her hands under his jacket onto his ribs. "It's incredibly dangerous, though."

"Dangerous? You felt pain?" he asked, and his worry made her wish she could kiss him.

"No, nothing but pleasure, I promise." Glancing around, she made sure that no one was standing too close, but she lowered her volume even more anyway. "What would you have done if I came?"

"I'd have been incredibly disappointed to miss it," he said. "Because your pussy squeezes me so tight when you climax, I'd have missed out on a treat."

He was flirting with her in the most explicit way, in the most public of settings. He had to know that it wasn't just the media who were scrutinizing him, it was all of his corporate colleagues and peers, as well. But he didn't care, he was focused on her, distracting her, making her feel good to distract her from her apprehension.

She smiled. "Talking like that doesn't help to cool me

down."

"I kept it brief and the intensity low. I wanted you to feel it before I took you to the edge."

Anticipation ticked her heart. "There's more?" she asked. It had been about all she could take in this public setting to feel like his fingers were caressing her in the most incredible way that usually only took place when there wasn't another soul in sight.

"A lot more," he said. "And you should get used to it. I like turning you on, shy. It tests my control to do it in a place like this."

So that was what he was doing. Control turned him on, and knowing that she was ready for him, craving him, while he was forced to restrain himself. It gave him back some of that excitement. She hoped it wasn't punishment, she hoped he didn't use these people as a way to constrain himself.

"We could go somewhere," she said, sliding her hands up his chest to link them at the back of his neck. "This is a hotel. I'm sure you could afford a room. Did you bring your credit card?"

"I think they'd spot us," he said. "We're supposed to be networking, making connections."

Pushing onto her tiptoes, she knew she couldn't taste his mouth, but that didn't stop her from getting close. "I'm thinking about making a deep connection, lord," she murmured. He wasn't the only one who could play with innuendo. "Connecting with you in the most complete way."

He began to lower and she thought he might kiss her. If he broke the rules of decorum, she wasn't going to argue.

"You do make a beautiful couple."

The voice to their left startled them both. People had been approaching all night, and given their current proximity, they were probably still the focus of a lot of eyes right now.

"You bastard," Zave said and began to turn.

Devon tightened her grip. "Not here. He's shown up here like this because it's so public, right, Thad?"

He was wearing a tux and was as coiffed as everyone else here. He would probably have received an invitation before the Mexico mission. Technically, he was family, so no one would have refused him entry.

"You've got some nerve showing up here," Zave said. "What is it you want, turncoat?"

Arousal became panic; Devon didn't know how to control this confrontation. "You were warned," Thad said and took a flash drive from his pocket. He didn't even try to offer it to Zave, he just reached over and popped it into his pocket.

"What the fuck is that, some virus to eat our system? You think I'm dumb enough to—

"Instructions," Thad said. "It's instructions. I was told to come here and deliver it."

"You're running Saint's errands now? That was worth shitting all over the rest of us for?" Zave asked. "I should've put Rave on a rooftop tonight. If we thought you'd be so stupid to—"

"If we thought Raven was on a rooftop, I wouldn't have come."

Zave sneered. "Don't you get it? That's why they sent you. You're expendable. Saint can't come. Mitchell can't come. Fuck sake, this room is swarming with CI employees, and they're both supposed to be dead. Leatt's a nobody, but he's shown he has abilities. He can think on his feet. Caine was a good get, how did you manage that?"

It wasn't anger alone that flavored Zave's words. There was a disgust and a resentment that made Thad's betrayal all the more potent. "Caine's worked for Saint before, when he was legit."

Her husband was tense and angry. Devon hated what this unexpected argument had done to their night. "I know that," Zave said. "I was in the same fucking meetings that you were. Did you forget sitting around Rave's dinner table the night you met Zar? You fucking prick."

"Yeah, and you all hated Caine that night," Thad said, arguing back, showing some fire. "Raven was ready to take him out, and how many months later was it that they were working together to take down Cuckoo? People switch sides in this game, Falcon, it's what they do. Everyone's out for themselves."

"Not the Kindred," Zave said. "No one has ever

walked away, except you. Is that what you want to be remembered for? Trailblazer betrayer? You will taste Maverick's rage, you know that. I don't give a fuck who you are."

Thad lunged forward. "And is Rave gonna tell my mother what he did? Is he?"

Zave lowered his head and without blinking he returned the rage radiating from Thad. "Yes, he will and I'll be standing next to him, Zara too, and we'll tell her how we took you down, and Saint, and your fucking Daddy, and I bet she'll be proud of every fucking one of us."

Thad looked at Devon as if she should calm Zave or tell him to temper what he was saying, but she wouldn't. Bess would never be happy to see her son die, Devon just knew it, she didn't need to be told. But there wasn't a chance in hell she was going to make Thad feel better or reassure him in any way. There may come a time when they had to take him down, and it would be on Raven to do that.

"You shouldn't have got in our way," Thad said, moving a few inches back. "Dempsey was ours."

"And instead you stole a kid, a kid who worked for Sikorski, a kid who's useless to you. Swift never taught him shit. You want to do what you're doing then do it, I don't fucking care. But Saint's a fucking idiot if he thinks he can mimic the Kindred and achieve more than us. You don't need to fill every Kindred position. All you need is focus and determination."

"Giving us tips?" Thad asked, disbelieving and snide. "You think we need your instructions? Typical fucking Zave, you think you know so much better than everyone. You and Raven and your little secret talks and Swift, always swooping in there to save everybody's asses, doing all the leg work while the rest of us just sit back and watch, waiting to be handed out grunt work. All of you are arrogant fucking pricks who deserve to be shown you're not all that. You're nothing special. You've just had a run of luck."

"A run of luck?" Zave asked. "It's called hard work and like I said, focus, determination. We never thought we were special. We never thought we could rule the world. We made a difference where we could—"

"Thinking small," Thad spat back. "Fixing one problem at a time. One man. One job."

"You want to raise a fucking army?" Zave asked. "It doesn't make sense. I can believe Mitchell is that arrogant. Fuck, we all know that Saint is. You want to talk about people who think they're special, look no further than Grant McCormack Junior, the boy who always thought he was better. The boy who even when we were kicking around in diapers wouldn't get mud on his shoes. Do you think that's the guy who's going to make a difference in the world and think big? Why? Because he's squirreled away some money? Stolen a few supplies? What is it that Syn even want? Are you just going to keep plugging away until you have a million men standing behind you and then what? You want land? Your own fucking country? Your own planet? It won't ever be enough, and you turned your fucking back on everyone who would stand beside you, everyone who would have laid down to die for you. Fucking us meant fucking yourself. You're here because you're expendable. You're of no use to them."

"I'm of use to my father."

"Your father who took out mine and Raven's? He'll destroy anything to get what he wants, which is just the same as what Saint wants, the same as what Leatt wants. Power. You never wanted power."

"Maybe I did," Thad said. "Maybe I just never got the chance to taste it because I was always running around after you, after Raven. You guys never respected me."

"What the fuck did you want? You were given access to everything you ever wanted. Did you want us to pat you on the head and tell you how amazing you were?"

"I wanted you to trust me," Thad said. "Any time shit hit the fan, it wasn't me you turned to, even when I was right in front of your fucking face. You'd go to Raven on the other side of the country or call and he'd be here in a day. If I needed anything, I'd wait a week and a half."

"So you just weren't invited to the cool kids table? Wow, maybe you and Saint are suited."

"Saint?" Devon asked, getting her first chance to

speak.

Zave glanced at her. "It's what we called Grant McCormack when we were kids because he would never do anything wrong. He followed the rules, and he was the perfect child who tattletaled on the rest of us."

And wouldn't get mud on his shoes, she thought. The men returned to glaring at each other, and she took it on herself to break the stalemate. "If you've done what you came to do, you can leave," she said, moving in at her husband's side to slide an arm around his waist. "Or we can have security remove you."

"And cause a scene?" Thad asked. "I'm family, think of what the media would say to that. I don't think you'll do that."

"Think again," Zave said, fixating on Thad. Raising an arm, he summoned three men who approached as if from absolutely nowhere to close around the doctor. "My cousin's had too much to drink. I think you should escort him out. Make sure he gets a ride home. Thad, if you come near me or my wife again, you won't receive this same generosity."

He nodded once, and the three men began to take Thad out. The doctor had said that his removal would cause a scene, but it didn't. People noticed, but Thad didn't kick and scream, so they just whispered at each other as they had all night.

Devon could only watch the progress of Thad's escorted departure for a short distance, but Zave had height that allowed him to see farther. Remaining silent while he watched the progress she couldn't see, Devon waited for her husband to confirm that the unwanted guest had gone.

Which he did when he looked down at her again. "Are you okay?" he asked, stroking her arms and her shoulders. "I should get you home."

But she took his arm and drew him to a stop before he could get more than a couple of steps. Prioritizing her meant he didn't address a potential hazard handed to him by a man they could no longer trust. Devon wouldn't let him risk ignoring that threat. "That thing he put in your pocket, is it dangerous?"

"I don't know. But I'm not touching it. We'll lift fingerprints, do physical forensics on the thing before we let Swift do a digital sweep."

"Swift isn't here," she said, but he brushed his thumb down her cheek and took his phone from his pocket.

"Thad was right about one thing." Zave dialed his phone. "If I need something, they'll be here within a day."

Zave didn't worry about civilities after he decided they were leaving. He spoke into his phone for a few minutes, then put an arm around her and took her out of the ballroom, ignoring anyone who tried to intercept them.

Devon was relieved to be back in the limo but worried about the tension her husband exuded. There was nothing they could do until the others arrived, and it hurt her right down to the tips of her toes that Thad had come and ruined what was supposed to be a wonderful night.

Devon had known it was going to be tense for them because Zave hadn't been out in public for so long, and she was a complete newbie. But it wasn't supposed to be about the Kindred or about Syn and peril.

She and Zave had been tasked with keeping up appearances, that was what the night had been about. That and just being them, just being married and together for a while. With his new toy and her experience of being pleasured by him from afar, he'd promised her that the night was supposed to end on a positive note, not like this.

Since they left the hotel, he'd been sitting with his elbow on the sill of the door with his knuckles over his lips, growling at the view he probably couldn't decipher beyond the window. Twisting her body toward his, she stroked both hands around his thigh, from the top to the inside.

"Lord?" she said, and his hand dropped from his mouth. "Show me what it can do."

This request was enough to make him turn. "Not tonight, sweetheart," he said, brushing a knuckle down her cheek. "I have business to think about."

"KC is fine. The merger is going ahead." He had to see through her deliberate attempt to divert him, but he didn't let her get away with it.

"Kindred business."

"The Kindred won't be here for hours. Didn't you say they would arrive in the morning? Do you plan to brood all night?" she asked. "Do I need to do a Bess and slap you to remind you that we're not letting them take over our lives?"

The harsh set of his brow softened a fraction, and he leaned forward. "Keep driving, Phil. We're not ready to go home yet." Twisting, he pressed the button to raise the privacy screen, ensconcing them in a secret shell. "You like the toys," he said, and she nodded. "You once told me you felt like an experiment."

He was stroking her face, the side of her neck, her shoulder. The beautiful dress she wore was red satin covered with a red and black lace that made the gown more exquisite than any she'd worn in the past.

"It amazes me," she said, tipping up her chin. "That a man as incredible as you spoils me like you do."

He slid the back of his fingers over the swell of her breast and allowed them to descend to her hip. Gathering her skirt, he exposed her thighs and stroked them with the flat of his palm. "And it amazes me I found a woman so forgiving, one who understands me when I can't understand myself."

He was so thorough in everything he did, so curious, not only about his technology and machines, but about her body, about each freckle, each crevice and rise. He scrutinized how every inch of her reacted to his varying caress. Pushing one knee away, he opened her legs wide. Hooking his strong calf over her shin, he touched her.

"Let me take them off," he said, skimming his fingertips up the delicate flesh of her inner thigh.

"No," she said, dropping a hand onto his before it could reach the lace of her underwear. "I want to know. What could you have done to me?"

"This is the beginning, shy. You will feel everything you want to feel, and if you like it, you can experience it again and again."

Over time she'd get used to being in crowds again, just as he would. They wouldn't need these games to distract each other. Although Devon wouldn't give up their trust and wouldn't discourage his public displays of secret affection.

Now that she'd seen him in action, she understood. She wasn't the only one dealing with anxiety in these groups where expectations were high. Everyone stayed quiet when Xavier Knight spoke. But he didn't want influence, he didn't trust that he deserved it or that his decisions were sound.

This was probably why he relied on Cedric to make many business choices while Zave focused on the tech that he was confident he knew. With regards to the Kindred, his relationship with Brodie gave both of them a crutch, one that they now knew Thad resented.

"What would you like, my shy?" he asked, and although she was ensnared by his gaze, Devon was aware of his hand leaving her leg and snaking its way into his pocket. Again, a silent buzz moved through her. She hadn't heard him flip a switch or press a button. She didn't hear a motor or anything that would suggest vibrations, and yet, she could feel them.

Pursing her lips, she whimpered. "That's amazing."

"Slide your hips to the edge," he murmured. "Close your eyes."

She did both, and he must have taken his control from his pocket and maybe switched hands because his hand returned to her thigh as the other arm coiled around her back and brought her head onto his shoulder.

The heat that moved around her clit in delightful swirls made her swell and grow ready to accept him. "How are you doing this?" she gasped in a whispered exhale. "How…? How does it work?"

He drew circles on the inside of her knee that mirrored those whirling around her clit, and the pressure grew, wringing more juice from her passage. Zave turned his lips against her hair. "It works on the same concept as our earpieces and draws its power from your body."

So the hotter she was, the hotter it got. Devon liked the sound of that. "The elements inside react to the heat, and they undulate at different frequencies that stimulate you exactly as I tell them to."

All of her was enlivened, the pressure, the heat, the

vibration, every inch of her was exposed. Lifting her hips, she invited his hand higher as it ascended her inner thigh. "Oh God, Zave," she whispered as the pulse became a thrum, became a beat, and the bass in her core thumped so hard she wriggled against it.

He touched her panties and whispered into her ear, "You've soaked right through these. Take them off."

At his mercy and used to following his commands, she did exactly as he requested in a hurried, undignified wriggle. But she was already moaning and gasping in short, shallow pants that she knew were a prelude to the crescendo. When her ass hit the seat again, he pushed her legs apart as they had been before and drove two digits inside of her. She screamed and bucked up, grabbing hold of his lapel.

"Oh, yes! Yes!" she called out as he finger-fucked her in the back of this premium vehicle that was driving aimlessly through the city streets, giving him time to bring her to climax.

Her whole body was vibrating, not because of the devices that were still stimulating her, but because the impact of orgasm wouldn't subside as he turned up the intensity.

"I can't take any more," she said and opened her drowsy eyes to find his lingering just above. Her head lolled to his shoulder.

Zave dropped his lips onto hers. "What did I tell you before we came out?" he asked. Taking her hand from his lap, he slid it up and pressed it against the erection he'd freed at some point.

Filled with desperate need, she leaped up, ready to climb aboard. But he sat her down and came over her, resting a knee on the seat between her thighs. "Close your eyes," he said.

The heat didn't lessen, but the vibration seemed to slow. Although he slid his fingers down through her slick flesh, she didn't realize that he'd removed the toy until he sat back down and tossed the strips to the floor.

She was disappointed that her experience with their newest game was over until she saw that her husband was seated, ready for her. Devon climbed astride his lap and sank down onto his dick. "Oh, lord," she said, rising and lowering in the cramped space of the back of this car.

Although they weren't restricted at either side, it took her some time to get used to the ceiling height, although Devon learned quickly how the roof could give her valuable leverage if she laid her palms upon it. Freeing the underarm zipper, Zave helped her arms out of the dress and pressed her hands back to the ceiling. As she rode him hard, he kissed and licked and suckled on her, pushing her into another orgasm.

If she had tried to make love with him or stimulate him on her own, he'd have put up resistance given that he'd been in such a bad mood. The toy had helped her to win more than just her own pleasure. Zave had a compulsion to fulfill her every request, and tonight was not an exception. By giving her what she wanted, he too got the chance to find oblivion.

Devon was so proud of him for facing his cousin, for telling the truth, for resisting the urge to scream at Thad or pummel him. Whatever was on the device that Thad had given them, they would learn all of that tomorrow.

But she wouldn't be fulfilling her duty as his wife if she allowed him to brood and sulk all night. When he seized her waist and yanked her down, he spilled himself into her, and Devon knew his release was more than physical. She didn't rush away from his lap, even after they were done. She stayed here, stroking him and holding him. Her body stayed limp on his.

As he held her, she felt his need for more than just sex, he needed her comfort and reassurance that he wasn't alone. As much as he might believe he deserved to be punished, his subconscious didn't want to be abandoned.

Devon was happy to stay in his lap, even as Zave ordered the driver home. When she had to, she would dress and they'd go upstairs to bed where she hoped they would enjoy each other again. But she wasn't budging from this spot on his lap one second before she had to.

# THIRTEEN

"OKAY," TUCK DECLARED to the room, leaning back in the dining chair to link his fingers at the back of his head. "The good news is it's not gonna blow up the building."

Everyone gravitated back toward him. Devon and Zara had been standing on the balcony talking about bullshit, both of them aware that they were biding time until Tuck was done. Kadie had been chatting with them until Tuck began muttering to himself, and that was when she'd gone over to sit at her boyfriend's side.

Zave and Brodie had, as per usual, been whispering with each other. This time they elected to stand in the kitchen, not to do anything, just in prime position to keep an eye on everyone else.

They all crowded around Tuck, but he picked up the laptop and strode toward the living room on the other side of the staircase, where he put the machine on the entertainment center beneath the large-screen, wall-mounted television.

He turned on the TV, pressed a few buttons, and a few seconds later the screen matched the laptop display. Tuck stood up and gestured everyone over. "Sit down, you're gonna want to see this," he said, and it didn't take more than a few seconds for everyone to seat themselves in the living room on the couch and armchair around the TV.

"What's going on?" Zara asked.

As though this was a standard presentation, Tuck cracked his knuckles and took a breath. "They're not asking for weapons, and there are a couple of files on there which will mean something to you, Falc, but the schematics are crude, and it's nothing we couldn't deliberately sabotage."

"So why give it to us?" Zara asked, sliding further into her place on the couch between Devon and her husband.

Brodie was at the end of the couch, and Kadie was at the other end on Devon's other side. Zave was seated on an armchair beyond Kadie, and Devon wanted to go and sit with him but didn't want her comfort to be conspicuous.

"Why are we sitting around here if it just contains a couple of engineering plans? Unless it's about Game Time, do you think—"

"No," Tuck said. "This is incendiary."

"What does that mean?" Devon asked, and Kadie took her hand.

"It's a message," Kadie said, looking at her man, who was standing in front of the television.

Tuck went to tap a key on the keyboard, then paused in a crouch to look at Zara. "Rave, Swallow, I don't know which one of you we'll have to tie down, but you're definitely gonna want to see this."

Devon wanted to see it, too, if for no other reason than to learn what all the fuss was about. Zave touched a button that was built into the cube table next to his chair, and the lights dimmed as the panels she'd now become familiar with slid from the walls to cover the windows, plunging the room into complete darkness.

Tuck pressed another button on the computer and white noise faded up. There was a crackle.

A few seconds ago, this space had been benign. Despite the obvious class of the environment, they were just people standing in an apartment. Now it felt like a secret military bunker, like they'd hunkered down in a trench, ready for warfare.

With bated breath, Devon anticipated what their

enemy's first move may be.

A light flickered onto the wide television screen, and it illuminated the body of a man. They couldn't see his face. All around him was dark, but he was sitting in a chair wearing jeans and a blue checked shirt.

His hands curled around the arms of what appeared to be an executive chair. Devon didn't know who he was, and she wondered why he'd shrouded his face, at least until Zara broke the thick silence.

"It's Grant," Zara whispered, and Devon glanced around to see Zara dig her nails into Brodie's thigh.

"I wish I could be there to see your face, Zar," came the slow words from the shaded man on the screen. "I don't know whether to laugh or apologize. It's tough to think that just a few years ago we were worker bees in corporate offices. You'd never have envisioned this future. But I could. The only difference between my plan and this reality is where you are. You were supposed to be with Syn, not there with those cretins.

"But..." he said, raising his hands and slapping them onto the arms of his chair. "You've made your choice. I miss you. But I wouldn't have you here. He's changed who you are, and that woman is corrupt."

"The fucker," Brodie growled, and Zara dug her nails in deeper.

"I had to contact you to straighten out a few things. Our messenger didn't make things clear enough. Maybe, Devon, you didn't understand quite what you'd stumbled onto when you hitched yourself to the Kindred wagon. We knew your brother was a lowlife, but we didn't give you credit for quite how you'd insinuated yourself into the heart of my brilliant cousin."

Although his face was still in darkness, Grant's body turned, ironically, in the direction of where Zave sat as if he could see him. It wasn't a drastic move, it was subtle, but enough to set her on edge. "Zave, you could've made an excellent member of our team," Grant said. "I'm sorry we didn't mobilize quick enough to show you our abilities. Of all the people I imagine are in that room with you now, you are the one we would welcome. Your brilliant mind made KC what it is and bailed CI out more than once. I doubt you knew it, but our fathers worked more closely together than either you or I realized. They used both of us, just like they used Frank.

"But that doesn't matter now. Syn are about the future. We have an objective, one I won't share with you. We require technology that will have to be built and programmed. The schematics are on this device, and we will expect delivery within ten days."

"He has no shame," Kadie muttered.

"I can hear your ridiculous, righteous objections, but they mean nothing to me, and my objective will not harm any of you. The bottom line is the Kindred owe Syn. By sparing your lives, we're doing you a kindness, and we're only willing to do that if you comply with our demands. Albert Sutcliffe was an easy mark, one who was meant to be a stepping stone. Taking his compound and the supplies he'd amassed, the weaponry, it would've set Syn in a strong, starting position, given us a valuable foundation."

"I hope he talks more about how we fucked him," Brodie grumbled with satisfaction.

"Given the Kindred's interference, you can understand why we resent any possible future involvement you may have that is not sanctioned by Syn. Over time, you will see that Syn are not the Kindred's enemy. Although, that may change if you deviate from our requests."

"He wouldn't be Saint without a superiority complex," Tuck said, folding his arms.

"Brother, you stole from me." Grant kept talking. "You stole the compound and bartered it to an insignificant ally. You double-crossed me, emptying the bunker that contained bounty meant for Syn. But my hatred for you is rooted in our past. You know there is no salvation for us. I despise you and everything you stand for. The final straw was when you took from me the woman who was supposed to be on my side."

Brodie began to stand, and Zara slapped an arm on his chest to hinder him enough that she could leap into his lap. "Stay put," she commanded, and he shoved her aside so he could continue to watch the screen with her on his knee.

"You are to stay away. This mission is for Zave and for Tuck, they will repay the Kindred's debt. If they do, we will return the boy and you can keep Dempsey. We shall go our separate ways. If you do not, we will follow through on our threats to ruin the Kindred. We will share evidence of Raven's misdeeds and Falcon's. Oh, and of course, the boy will die. All of you have something to lose."

"We're not the only ones, fucker," Brodie snarled.

"Mitchell tells me how I should maintain my business acumen; how important it is to maneuver in these negotiations and to maintain a level of professional detachment. Zara, you remember our meetings? The late nights in the office, the meals we shared alone, the intimate conversation."

Brodie tried to rise again, and Zara dug her heel into his foot. "He's trying to get a rise out of you, beau. There's no one here for you to shoot, so stay down."

Grant paused. "You have already lost Art, Kindred. Your revered chief is gone. We have taken your doctor; Thad stands with us. How many more men can you lose and still function? Our numbers are growing. From the Sutcliffe mess, we learned who Leatt was, watched him, groomed him, and brought him into our fold. He's valuable. As is Griffin Caine, my brother's greatest enemy." Devon heard a smile in Grant McCormack's voice. "He will prove most valuable. His hatred of my brother almost matches my own. And he is another man, Zara, that you have lost because of your loyalty to the man you share your bed with."

Devon didn't know Grant McCormack well. She'd met him and heard stories of him. What she was learning now was that he liked the sound of his own voice, he was enjoying this, and believed in his own importance. It was clear that he liked wielding power and that he liked hurting others.

"Back to business," Grant said, clearing his throat. "The details of what we need are on the USB drive. You will have to work hard. We know it will be your instinct to tamper with or ruin the devices, but not all of our people will be at the handover. We will protect ourselves. The information we have will be encoded to send to authorities automatically unless Mitchell or myself is there to deactivate the message. And the boy, it's up to you if he lives or dies. Mess with us, and we won't give you a second chance. We will put a bullet in him if you do anything we don't like. He's expendable. Almost as expendable as the women who sit there with you. Even Zara, who I once would've given my life to protect."

"Yeah, right," Tuck said. "He only protects himself."

"You mean nothing to me now. Just as Devon means nothing, and Kadie means nothing. Your females have no value, and they are easy targets. Hurt us again, and our primary mission will be to destroy everything you love. If you think we are incapable or you believe yourselves superior, think of where we are now. You're talking to a dead man who you were all convinced was gone. I didn't even have to commit a crime to fake my death. You orchestrated that for me, usurped my company, sold it to our cousin. If I stroll into the FBI and tell them I've been kept prisoner, your crimes will send you to their deepest pits for the rest of time. They'll uncover the Kindred, all of their work, but it won't seem good. We will make sure you are seen as the most evil, despicable criminal organization who are working underground in this country, killing and raping for your own gain, thinking of nothing but yourselves and your own sick wants."

"We're sick?" Tuck muttered.

Grant exhaled a laugh. "Something for you to think about as you fall asleep tonight in his arms, Zar. I can turn him into the most hated and notorious man in the world, and what will you be left with then?"

The next pause was so long that Devon thought the video was finished. But Grant moved, sitting forward in his chair enough that his features were caught in the edge of the light giving them a smoky hue. So, while they were not entirely distinguishable, they made him seem like a ghost, hidden in a shadow, staring through the night, pouring his evil purpose into each of their souls.

"All you had to do was toss me the keys, Zar. Your life would've been so different…"

His voice faded off into a whisper so soft that his lips

didn't move. The image froze and faded to darkness, plunging them into the same abyss.

Devon wasn't going to speak first. It wasn't her place. Grant had referred to her, but this was a message for the Kindred veterans. Kadie squeezed her hand, and Devon remembered that she'd been clutching it throughout the message. After another few seconds, there was a click and recessed lighting flared on around the coving in the room.

Maybe each of the Kindred were waiting for the others to speak. Zara stayed on Brodie's lap with his arms loose around her waist. Kadie was looking at Tuck who stood next to Zave's chair, and Zave was staring at the floor.

"We should get to work," Zave said and got to his feet. Tuck actually took a step toward him, as if he was going to follow, and that was when Kadie leaped up and rushed into Tuck.

"You can't do what they're saying," Kadie said. "You can't give in to them. It's scaremongering, they're threatening you!"

"What do you want me to do, Toots? If we do nothing, your pet will die. Do you want them to kill your pet?"

Kadie's hands dropped away from his body. She sidestepped, Tuck kissed her temple and patted Zave's shoulder once, which prompted him to move again. Devon wasn't going to give up so easily.

"What about Bess?" Devon asked, and the men stopped again. She had to get up to turn and see them in the space behind the couch. "We have to bring her here."

Zave nodded and took his phone from his pocket.

"Won't she be more at risk here?" Kadie asked.

"She's more at risk out there on her own," Devon said. "If Thad's in town, the rest of them could be."

She had thought about Bess last night before she and Zave got intimate in the car. But she couldn't believe that Thad could hurt his mother. So if he'd chosen to go and talk to his mother, maybe Bess could get him to see sense. At least they would both get closure.

Mitchell had promised that Bess wouldn't be hurt. But in light of this development, Devon didn't think it was right that she be left out there alone.

Zave put his phone back into his pocket. "Security will pick her up, and she'll be here within the hour," he said.

Typical that Zave should send men without warning Bess they were coming. Devon wasn't going to let Bess be scared by the sudden arrival of strangers. She'd give her a call and let her know what was going on. Everyone was moving again until Zara surged up.

"Swift, there has to be a way to get in touch with him," Zara said.

Tuck turned. "Why do you want to get in touch with him?"

Grant had said that the details were on the USB drive, and Devon took that to mean the meeting place would be on there too. She doubted that Syn would be as dumb as to give the Kindred a map to their base, though. But Zara had to be talking about the man on the tape, the one she'd been close to at some point. Getting in touch with Grant would probably be impossible. Even if it wasn't, Devon questioned the merit of reaching out to the sociopath.

Squaring her jaw, Zara deliberately kept her attention away from her husband. "Because I can talk to him," she said.

Brodie slowly rose from the couch, and Devon wasn't the only one who shrank back. "You're going nowhere near him," Brodie grumbled. "I am not going through this shit again. You heard what he said. You mean nothing to him."

"I have to try," Zara said, assured in her determination. Devon had to give her points for courage. "I know Mitchell. I know Caine. I know Leatt—"

"All of them?" Brodie asked. "You want to stroll right into Syn HQ and say, 'Hey, remember me? I'm the girl you all liked once.' The last person we'll send into that room is you."

"Why?" Zara snapped. "Because you love me more than Falcon loves Finch or Swift loves Dove? You can't put a measure on that, I'm no more valuable than they are. I have connections, remember? It's why I'm useful to the Kindred."

"Not anymore," Brodie said. "I'm not keeping you away from Syn because you're more important. Damn right, you're more important to me, but it's because you have history with every man in there that you have to stay away. They all have reason to want to hurt you. The rest of us can hold our own or won't provoke an emotional reaction. The last time you saw Leatt—"

"Was in Purdy's," Zara said. "And he was friendly. He promised not to hurt me."

"Caine said something like that to you before he saved your life and wiped the slate clean. You and Thad were thick as thieves, always laughing and playing. Did you have a fucking clue what he was going to do?"

"Of course not!" Zara said. "Grant talks as if he's the leader, but he's not. He's under Mitchell, who always admired me in his own kind of way."

"He didn't admire you enough to bring you to the inside," Brodie said.

"He tried to," Zara said. "If Devon's story is true, Mitchell told Grant to bring me in before I ever met you. It was Grant who chose not to do that."

"You're fighting over nothing," Tuck said. "Number one, we don't have a fucking clue where they are. Number two, there's no way that you can reason with them, Zara. They won't listen. Mitchell and McCormack have been planning this for years, and they were doing it right under your nose. They're not going to be swayed because you ask nicely."

Kadie went over and swatted his chest. "At least she's trying. All you're doing is waving the white flag. The big bully comes on the TV and tells you to bend over and you unzip your fly. That's not the Tucker Holt I know. He threatened my life, did you hear that?"

"Yes," Tuck said. "That was one part of his rant that I heard pretty fucking clear, Toots, and that's exactly why I'm gonna do what he's telling me to do. I don't give a shit about your pet. I give a shit about your life. As soon as Syn send Raven and Falcon down the river, do you know who'll be in the cell between them? Me! Because I've been there for everything, my fingerprints are all over it. And what happens to the three of you when we're in the slammer, huh?"

"Hot shot—"

Tuck strode away from Kadie to get into a central

position between the door and the back of the couch. "Devon has a fucking island to run to, but it's not gonna keep her safe. It'll be a flashing fucking target. They'll know exactly where to hit. They know exactly where she'll be and that she'll be all alone. They don't even have to crack security, even if Devon was willing to be a prisoner in the house for the next thirty or forty years until the rest of us get out of jail. All they need is an aircraft, a couple of explosive devices that will make it look like an accidental fire. Who's gonna investigate, huh? Who? I'd be surprised if anybody noticed the house had been burnt to the ground."

Kadie tried to soothe him by raising her hands. "Calm down."

But he wasn't done. "And you, Toots, where are you gonna go? Are you gonna join Devon on her island? You'll end up going down with her. Are you gonna stay in the manor with Zara? That would work, except it brings us to the greatest problem of them all." Tuck turned around and balled his fists on his hips. "There's no way Ms. Zara Bandini is gonna sit down quietly and wait for her man to do his time. You're gonna get pissed, Swallow, and you're gonna do exactly what you just did. You're gonna convince yourself that if you can get in Grant's face that you'll make him see the error of his ways. When you wade in, you're going to take my Kadie with you," Tuck said, pointing at her. "And Devon's not gonna be left out, especially when you pull Rig in with you. You're going to get your own little troupe going. Meanwhile, the three of us are gonna be banged up, telling all of you to sit on your asses, knowing that not one of you is gonna listen!"

Devon might have expected Brodie to leap in and tell Tuck not to speak shit about his wife. But Tuck wasn't angry, he wasn't resentful, or being hateful. It was like projecting the narrative forward and even Zara didn't object.

"Okay, so we have to admit that they've positioned themselves well and they have Thad, who might not have been active in the field with the Kindred but he was always present during our strategy discussions, and he knows what tech we have. We have to assume he's told them everything."

"He might not," Kadie said. "He'll keep some

information to himself if he's smart. It gives him leverage."

Zara shrugged. "Maybe. But we can't be sure of that. We need to catch a break."

"Well, that's an excellent fucking strategy, baby," Brodie said and sank back onto the couch where he folded his arms. "We'll all just sit fucking here and wait for a break to find us. Excellent. I'll bet good luck is about to knock on the front door. Maybe I should run out for beer before it gets here."

Being snide wasn't helpful, and Devon could sense an argument brewing. Once again, her own man was saying little, but she knew Zave was absorbing everything that was being said. They all stayed quiet, in their own little bubbles for a second. But their reflection was shattered by a knock at the door.

# FOURTEEN

DEVON'S CHIN CAME up and she saw that everyone was as startled as she was, everyone except Zave who just started toward the door. "That's quick for Bess," Devon said.

Zave looked through the peephole, and for the man who was always unruffled, Devon was stunned to see surprise on his face when he whipped around and looked at Zara to point at Brodie. Zara kicked her husband's shin without making a sound, nodded up, and without words, Brodie knew he had to mobilize.

Brodie was on his feet and heading toward the door without a whisper of a sound. Pulling a gun from the back of his waistband, he put his back to the wall behind the door. Nobody knew who was on the other side of that door, except Zave. Whoever it was demanded that the Kindred's assassin be ready to earn his title.

Zave held up three fingers, counting them down. Brodie used the cover of Zave unlocking and opening the door to load a round into the chamber of the semi-automatic weapon he held in both hands at chest height, pointing it to the ceiling.

Zave opened the door, and she wanted to see who would come in after he backed away. As soon as she saw

Caine, Devon gasped. Zave slammed the door, Brodie extended the gun and pointed it to the back of their guest's head. Caine lifted both hands in surrender out to his sides, and he fixated on Zara.

"I got your call, sexy," Caine drawled. "Thought you were giving into those animal urges when you demanded some alone time. Your boyfriend's got a little jealousy problem. He's always been threatened by me; he can't handle our love."

"Get on your fucking knees," Brodie snarled. "I'm gonna blow your brains out right here."

Caine lowered to his knees. "Bring your pussy over here, Bandini. I'll show your boyfriend how to get the most outta you."

"Beau," Zara said. Hurrying around the couch, she shot across the room. But Brodie moved around, and keeping the gun trained to Caine's head, he blocked Zara from getting too close.

"He could be armed," Brodie growled.

Zara didn't seem to care about or acknowledge Caine's innuendo, as she was more focused on chastising and calming her husband. "His hands are up," Zara said.

"He could be wearing a wire."

"Well, the only thing that's been revealed so far is that you're an arrogant fuck, and that's no secret, and…" Zara said and narrowed her eyes on the man on his knees, "what are you doing here, Caine?"

"What I always do," Caine said. "I'm looking for a better offer. All you have to do is match Saint's and you've got yourself an inside man."

Devon didn't know whether to believe it, and neither did the others because they exchanged measured glances. But she couldn't see Caine's face until Brodie moved further around, until he was once again behind Caine. Brodie made eye contact with Zave, with Tuck, and then Zara.

Zara was still looking at the man on his knees. "Would you look at that?" Zara said, folding her arms. "I think we just caught a break… It strolled up and knocked right on that front door, beau. Did you see that?"

\*\*\*

IT TOOK ABOUT an hour before Brodie would let Caine sit down. He was allowed off his knees after ten minutes but kept by the door, and the weapon was pointed at him constantly. Devon thought that it showed quite remarkable restraint that Brodie didn't accidentally on purpose trip and pull the trigger. The tension between these men was visceral.

Bess had arrived a while ago and been shocked by the scene, but there was no time for explanations. When Zave showed her to her room, they were gone for more than a few minutes, and then he came back and Devon hadn't seen Bess since. She understood Zave's want to keep his aunt far away from Caine.

The rest of them were in the apartment's living space. Kadie brought Caine a drink from the kitchen and put it on the dining table in front of him where he'd been allowed to sit. Kadie sat beside him. Zara was at his other side. Devon went over to stand behind Kadie because she was fascinated by this man and how he'd had the courage to walk in here, given that he was supposed to be allied with Syn, and all of the men in this room were his enemies.

Brodie was leaning against the wall behind him, just at the edge of the kitchen. He had his arms folded, and the gun hung loose beneath his arm.

Caine sat back and went for his pocket. Brodie leaped forward, chambering that round again. Caine must have heard it because he held up his hands. "Just going for my cigs, Rave. Cool your jets." Caine looked at Zara. "Is he always so quick to fire? Must lead to a lot of disappointment for you."

Kadie put her hand in the jacket pocket he'd been going for on her side. She took out his cigarettes and his lighter, opened the pack, and took one out, showing that there was nothing sinister inside the carton.

"You know what I notice?" Caine asked, picking up the cigarette and putting it between his lips to light it. He took a long draw and then exhaled toward the ceiling. "I notice how twitchy all you guys are. Rave, back there..." He nodded backwards. "And you two..."

Zave stayed near the bottom of the stairs, glaring, almost as intent as Brodie was. Tuck paced toward the covered window and back again, the length of the table to the kitchen and back around. He was a caged tiger, he needed to do something but couldn't leave this confinement.

"You're a piece of shit," Brodie grumbled.

Caine didn't respond and continued his thought. "All you twitchy fuckers, glaring at me, pointing your guns at me, ready to take me apart." He took another draw. "You know what I see?"

"What do you see, Caine?" Brodie growled from behind him.

"All your fucking women love me."

Even Devon hadn't noticed it, but he was right, not that they loved him but that they had no fear. Zara was so close to him that her arm brushed his and her foot rested on the high crossbar of his chair, making her shin come into periodic contact with his thigh.

Kadie had angled her chair so she faced him, her body fully exposed toward his, and Devon stood behind Kadie with her elbows on the back of the chair. He switched his cigarette to the other hand and rubbed Kadie's knee, which made Tuck stop, but before the hacker could object, Caine switched fingers again and leaned over to kiss Zara's cheek.

"Stop it," Zara said and leaned back to look at Brodie. "Don't rise to it." She was clear in her commands.

Caine's eyes slunk around to Devon, and he winked. "You can come sit right here," he said, leaning back and stroking his thigh. "You and me got no rules. You're the only gal here who's slept in my bed."

She straightened and saw Zave's jaw tick. "You weren't in it," Devon said, "and it wasn't by choice."

"That's what they all say," Caine said, amused by his own joke as he took another draw of the cigarette. "We can sit here all day; we're achieving fuck all."

As relaxed as Caine was, the others were still uptight. "Then why are you here? What do you hope to achieve?" Tuck asked.

"I didn't do so bad on the mission that saved your boy's ass, did I? Howie, right? That boy gets himself in a lot of trouble. I saved your girl and his," Caine said, resting an arm along the back of Zara's chair. "I don't feel much gratitude from you fuckers."

"Maybe that's because you knew Grant McCormack was alive and you never told us," Zara said, kicking his shin beneath the table.

"I was as shocked as the rest of you," Caine muttered.

"Were you?" Zara asked, taking no shit. "You were in Sutcliffe's compound with us, Caine. You saw Leatt put those bullets in him. When we left, you were still there. Are you telling me you didn't see Grant move?"

Caine inhaled. "Leatt told me to split, and I did. Far as I was concerned, Saint was gone."

There was so much history here, and it was hard for her to keep track of everything that these people had been through together. Caine was deep inside, yet not in the Kindred and certainly not trusted. As far as she could figure, everyone who was part of this mess was here for a reason, nothing was a coincidence.

"Are you related?" Devon asked the inappropriate question. But it seemed only relatives and those closest to the Kindred knew Grant as "Saint."

Caine laughed. "Not a fucking chance. Why, baby? You like keeping it in the family? I can be your brother, your cousin, your daddy, anything you want me to be, babe. I told you I'd share you with the doctor. I'll share you with the genius too."

Zave did better than Brodie at not reacting to the jibes. But Devon could tell that he was growing tenser.

Zara moved the conversation on, probably trying to prevent Zave and Caine from coming to blows in the same kind of way she calmed Brodie with distraction. "So how did they get you?" Zara asked. "I haven't seen you since you left Sikorski's place. The last time you called me, you were in Hong Kong."

"So was Mitchell," Caine said. "I didn't even know the fucker when he walked up to me. I still don't know how he found me. I don't give a fuck."

"You don't give a fuck about anything," Zara said.

Caine made eye contact with the woman beside him.

"I give a fuck about plenty."

Something went unsaid between the pair, and Zara took them back to the point. "So he approached you?"

"Yeah," Caine said. "And it was your doctor that told him to do it."

"Bullshit," Brodie said.

The startling outburst made Devon look at the sniper, but he was focused on Zave, who was once again looking at the floor. Brodie probably believed it of Thad. She certainly could and he was cynical enough. But it was toughest on Zave, who'd invited the man into his home on an almost daily basis, to find out he'd been plotting for some time.

"Is that what you came to tell us?" Brodie asked, shoving away from the wall to swagger around the table. "You came to tell us that Thad is a rat? We knew that. But he wouldn't vouch for you in a million years. No member of the Kindred would."

Brodie put his hands down on the opposite side of the table from where Caine sat, the gun still conspicuous in his right hand and his forefinger resting over the trigger. Devon looked to Zara, and she knew she wasn't the only one focused on the newest Mrs. McCormack. If anyone in the room would vouch for this man, it would be her. Maybe it was her friendship with Caine that had made Thad think he could be a good guy.

"It doesn't fucking matter," Caine said. "Don't you get it? How I ended up with them doesn't. Fucking. Matter."

"I'll tell you what fucking matters," Brodie said.

Caine wasn't intimidated by the growl in Brodie's eyes like she was. He stayed loose as he finished his cigarette. Flicking most of his ash to the floor, he then dropped the butt into the liquid Kadie had put in front of him.

Caine swiped the glass aside and linked his hands on the table to glare at Brodie. "Are you gonna take the risk of sending me out that door without asking what I know?" Caine asked. "It's not like we don't have reason to hate each other. But I'm not here to save your ass."

"Then why are you here?" Brodie spat. "You sure didn't come running because Zara called. You never even spoke to her, and she didn't leave a message."

"Watch her make the call, did you?" Caine asked. "Are you that insecure, Rave?"

Zara groaned out impatient frustration. "Stop taunting each other!" Standing up, she chastised them both. "It's pathetic and it's juvenile. Lives are at stake and you two are sniping? Haven't you learned by now that it doesn't matter whose dick is bigger? What matters is that we take Syn down."

"And we're not gonna ask for his help to do that until we know what's motivating him," Brodie said.

"Do you really care?" Zara asked her husband.

"Yes," Tuck answered. "Because he'll be working both sides. This is Caine, for fuck sake."

Caine wasn't insulted. "They don't know I'm here," he said.

"And they just let you saunter out the room without word?"

Caine sneered. "When I want to leave a room, I get up and walk out," he snapped at the hacker. "I'm not a pussy like you, I don't need to ask no cunt's permission. I don't have a woman carrying my balls in her purse like you fuckers do. Or a master who puts me on a leash." Caine glared at Brodie again. "You guys get so stuck on your chief's fucking rules, on the way Art did things." Caine shot to his feet, shoving his chair away from behind him when he locked his knees. "Look around you, do you see Art? He's fucking dead! They played it well, Syn blindsided you, and now they're holding all the fucking cards. You guys are running around trying to mop up spilled milk, wondering how the fuck all this happened on your watch! You want to know how it happened? Him!" Caine tipped his chin toward Brodie. "All this is his fault."

Zara wasn't taking that. "Shut the fuck up," she said, jabbing his chest with two knuckles. "This started long before Raven ever picked up a gun. This started when all of these guys were just kids. It started with Frank Mitchell and his greed. He orchestrated Brodie's parents' death because he wanted to control Game Time. He got scared. He ducked for cover, and it wasn't until he saw Grant's potential that he realized his dream wasn't lost. All it took to get it was destroying Falcon's parents! That's all he's ever done; he destroys everyone who gets in his way."

"That's a lovely story, really," Caine said, patting his chest. "It gets me right here, goosebumps, really, huge sympathy for these grown men and their mommy issues."

"Caine," Zara whined.

But he turned on her. "Mitchell is a maniac. A man with big ideas who trained Saint to believe in the same fucked up ideas. Do you think he'd have gotten this far without Grant McCormack? You said it yourself, he couldn't do it alone. He wussed out of it until he had Saint backing him up. Saint's the real brain. Don't act fucking surprised about it, either," Caine said, thrusting an arm behind him to a four o'clock position without taking his eyes away from Zara. "Your Falcon is one of the smartest men in business today, and your hapless hubby, well, he's come up with a half-decent strategy or two in his life. It comes from Art's side. From Bess, Melinda, Philippa, they're the brains. They always held the reins. Why do you think Brodie puts up with you when all you do is nag his ear all the time? You're just like Melinda."

"You're not the first person to say that to me," Zara said, drawing her eyes away. "Does that matter? Does it matter who's the smartest or the quickest or the—"

"Yes," Caine said. "Because you guys aren't looking at this right, all you see is Syn's slick move. They have me and Leatt, Thad, Mitchell. We outman you."

Brodie snickered. "I get that you're not academic, fuckwit, but there's six people standing here and only five in your seedy motel across town."

"Right," Caine said, turning to Brodie before he nodded at Devon and Kadie. "That pair count as one if you're lucky. Sorry, darlins, you're easy on the eyes while we're laying around, but you just don't have the experience, and your men have kept you shut up for too long."

Devon couldn't argue against having a lack of experience. Her brother had kept her shut away from as much of the evil in the world as he could too. "You don't know what you're talking about," Brodie said.

"You can call in Rig," Caine said. "He'll bring a

couple of guys, but if you're talking about getting dicks lined up on opposite sides of the battle lines, well… it's all gonna be about ponying up the dough, and then you're gonna have a full-blown war. Where the fuck are you gonna do that and stay covert?"

"You said we were looking at this wrong," Zara said. "How should we be looking at this?"

"Someone who appreciates me," Caine said, winking at her. "It comes down to those minds. Falc, Rave, they share the blood, just like Grant and Thad."

"So it's going to come down to a battle of the cousins?"

"Yeah," Caine said. "And you guys have got the advantage because the only one who used that brain for strategy, combat, conflict like this, was Art. And who did he train?" Caine looked at Brodie and then at Tuck. "You have to use that."

"Admitting that you're fodder?" Brodie sneered.

"I'm muscle. You think I'm gonna work up a sweat for Syn? Fuck that. When I got Mitchell's offer, I was doing fuck all else. They offered me money and creature comforts." Devon took that to mean hookers and hotel rooms. "But I didn't sign no contract or agree to die for these guys. You know me, Zar, I like to watch, and I figured whatever they were cooking would clash with the Kindred one day."

"So you went in there to look out for us?" Zara asked, understandably dubious.

"I went in there to look out for me. Free digs and every demand catered for? Ha, who wouldn't take advantage?"

"They gave you the offer and you thought, 'Why not use these people's resources?' Was that it?"

"Something like that," Caine said.

"You could've picked up the phone," Zara snapped. "You could've told me what was happening."

Caine smiled that slow, sinister smirk that he wore so well and touched a fingertip to Zara's nose. "Now where's the fun in that, button?"

Zara took his finger away from her face. Keeping hold of it in a fist, she made eye contact with Brodie. "We don't have to trust him to use him."

Caine bowed to murmur in Zara's ear. "You can use me for anything you want, sweetheart. But first I say, let's order something to eat. I've got another couple of hours before I have to saunter back into that room."

Watching the men's power play intrigued Devon. Caine wasn't really hungry. He didn't care about the food. He just liked to delay things to give himself more time to watch the Kindred. So while the others accommodated him, Devon went to Zave, who'd been quiet for quite some time.

She went up close, and Zave didn't even react to her proximity. Pressing her palms against him, she tried to get him to make eye contact, but it took her a good ten seconds to achieve her aim. "Do you think he's gathering intel?" she whispered. "Could Syn have sent him here to find out what we plan to do?"

"Yes," Zave said, glancing at the table.

# FIFTEEN

EVERYONE WAS BUSY. Zave put an arm around her and guided her up the stairs into their bedroom, where he closed the door. The brilliant light up here was jarring after being in the dark lower floor of the apartment for so long.

The privacy panels were good, she had to give them that. It seemed like the middle of the night down there when it was actually only the middle of the afternoon if the sun up here was an indication of the time.

Zave took her over to the bed and sat her down before hunkering in front of her. "Do you want to go back to the island?" he asked. "Now that Bess understands what's going on, I'm sure she'll go with you and you can—"

"No," Devon said.

"You don't have to be afraid. I can have security on the island at all times. It will be a fortress. We can have choppers in the air, no one will be allowed to approach. Security will be armed, and they'll take down anyone who threatens you. Are you concerned about what Swift said?"

"I'm concerned about what Caine said," Devon admitted, brushing her fingers through his hair and down his jaw. "And I'm concerned about you. You've been so quiet today. I don't like it when you go into your own head and leave me out here alone."

"You're not alone," he said, curling his hand around hers.

"The Kindred will need to come up with a plan."

"You can be a part of those meetings if you want to. Don't listen to Caine when he says you're not valuable. You are. You're the most important person in this apartment, in this building, in this world."

"To you," she said, smiling, because it was nice that he was taking some time out to reassure her. Slipping off her shoes, she pushed back on the bed to lie down. "Will you lie with me?"

He glanced at the door. "We have to be around to hear what Caine has to say. It will be important, and we may pick up on something that the others don't. Kindred strategy meetings are largely about brainstorming," he said and stood up. "Sometimes there's an obvious course of action or someone has a specific plan they'd like to follow. But situations like this, when there are so many variables…"

Devon sat up and reached over to take his hand. "It will take time for him to decide what he wants to eat and time for the food to be delivered. I'm not asking you to make love to me, Zave. I'm asking you to lie down and let me comfort you a minute."

He couldn't argue with logic. Caine would make more jibes, Brodie would rise to them, and Zara would be telling them to cut it out. But it was unlikely they would miss any earth-shattering revelations in the next few minutes. Caine was holding on to those secrets so that he could release them when they would be most valuable. He made no secret of his passion for monitoring people. Absorbing reactions to shocking news would be like a drug to him. Caine had done nothing except try to shock her when they'd met, like he got off on the idea that his words were unsettling.

But the more time she spent with him, the more she doubted how vicious he was. Caine said these things and his language was coarse, but he seemed too laid back, lazy almost, to actually follow through on the threats. He hadn't cared when Brodie's gun was trained on him. Caine, Devon was sure, was dangerous, but it would probably take quite a lot of pushing to make him exert the energy of actually killing somebody or hurting them.

Zave had finished his reflection, and he came around the bed to crawl on beside her. He lay down and gathered her body against his. Immediately, she felt better when both of them relaxed.

"This is a perk of being married," she murmured into his chest. "We don't need a reason to hold each other or have expectation that things have to go further than this. Your mind is so complex, such a complicated place, that I could never understand all your thoughts. It's my job." Devon stroked the small portion of his chest that she could reach while locked in the circle of his arms. "To slow everything down for you, to simplify it. You have to forget about the Kindred, about Syn and all the people downstairs. You have to forget about the island and the threats and what might happen down the road. Close your eyes and live for this exact minute when all you are is a husband holding his wife, enjoying the heat of her body and the softness of her skin.

"You're a man with a woman who loves him with all of her heart. I don't want you to be Falcon right now. I don't even want you to be Xavier Knight, KC CEO. You're not Thad's cousin or your father's son." Tipping her head back, Devon rested her hand on his cheek. "You're my lord, that's it. That's all. You're the man who wouldn't make love to me until he was sure he wanted to marry me. The man who kissed me outside my bedroom because it just felt so right, even though it was completely illogical." She grinned when he lowered to kiss her again. "Forget everything else, Zave. Forget where we are and why, and just be here with me, right now. Can you do that for me?"

He drew her head against his chest and kissed the top. "Yes, shy, I can."

Comforting her husband was a luxury he didn't often let her indulge in. Devon wanted the freedom to do whatever she wanted to with the man she'd pledged her life to. She could lie here in his arms and let him breathe through his worries, but she knew him too well to think he was just going to let it go because she'd said a few soothing words.

Devon couldn't blame him for being preoccupied. There was a lot of pressure on the Kindred, but beyond that, Syn had singled out Zave to do their work. From everything she'd seen so far, it looked like they were going to have to comply with what Syn wanted them to do.

If he gave these people he didn't trust his technology, tech that he'd only ever made for Kindred purposes in the past, and then they did something that hurt innocent people, she wasn't sure he would come through that.

Zave had gone to the extreme of shutting himself away on the island when he'd lost his parents through no fault of his own. And when they'd lost Bronwyn, despite again not doing anything to invite that tragedy, Zave had retreated even more while taking serious risks to save other women.

Syn were doing damage on a larger scale to strangers. She could only assume the worst when they'd been given no specifics. Men like Frank Mitchell and Grant McCormack weren't righteous, despite what they tried to assert.

His arms had relaxed enough that she could skim hers down his ribs. Loosening his pants, Devon tipped her head back to make eye contact again. "I can give you your toys if you want to play," he said. "But I have to get back downstairs."

"In a minute," she murmured, boosting close enough to kiss him. "I want to play with something else."

She wasn't interested in her own pleasure now. All that she cared about was his, and her voice wasn't as sensual as his was to her when she was being pleasured, so she didn't try to say anything to enhance the moment. All she did was take his dick out of his pants and massage it inside her fist.

Devon found he was already erect, and it was flattering to know that just being this close to her caused his arousal. Although she desperately wanted to do this, her heart was pounding in fear that he may tell her to stop at any moment.

Inching south, she knew it would be impossible for her to suck him off without him noticing that's what she was doing. But she tried, like she had on the night they first kissed, to be subtle, as if any jerky movements might cause him to withdraw.

Sliding from his arms, Devon managed to push him onto his back, and maybe it was the stress of the day, or his overwhelming need, but he let her take him into her mouth. Devon dipped low, trying her best to watch him for as long as she could. But when his eyes closed, she didn't ask him to look at her. She wanted him lost, wanted him so deep in this moment that just for a minute or two at least, she could make his world seem right again.

Dipping down, she took him deep until his engorged head rubbed on the back of her tongue and nudged into her throat. Devon wanted to do this more often because now that they were married, she was the only woman alive allowed to do this. It was a testament to how far he'd come from being the man who had once refused to kiss her because he didn't deserve the taste of her lips, to now letting her tug his dick against her breast as she stroked her thumb over the apex every time she reached it.

She wanted sex because doing this, having such power over this incredible man overwhelmed her. He needed this, and he'd learned he was allowed to let her tease his body. So often he prioritized her needs, and many times, she'd fought with him, begging to be an equal. At times, she could tell it pained him, but he was doing his best to involve her in every part of his life.

Pushing him into her cheek, she fondled his balls and drummed her fingers on his shaft in a rhythmic, coiling motion. He hissed and as she pushed him deep into her mouth, she dug her nails in against his groin, and his hips rose as he reached the limit of what he could bear. His seed spurted into her throat, and she swallowed his release, hoping it would alleviate some of his burden.

No sooner had she licked her lips than he was drawing her up into his arms, putting her onto her back, but she laid her hands on her chest and resisted his kiss. "You have to go downstairs," she said, smiling and stroking his jaw. There was a feral need in him now, and he cradled her breast, ready to reciprocate. She lifted her arms up around his neck and tucked her face against him. "How many times have you spoiled me and not let me return the favor?"

"I like to return the favor."

His murmuring voice coupled with the gentle rise and fall of his chest betrayed that this wasn't another act he'd add to his list of things to feel guilty about. It shouldn't be that way; she should be allowed to pleasure him without it taking on greater meaning than the moment. "I know, but right now, you can't," she said, kissing the underside of his chin. "Go back down to the others, lord. Finish what we started."

Pouncing off the bed, there was a spring in her step as she headed for the bedroom door. He had to hurry to catch up with her at the top of the stairs. Devon couldn't let him come up with a reason that he had to reciprocate. What she'd done was no big deal to her, it was a basic comfort meant to destress a man she loved. But to him, it meant the world.

They'd just reached the bottom of the stairs, when there was a knock and Tuck went to bring in the boxes of food, which he dumped onto the dining table for Kadie and Zara to begin handing out.

"You get quick service up here," Caine said. "Bet you tip well."

"You ordered from a place a block over," Zara said, tossing a takeout tray onto the table in front of him. "And I put all this on your credit card."

"That's cool, I've got a buddy who zeroes them every month," Caine said, popping off the lid of his food and pulling out a plastic fork from the underside. "I can keep you like a queen."

"I still have my gun," Brodie said from the kitchen.

Nothing could make Caine lose that cool confidence that irked the men and intrigued the ladies. "When are you going to start talking?" Zara asked. "Tell us what you know about Syn's plan."

"So far, all I know is they have a list," Caine said, "of people they're going after, some to kill, some to recruit. It's all part of their plan to mobilize for the big work, as they call it. They're treating these guys as kind of a training and morale exercise."

Monitoring the room and the mood, she and Zave made their way to the group. "Have you seen the list?" Zara asked.

Caine shook his head, his mouth full of food. "No. I never asked to. Why would I? I don't give a fuck. They can kill anybody they want to, it means fuck all to me."

It seemed he wasn't much of a forward planner, though it was possible he was just that laid back. Zara didn't berate him, just explained why it meant something to the Kindred. "If we knew who was on the list," she said, "we might be able to figure out where they're going to be next."

But he wasn't understanding, he was smug. "I could tell you where they are right now," Caine said, and everybody stopped what they were doing.

Zave and Devon had just sat down at the table when Caine revealed that truth. Despite not being around to order food, there were takeout trays at their places waiting for them.

Impatient, Zara prompted him. "So tell us," she said. "And we can end this now."

Caine was skeptical. "Are you gonna go in and shoot them all?" he asked. "Don't forget your boyfriend is related to fifty percent of the guys in there. Seventy-five if you include Mitchell, although, I don't know how that works out."

His attitude wouldn't be appreciated by most of the people in the room, but he had a point that they had to come up with a plan before storming anywhere and that would mean facing some tough questions about what to do with their relatives. These weren't strangers who could be taken down without breaking a sweat; the Kindred had blood in that room.

Caine wasn't going to make this an easy grab for the Kindred, maybe because he enjoyed watching people squirm or because he had loyalty to his Syn friends. Devon didn't want him to get too much satisfaction from the power he was holding.

"Thad says that they're doing important work; that they're going after the cartels," Devon said. "Is that true?"

Watching people was his thing, and it was clear how much he liked to scrutinize those around him when new information was shared. If he wasn't a thug, he'd have made a good politician because he managed to respond without answering her question.

"Why? You wanna come back with me and join our cause?" Caine asked. Except he would know about her experience with those bastards, which would explain why he wasn't affected when she shook her head. "We'll take care of your pussy over there too, if that's what you're worried about."

"Enough," Zave growled.

The word was enough to make Caine shrug and move on. "Like I said, I haven't seen the list. I know they started a war down there at that meet. I don't know how long it will take your cartel buddies to get their shit together again. They put you through some crap, huh, honey?"

Devon focused on her food and was surprised to feel Zave's hand cover hers. Comfort would only bring her emotions closer to the surface, and she didn't want to appear weak in front of this audience. "Did we get something for Bess?" she asked. "I don't want her to feel like a prisoner."

Zara lifted another box. "Yeah, I'll take it to her."

Devon stood up. "Let me do it. You guys are talking business; I don't need to be around for that."

Devon took the box from Zara and headed for the room they'd sent Bess to. That the woman had stayed out of the way, without asking any questions, made Devon worry that their caretaker was more upset about what was going on than she'd admitted to anyone.

Knocking on the door, she went inside to find Bess sitting on the bed, holding a book. But she wasn't reading, she was gazing out the window that covered the wall opposite the bed. A glazed door led to the balcony that stretched to the living room, but it was locked.

Bess smiled when she saw Devon. "This is a role reversal," she said, patting the bed.

Devon went over to put the box on the bedside and took a seat facing her friend. Usually Bess was the one bringing her food and comfort. "Caine wanted to order food."

Bess glanced at the box and was still trying to smile, but Devon knew something was on her mind. "Why is he here?" she asked.

"I think that's what the Kindred are trying to figure out," Devon said. "The only one who really seems to trust him is Zara. Kadie's not afraid of him. But none of the guys like him."

"There's a lot of history," Bess said. "Caine saved Zara's life and Kadie's, too, during a Kindred mission when they were pulling Howie out of captivity."

Most aspects of Kindred history were complex, and relationships were complicated. Devon felt for the poor kid who'd already been a pawn used against the Circle once. "And now he's trapped again."

Focusing on a negative would remind Bess of her own worries. She reverted to her usual role of worrying about everyone except herself. "Where's Dempsey?" Bess asked. "I've never met him."

She'd come here to support Bess, but Devon considered the woman a friend and didn't mind asking her to fill in a few blanks. "He's Kadie's cousin, right? Kadie said he was staying at a hotel somewhere, I think they want to keep him out of it. Unless they need him, I suppose. I don't know much about him."

Bess explained why he was being held at arm's length. "They don't have the time right now to initiate a new Kindred member. Swift still has to do his due diligence even for one of his oldest friends. Dempsey never knew the truth about what Swift does, he ran Swift's legitimate company with Kadie. Kadie only found out the truth after she and Swift split up and she went looking for him."

"Sounds like an interesting story," Devon said, pulling her bare feet onto the bed to cross her legs.

"All of the Kindred stories are interesting," Bess said. "I just wish they all had happy endings."

Tuck and Kadie had a happy ending in that they were together. Bess didn't have much of one. The boy she'd raised on her own after being knocked up during a frivolous affair had scarpered to run to the father he'd never known. That would hurt any mother. But to know he'd betrayed everyone they both cared about, betrayed her family to run away to the paternal side to do harm, it had to make the deception sting more.

"I'm sorry we had to take you away from Thad's apartment," Devon said. "We just didn't want you to be out there on your own."

"I understand." Bess leaned forward to take her hand after putting the book aside. She didn't even look at the food tray. "I couldn't settle there anyway, I tried my best. I expected to find some sort of note or message, but there was nothing, and then I tried to go through some of his things to find out if maybe he was being coerced or blackmailed and…"

Bess didn't finish the sentence. "You found nothing?"

"It was eerie. Everything was so normal. Nothing seemed staged or hurried or cleaned up or erased. His sneakers were still in the closet by the door. His stethoscope lay with his hospital ID. Sometimes he worked at the free clinics, he volunteered, so he'd always bring his things home. I suppose it came from the Kindred, too, the always be prepared, never leave evidence… those things were engrained in him… At least, I thought they were."

Difficult as it was for Bess to talk about, Devon was encouraged that her friend trusted her enough to open up and be honest. "I know you might not believe it now, but it will get easier."

"He's my only son," Bess said, and when her gaze drifted toward the window again, she didn't even attempt to smile. "I love Zave and Brodie, and I feel awful that they lost their parents. With Art gone, it's just occurring to me that I'm… alone."

"You're not alone!" Devon moved up the bed to get closer to Bess. "You have me and Zave, and Brodie and Zara, right out there. We're family."

"I know," Bess said, "but your children won't have paternal grandparents." Or maternal either, Devon thought, but now wasn't the time to bring up her own family troubles. "The Kindred was a part of Brodie's life from a young age. Zave was forced to grow up when his father started KC and thrust him into the professional world too early. Those boys had extraordinary lives, Grant did too, taking on the responsibility of CI while finishing school and dealing with the grief of losing his parents. I know it sounds horrible of me now, but there was always a part of me which was a little bit smug because Thad had as close to a normal childhood as I could give him as a single mother. Mitchell did send money, but I was always employed, I tried to instill a strong work ethic into him... We visited sometimes with his aunts, uncles, and cousins, but for the most part... he went to high school, he went to college, he went to med school. He got a job at the hospital and met Bronwyn, it was all normal.

"After my sister, Philippa, died, I spent more time with Zave. But Thad was grown then and he didn't need me, he was working hundreds of hours at the hospital. I was glad to have someone to take care of. But I always assumed that one day, you know, he would get married and have children, and settle down and..."

"You would be a grandmother," Devon said and a warm smile flickered onto Bess' face before her focus fell to the bed.

"I thought I knew him, Devon. I thought I knew who he was and I thought, even with him all grown up, that he respected me."

Bess had lost so much, not only her son and her faith in reality, but the future she'd taken for granted. "He does," Devon said. "He has to."

But she couldn't possibly know that, and she couldn't fault Bess for thinking otherwise given everything that Thad had done recently.

"I don't know what his future will be. And it's ridiculous, but as a mother, that keeps me up at night. He went into dangerous situations with Zave and Brodie, and I worried for them all, but not like this. Since he was born, I've always known roughly where he is or what he's up to, at least. There's always been a person I trust watching his back. Through his life, I've known what city he was in. I've always been able to pick up a phone, I've always been able to get in touch with him... now I can't."

Devon's heart broke when she saw the fat tears

bleeding from Bess's lashes. The woman had struggled to hold it together, there was concealer smudged beneath her eyes, and Devon had never seen her wearing makeup. The sparkle that had always beamed out of her expression, that eternal optimism, was gone. She was grieving her son as if he'd lost his life, and in many ways, he had, and the relationship they had was broken. It wouldn't be easily fixed.

"I don't know why he's doing this."

Offering comfort wasn't easy because Devon didn't have any answers, but she couldn't leave Bess hanging and had to give her something. "You know, he told me to tell you he was sorry. He does still love you."

"But what can I do for him?" Bess asked, sounding more desperate than Devon had ever known her, and it made sadness well up in her own eyes. "I know he's a grown man, but as a mother, I want to be able to help him. I want to be there for him. I want to know that my baby can always come home to me."

Devon couldn't say much more to comfort her, so she just lunged forward to pull her into her arms, and as Bess had said, their roles flipped because Devon hugged and soothed as Bess sobbed into her. It wasn't right that Thad was doing this to a woman who'd dedicated her life to giving him everything he ever wanted or needed. It was selfish and unreasonable.

But she did believe what she'd said that Thad did still care for his mother, and this wasn't about any resentment he had toward her. How could anyone resent Bess? It wasn't possible. But that was little comfort to a woman who just wanted to reach out to her child.

"I just wish he would've talked to me," Bess said when she began to calm down.

Devon stroked her hair from her face and kissed her cheek before hugging her again. "Caine could get a message to him."

But if he did, that would mean betraying that he'd been here. So unless he was willing to admit to Syn that he'd been here, that wouldn't work. They couldn't rely on Thad to keep the secret.

"A message?"

Zave had said something after her return to the island that might not have occurred to Bess. She didn't want to put ideas in her friend's head but had to be honest. "There's one other thing," Devon said, taking a deep breath because she was hesitant to make the suggestion.

Bess moved out of her embrace. "What?"

"Caine is going back there. He won't tell us where the base is. So if you were to go there, they wouldn't let you leave again. I wouldn't even suggest that you go, but Mitchell did promise nothing would happen to you. Thad did too. I don't think any of them resent you and Caine seems intent on supporting Zara, so he may be able to protect you."

"You think I should go to Syn?" Bess asked, exuding nothing but shock. "I don't want to join them. I don't want to be any part of—"

"I'm not suggesting you join them or spill Kindred secrets. If it was up to me, I'd tell you to stay here and let us look after you. But if you want to talk to your child, it may be the only way to do it. We don't know where they are or how long they'll be in the city. It's up to you. I won't tell the others I made the suggestion, yet. Think about it. Caine said he didn't have to leave for another couple of hours."

It was a massive decision for Bess to make. Devon hoped Bess would stay here. But she understood what it was to yearn for the chance to talk to someone, communicate, to reach out to them one last time.

Once Thad left the city to start on this mission of eliminating those who'd upset Syn members, they could go to any place in the world. If Zave was right that Thad was expendable, he may be the first man sacrificed if a situation called for it.

Though there were probably people in this country Syn wanted to get through first, but it would be like looking for a needle in a haystack trying to find men who had to be covert or risk exposing the truth about their faked deaths.

Devon sat straighter as Bess was contemplating what she'd said. "I'll come back in a while," she said and scooted off the bed.

"Is everything all right?" Bess asked.

Devon nodded. "I just thought of something I need to tell Zave, but don't feel like a prisoner in here. If you want to come out and join the others, you can. I'm so glad you're here."

Smiling before she left the room, she tried to subdue her adrenaline rush, but once the door was closed, she darted up the hallway. Everyone was talking when she got there, but she didn't hesitate in marching over to stand between Brodie and Swift and Tuck who were seated opposite Caine.

"My brother will be on that list," Devon said. Caine's chewing slowed. "Won't he?"

If Syn had been pissed off at Rig enough that they ordered she be kidnapped to teach him a lesson, they'd be pissed off enough that the original plan hadn't worked and may take another swing.

"Probably," Caine said, not bothering to swallow.

She looked to her husband. "We have to do something. They said that they set things up to happen automatically. What if they've sent somebody after him?"

Zave turned to Brodie, who got up to head for the phone. "I'll call Rig, he'll be fine," Brodie said.

He dialed and waited, and she didn't want anyone to speak until she heard him acknowledging her brother. She waited. And waited. And nothing happened.

Brodie hung up. "He didn't answer," he said and put the phone on the kitchen island to come back to the table as if it was no big deal.

Caine didn't have enough compassion to be upfront with them, and she felt guilty that she hadn't queried her brother's safety already. "Have they hurt him?" she asked Caine but moved toward Zave because she didn't have the time to play games. "I have to go to him."

She turned to head for the bedroom, where she intended to pick up her passport and her overnight bag. But Zave got in front of her before she reached the stairs. "You can't fly commercial, they'll find you."

She didn't need him throwing up more obstacles, she just had to get to her brother. "How? They don't care about me. They don't have a computer pro—"

"Searching a flight manifest isn't difficult," Tuck said. "And they have Howie. If they've got a weapon to his head, God knows what he's doing for them. He didn't hold up too well against Sikorski, and I'll admit Saint isn't quite on that level, but the kid is just a kid."

What did they expect her to do? Sit on her ass? "I don't care," Devon said. "I can't just sit here."

She tried to get past Zave, but he snatched her arm. "They threatened your life, Devon, you don't leave my side."

Assertive as he was, she wasn't going to give up, although she was open to being reasonable and finding solutions. "I'll take security," she said. "I'll have Petri fly with me."

But her husband wasn't interested in breaking barriers, only placating her. "You need to calm down," he said. "So your brother didn't answer the phone one time, so what? He could be busy."

"He could be taking a shit," Caine offered, but the suggestion wasn't helpful.

"It could be anything," Zave said. "Maybe he's just not in the room. Maybe he's on the other line. Maybe he's in a meeting with his gang. Let's just finish our food. Get some more answers. And we'll try him again in a while, okay?"

They might think this was no big deal and she should just chill out. But Devon was fraught now that she'd realized her blood was on Syn's hit list. "We can't just leave him out there."

"We won't. We'll think of something."

Rig would have to be part of whatever plan the Kindred was going to come up with. But that strategy meeting wouldn't happen until after Caine left. Her strong reaction may have been ill-advised because if Caine was working both sides, she'd just exposed a weakness. But it wasn't a leap that she cared about her brother or that he cared about her. Syn already knew that.

She let Zave take her back to the table and sit her down. Suddenly, her food didn't seem that appetizing.

"This is good chow," Caine said.

Devon couldn't believe how he could happily scoff so much when she felt so sick. Zave took her hand, curling his fingers around hers as he speared more of his own lunch into his mouth. Sustenance was important, but it was impossible to eat when the food felt like sand in her throat. Her brother was out there, and she didn't need to see Syn's list to know that he was on it. Until she heard his voice or had him with her, Devon wasn't going to settle. She'd give it five more minutes, and then she was phoning again.

# SIXTEEN

SHE'D BEEN TOLD that he was safe. Initial relief became impatience as all she could do was wait the day it took them to get him here. Brodie had told Rigor to come to them, and at her request, Zave had sent security to escort him. Rigor would hate to have a bunch of guys surrounding him like he was in some way vulnerable, but Devon wasn't willing to take the risk with his safety and would be happy to let him argue with her about it.

It didn't help her impatience that everyone else seemed to have things to do. Bess had taken to the kitchen, as on the island, household chores helped to distract her from what was going on. Kadie and Zara had gone out to gather supplies, Brodie was in one of the bedrooms with Tuck and Zave, either helping with the build or whispering. Devon didn't know which was more infuriating.

"He'll be here any minute," Bess called from the kitchen where she was cooking, though there hadn't been much for her to cook with. Grocery shopping was low on the to-do list.

Leaving the couch, Devon went over to the kitchen island, keeping out of Bess' way, but appreciating the chance to vent. "Until I'm looking at him, I won't be sure about that... We should never have let him leave. What were we thinking?"

Bess kept stirring the pot on the stove. "It's difficult to predict which turn Kindred missions will take," she said. "He wanted to go back to his own life, and everyone thought it was safe."

"Well, it wasn't," Devon muttered.

She'd assumed that Rigor was still with the Kindred when Zave called them back here, though it hadn't occurred to her to single him out and request that he join them. With Dempsey safe and Howie not being Rigor's problem, he'd have gone back to his own affairs, probably acting like his empire would collapse if he wasn't around to hold it up.

Rigor's "empire" was insignificant and hadn't been built on doing work like the Kindred did. Devon wished she'd been more vocal about his choices. If she had been, maybe they wouldn't be here now. She'd left her brother to his own destiny and allowed him to keep her out of it. She'd failed to see her role in his life as that of his conscience. If she had spoken out, pushed her way into his life, maybe he wouldn't be a target for groups like Syn. Maybe he wouldn't have gotten involved with the Kindred either, and then neither of them would be here.

Turning to rest on her elbows, she observed the sumptuous, modern apartment that she now called home. "Men like your brother take risks every day," Bess said. "He lives a dangerous life."

The people he did business with, and those he hired to do business for him, were often selfish and fickle. Devon knew there was always a possibility that Rig would be hurt by those who were in and out of his life. Naively, she'd always believed him capable and skilled. That was until she met the Kindred and she saw what real skills were.

Rigor was vulnerable, he would never admit it, but he was low-level. There was no finesse to what he did. She'd been able to tell in the KC office that he admired Brodie, although again, his ego would never allow him to admit it. What she should do was talk to Zave about Rigor becoming more involved, because if he was going to be a criminal, she'd rather he had the closer protection of the Kindred than be out there with people she wouldn't trust to look out for him.

Zave would resist, as the Kindred were particular about who they accepted into their ranks. But technically, now that they were married, Rigor was family. Pondering the merit of this argument and the likelihood that it would work, she almost missed the knock at the door. When it sounded again, louder this time, she pounced upright and gasped.

"Rig!"

Pulling open the door, she expected to be greeted by an angry brother or at least a frustrated one. But Rig was great at throwing curveballs. "Where's Rave?" he asked, swanning past her into the apartment.

Closing the door, Devon guessed there had been more conversation between the men than she'd been privy too because he wasn't asking her questions, and it wasn't like him to be so accepting without explanation. Rig seemed to be hyper, but in a "I'm ready to get the job done" type way, rather than a "I'm ready to start kicking ass" way.

Offended that he would rather see the sniper than his sister, she said, "It's nice to see you too." Folding her arms, she watched him pace around the open-plan space, taking note of Bess and what she was doing before heading into the living room. "I've been worried about you, Rig."

Distracted though he was, it wasn't her safety that was in the forefront of his mind. "You're with the Kindred. What do you have to worry about?"

That was a change in tune from the last time she'd seen him in Zave's KC office, and she wouldn't be fulfilling her sisterly duties if she didn't remind him of that. "I thought I was in danger here. I thought you were pissed at me." Her thoughts about questioning his moods and choices seemed to have translated into action.

Taking his place in front of the TV, his frown said he wasn't in the mood to be held to account. "Yeah. I'm pissed that you haven't answered my question."

But he hadn't answered hers either, and that he could skip over his previous feelings about who she was spending her time with made her feel out of the loop. Something had to have been said to him, to have been explained, for him to just be okay with it now, and she wanted him to tell her what it was.

"You were ready to pull me away from here," she said. "At KC, you demanded that I leave my husband."

As soon as she used the word, she kicked herself for reminding him of her nuptials. He was happy that she was safe with the Kindred but probably not happy she'd gotten herself hitched without word. "Before I knew he was your husband," he said and scowled. "How the fuck could you get married and not tell me? Don't you think that's weird? That he cut me out like that? You can't blame me for being suspicious when it was kept secret."

From his point of view, maybe. From hers, he'd never been that involved in her life. Although, it could be argued that there was no precedent for this situation, as neither of them had made such a lasting life decision before.

Maybe a confession would make him feel better. "Zave wanted you to be there. He was happy to wait and do it right. I told him that you wouldn't care. I picked the date."

From his blinking surprise, she worried that she might have upset him. "You think I wouldn't care that my only family, my baby sister, got married?"

The front door opened, and Zara came in with Kadie. Devon was grateful that the new entrants made him forget what they were talking about, so she didn't have to apologize or soothe his ego, whichever was the cause for his consternation.

"Rig, you're here," Zara said as she and Kadie dumped their bags on the table. Bess came over to help Kadie begin to unpack. "I'll get the guys. We have a lot to talk about."

Devon went into the kitchen to help Bess put the food stuffs away with Kadie, while Zara retrieved the men. No one wasted time on drawn out greetings.

Brodie gestured to the dining table, and then they were sitting down. "You saw the video?" Brodie asked.

Devon didn't know that the Kindred had shared Grant's home movie with her brother. But it was an encouraging sign of trust that they did. Although, the Kindred didn't care about keeping Grant's secret. He was the one who wanted to remain dead.

It wouldn't shatter their world if the video was leaked, if it was shared around, if it was sent to the media. Grant was the one who'd risked exposure by putting himself on film. It was obviously believed to be a risk worth taking, and he had shrouded his identity in the darkness. Although Devon imagined that either voice analysis or image enhancement could probably verify both who was on the tape and when it was made. But she was no expert.

"Yeah, I saw it," Rig said.

She kept her head craned in the direction of the table as she sorted the vegetables into the various baskets that Bess had brought from the walk-in pantry. The Kindred had a way of finding places to stay that had enough storage for everything they could possibly need to survive a siege.

Devon hadn't even noticed that there was a sliding door at the back of the kitchen. It was made to look like a false wall panel and hadn't been on the floor plan Zave had given her in his office. Maybe it had been planned as a panic room or something, but for now it was Kindred storage.

"What did you think?" Zara asked.

"The guy's got balls," Rig said. "Calling you all out."

Zave was sitting at the head of the table again, with Brodie to his left and Tuck to his right. Zara sat beside her husband with Rig opposite her. There was tension in the air. Devon couldn't decipher if it was caused by conflict or mistrust that lingered between those here or if it was because of the anger they all had about Syn.

Brodie wasn't so tactful about his opinion. "He's a fucking idiot," he muttered.

But Rig didn't get drawn into slinging insults, and she was impressed by how clear and determined he came across. "Do you have a plan?" Rig asked. "I'm guessing that's why I'm here, you need something from me."

Actually, he was here because she'd thrown a hissy fit and demanded that he be brought into the fold for protection. She expected one of them to point that out, which would make the tension rise when Rig realized he wasn't exactly welcome.

But nobody said that. Instead, assent came from Zara. "Yeah," she said. "They know you're here."

Tuck clarified, "If they're serious players, as they claim to be, they'll be monitoring flight manifests and may even have had eyes on you wherever you were and here too."

It was amazing, but Rig was undaunted. "So they know I'm around, and they want to take me down," he said.

Devon tried to keep her chin tipped down, acting as though she wasn't really listening in to what was being said, but all she was doing now was rearranging the vegetables that were already in the baskets. Bess and Kadie were behind doing the hard work, but Devon didn't want to miss a thing that was going on at the table a few feet away.

"Pretty much."

Again, without question or fear, her brother asked like it was no big deal, "And you want me to go for a walk?"

"More than that," Brodie said, clasping his hands to lean on the table. "We figure maybe you and your sister should have a blow out."

Rig's intent air took on a more serious hue. "All these years I tried to get you working for me, Rave, and here I am working for you," Rig said. "You want me to call these bastards out into the open where you can take them down, I'm game. But don't ask me to put Von in the firing line." Her brother pinned his attention on Zave at the top of the table. "So much for marrying her 'cause you love her. Did you come up with this plan?"

The plan, as much as Devon could figure it out, was to put Rig into danger. Syn wanted to hurt him, that was established. Syn were in town. If Caine was here, the rest of them were, too, and they had to wait around for Zave and Tuck to finish building the products they needed. So for now, Syn were sitting around, with little to do.

That Rig had just sauntered into town might seem a little too convenient, except his baby sister was here with her brand-new husband, so he had reason to be wandering the streets of the city.

"They're cocky," Zara said. "We've weighed the pros,

and Falc actually voted no to this plan. "The Kindred don't put their own in danger. We figure if we put you out there with your sister, they'll be salivating about the vulnerability and they won't see us coming."

He might not be afraid, but that didn't mean he wasn't up for taking precautions. "You gonna put Rave on a roof?" Rig asked.

Zara shrugged and glanced at her husband before fixating on Rigor again. "If that makes you more comfortable. But firing shots in the city streets is risky."

It would draw attention to the Kindred and would cause panic. Rig proved his priority was elsewhere. "I don't give a fuck about that when there's a chance of my sister getting kidnapped again. Do you think Syn will let her go if they get hold of her again? I don't… No, she stays here," Rig said. "I've got guys on a plane who'll be here tonight."

"They're not coming here," Brodie said. "You want to put your own men in a hotel, you do that, but you don't bring them anywhere near this apartment. If you do, I don't care who you're related to, I'll take you down myself."

Devon couldn't hold in her anguish any longer. "Hang on a second," she said, dumping the vegetables she'd been rearranging to storm around the island to the table. "You can't ask him to help you and then threaten him in the same sentence."

"I just did," Brodie said.

Zara put a hand on his forearm, probably to soothe him from leaping into confrontation, but Devon wasn't going to hold back. "I asked you to bring him here to keep him safe," she said. "Not to hurt him."

Playing mediator, as was often her role, Zara softened her husband's response with reassurance. "He won't be hurt," Zara said. "We've thought about it. He's the one they want right now, and Grant won't hesitate to take him down if he sees a chance. I know Saint is cocky, he believes he has the Kindred exactly where he wants them. He won't be looking over his shoulder, he thinks he's got us scrambling."

There was no denying the Kindred were not in a strong position at this moment. "He does," Devon said. "He does have us scrambling, and this is panic. You can't put an innocent man out onto the streets and ask him to trust you."

Rig snickered. "I've never been described as innocent before," he said, pushing out of his chair. "It's a buzz, Von. Who gives a fuck if they take me, what are they gonna do? Hurt me?"

He could be glib about his life if he wanted to, she didn't have any bravado to uphold. "Maybe," Devon said. "Best case scenario will be if they keep you locked up. Worst is they just kill you."

But he didn't seem to care, he didn't flinch. "And as long as I'm on their radar, that's gonna be true," Rig said. "I'm not walking around with a bullseye on my back. If they want me, they can come and get me. I'd rather get the shit done than stand about waiting for it to go down."

She couldn't believe how foolish that was, like he wanted to get his ya-yas in some adrenaline rush. But they were dealing with real stakes here. Her brother could die. The man she'd demanded be brought here for his own safety was about to be cast out as bait.

"Grant said he wouldn't hurt us," Devon said, frantic as she searched for an ally. The women in the kitchen were no longer unpacking, but they didn't join her or speak up, they just watched as she began to unravel. "He said that he wasn't after the Kindred, that as long as we stayed out of the way—"

"He's not Kindred," Brodie said, and she hated how he could be so blunt in his delivery of the facts that shattered her argument. Often, Zave's silence infuriated her, but she would take that over the cold, hard slap Brodie gave her every time he opened his mouth.

"Technicalities matter to Grant McCormack," Zara said, moving onto her feet, as well. "They want Rig and Rig is here. He's not Kindred. Grabbing him is not breaking the rules, Grant won't miss a chance to hurt us through a side door."

That wasn't good enough for her, but her brother spoke before she could voice further objection. "It's fuck all to do with you anyway," Rig said. "I choose to do this."

He could be so stubborn, but it was his double standards that made him a hypocrite and that was even worse. "But you choose to keep me out of it," Devon said. "I stood there and listen to you say that I'm not allowed to be hurt. But when I say the same thing—"

"It's not the same thing," Rig said with a scowl.

Except it was, he wanted to protect her, why shouldn't she reciprocate? "Why?" she demanded. "Because you're a guy and I'm not? Because I'm weak and you're strong? Because I'm vulnerable and you're capable?"

Rig folded his arms. "See, sis, you don't even need me to make the argument, you stand there and make it yourself."

Snide jibes might make him feel smug, but she didn't care about winning the fight, she cared about keeping him safe. "No, no," she said, shaking her head, and she grasped Zave's shoulder. "Tell him not to do this. Tell him this is a bad idea."

He turned to look up at her, but she wasn't encouraged by what she saw. There was no sympathy, there wasn't even pity. He was that stoic man who could keep himself outside the circle. He was an observer; he didn't have any intention of participating or bailing her out.

Maybe if she couldn't win the emotional argument, she could win the practical one. "How long would we wait?" Devon asked, going back to her brother. "You tell me I can't be involved, but what are you gonna do? Walk up and down the streets, waiting, expecting these guys to watch your every move, every minute? What happens after your guys arrive? Then you're not as vulnerable, maybe Syn won't go after him at all."

It was one thing to expect Syn to come for him after an event like a public argument that suggested a fracture in Rig's support structure. It was a different matter to expect everyone to be vigilant, at their best constantly, until Syn chose to make their move.

"We can make it happen," Zara said. "Grant's easy to manipulate, he always has been. That's why we're here now. Mitchell's made him pliant, open to the power of suggestion."

Zara was confident, but Devon didn't have a clue

what that meant. "I don't understand," she said.

"Caine," Tuck answered.

"Caine?" she repeated, and it was Zara she looked to for an explanation because she was closest to Syn's sniper.

"You know what he's like. If I ask him to poke at Grant a bit, he'll do it."

"For sport," Brodie said. "I actually envy the guy. Riling my big brother is a damn good time."

When he returned his attention to Zara, Devon lost sight of his expression, but she caught the exchange between the couple. Zara tried to appear unimpressed, but Devon read her concealed amusement.

Even when the Kindred were caught off-guard, they didn't wobble, they kept their focus on the horizon, on the ultimate goal, and came up with a plan. "Like we said, they'll have figured out that Rig is here by now. Caine's got a knack for getting into people's heads and stirring up shit."

So they were planning to have Caine provoke Syn into going after Rig. But what did that mean? She wasn't relaxed. This might seem like cold, hard fact to everyone else, but all she could think about was the possible human cost. "We'll be outnumbered," Devon said. "Especially if you plan to send him out alone."

Tuck responded, "They won't send out every man like Zara said. Saint's cocky. They want to whip Rigor out from under our nose and make it seem like a walk in the park. They think Zave and I are up to our eyeballs in electronics, trying to figure out their little prizes."

Zara carried on, "So at most they'll be expecting Rave, and if they send Caine to do a sniper sweep, we don't have to worry about him ratting out Raven."

"You've got a lot of faith in that guy, baby," Brodie said. "I'm still not convinced that we're not his sport."

Her husband's reticence didn't lessen Zara's certainty. "You weren't there," Zara said. "I watched him change when he listened to Cuckoo speak on that watch recording. Since then he's been different. And I think he's been manipulated for most of his life, he's been used and betrayed. Everyone's always looking for the next best thing. No one ever settles on him."

Pop psychology aside, Devon could feel sympathy for the guy without trusting him, and Brodie wasn't convinced either, though Devon doubted he was afflicted with any sympathy. "Because he's a prick," Raven said.

Zara sank down to dig her nails into his arm. "He trusts me because I'm the only person who's ever been honest with him."

Another Kindred tale lay behind Zara's conviction, Devon was sure of it. "For a reason," Brodie said. "You didn't do it 'cause he was such a cool guy. You did it because we needed to know where Game Time was."

Although she was still worried about her brother, Devon could recognize that Zara's faith was admirable, even if they weren't all as sure as she was about Caine's allegiance. "And after that," she said. "When he had nowhere to go, no one to turn to, no support, it was me he reached out to."

"To fuck with my head," Brodie said.

With all the animosity between the men, it didn't surprise Devon that Brodie was dubious; she was, as well. "So you're putting the life of my brother into the hands of a man who we can't agree to trust? We don't know whose side he's on," Devon said.

"Yep," Brodie said in his abrupt way. Despite the fact that it wasn't what she wanted to hear, he didn't try to soften or appease her, he just told it like it was. "And we're gonna make sure that prick brings my brother with him."

This was about more than just putting Rig in harm's way for the hell of it. "Why?"

Optimism, or maybe it was anticipation, rippled through the people seated at the table. "Because if we can draw Grant into the open, we can take him," Zara said. "And as soon as we have a hostage of our own, we can open negotiations."

"Negotia…"

Devon was so shocked by how casual they were with people's lives that she slunk back from the table. Her hand rose to her mouth as she tried to absorb the possibilities. The Kindred were thorough, and they were good strategists who took risks. And not small risks either, they took big risks that would either pay massive dividends or leave them decimated.

"And what do we do if you fail?" she asked when her hand drifted from her mouth. "What if Grant doesn't come?"

But the group didn't accept that as a possibility. "He will," Tuck said.

Devon wasn't so sure. "How do you know?"

As usual, the men kept their secrets, and it was Zara who tried to bring her into the fold. "Because he wants the adventure," she said. "He wants to be in the field. He wants to emulate his brother. Why do you think he was in Mexico? He didn't need to be. Mitchell's not quick and has no interest in getting his hands dirty."

Devon followed along, trying to come around to their way of thinking. "So he stays at home."

"Thad is not qualified. He's not gonna be in the field, what use is he?" Zara said.

Brodie offered a scenario but wasn't concerned about it. "Maybe he'll be kicking around in case someone gets hurt, but we're not worried about taking him down if we have to."

"You're not going to hurt him," Bess said from the kitchen.

Even Devon had to admit that she'd forgotten the woman was there. "We won't kill him," Brodie said. "But if he gets in the way, I'll put him on his ass."

Brodie was blunt with everyone, but Devon didn't like it when he was so honest with her. She expected, when she turned to Bess, to see the woman heartbroken.

Instead, she was shaking her head, not in the same desperate action that Devon felt drove her but almost like she expected nothing less. "I still expect you to look after him," Bess said. "You bring him to me if you can."

Brodie didn't reply, and although he had his back to the kitchen, he took two fingers to his forehead in a pronounced salute of acceptance.

Zara slid an arm around him to rest her head against his shoulder. "I don't think they'll bring Thad out, and if they do, I don't think he'll want a showdown," Zara said. "If he did, he wouldn't have shied away from answering to his mother or the rest of us."

She might have agreed, except he hadn't gone completely into hiding. "He showed up at the merger mixer," Devon said.

"A public place," Tuck answered. "Where he was on a clock and he knew he'd be flung out on his ass. Syn are gonna wait until Rig's isolated before they take him down. It will be on a quiet street, in an alleyway, maybe in a parking lot, somewhere where he's by himself. They'll rush out to grab him, and they're not gonna trust Thad to do that. Thad is a pawn, taken to damage us."

Which was another reason Bess was worried about him. "And because it never hurts to have a doctor on side," Brodie added.

Zara spoke up next, "Caine we can control. Mitchell won't be there."

"Leatt we can shoot," Brodie said, and there may have been some optimism in that tone like he would relish the chance to erase the man.

Without addressing her husband's perverse enjoyment, Zara concluded the roll. "So that leaves Saint, he wants to be Action Man anyway. With Caine's needling, there's no way he'll miss the chance to be there."

They'd thought about this, and they must have discussed it. Devon hadn't made more of an effort to be involved in the strategy meeting because she didn't think this would be the strategy. "I can't let you do this," she said.

Her brother was getting antsy but laid his attention on her. "You don't have a choice," Rigor replied. "They came for me by coming for you. I'm not gonna let that slide."

He was caught up in this moment, and the Kindred were seductive in their loyalty and determination. "So you're doing this for me?" Devon asked, but she wasn't fooled. "I don't believe it. You're not doing this to protect me, it's revenge and it's machismo. This might be normal to you guys, but it's not normal to me. I'm not gonna go along with it. Come up with a different plan, or as far as I'm concerned, all of you can go to hell."

Storming away from the table, she went up the stairs

and into the bedroom. Devon needed time to pace, to stress, to scream at nothing. Everyone was so sure that the plan would work, and it was a good plan because they needed some leverage and having a prisoner would give them that. They couldn't have a fake prisoner in Caine because Syn would see him as expendable in the same way the Kindred believed that Thad was to them and Leatt too.

They were just padding. Extra numbers. Men for Grant McCormack and Frank Mitchell to manipulate and direct. They wouldn't lose any sleep or spend any time trying to rescue them, they'd be written off as collateral damage. Standard breakage, factored into the cost of doing business.

The two main men were pivotal. If the Kindred could control one of them, they might be able to break out of this terrifying predicament.

Devon wasn't finished stressing when Rig burst into the room. "Get the hell out of here!" she demanded.

"No way! What the fuck do you think you're doing, speaking to me like that in front of those guys down there?"

So he was embarrassed? She'd hurt his pride? His dignity was bruised? She punched his shoulder. "I don't give a fuck what those guys think of you, and I don't care if you're pissed at me. Don't you get that you and me are the only family we have? If you go out there, they can't guarantee you'll live. I can't guarantee that this Caine guy won't shoot you. Maybe this is all a game to him, and he wants to draw you out. How the hell do I know?"

Rig threw up his hands. "What do you want me to do? Sit here like a pussy hiding? How does that help anyone?"

"It doesn't," Zave said from the doorway behind Rig. "Shy, we need a way out of this. The alternative is Swift and me giving them exactly what they want."

Somewhat deflated, she couldn't accept that their options were so bleak. "That's not the only alternative," she said, although she had to admit that she was no strategist and didn't have a better plan. "He's my brother. He's the only family I have."

Disregarding Rig even though he stood a foot to her left, Zave came to her. "I know what it is to lose family," he said. "If you tell me not to do this." He curled his hands around each side of her neck. "We won't."

"Fuck that," Rig said.

Zave ignored her brother and as usual, made her his focus. Putting her at the center of his universe gave him clarity, but she was still confused. "If we have to knock him out and send him to the suite on the island to protect him, we will," her husband said.

Their sniper wouldn't be quick to agree with tossing their plan out the window. "Brodie won't accept that."

Zave was enamored by her gaze. "Sure he will because his wife calls the shots he makes. He'll understand that mine does the same."

Finding his bluster, Rig injected his opinion. "I'm not going to no fucking island. I'm not going to no fucking cell."

Another voice rose from the doorway, "You'll go where we tell you to go." Everyone turned to see Zara observing them. "Give me a minute with Devon."

Zave kissed her head before grabbing Rig to give him a shove toward the door. Her brother wasn't getting a choice about leaving her with Zara. Once the men were gone, Zara closed the door.

Self-conscious, Devon squirmed. "I'm not trying to be difficult."

But Zara didn't care about why Devon was acting the way she was, at least, she didn't ask for explanations. Clear and calm, she smiled and shrugged. "Zave's right," Zara said. "I mean, we need this. More than maybe we've needed anything else. Because right now we have nothing to barter."

Glad that someone was at last acknowledging the Kindred were perhaps acting out of desperation, it wasn't enough to make her back down but was enough to soften her mood. "You're trading on my brother's life."

Zara didn't sugar coat the truth, and Devon wondered if she'd always been like that or if Brodie had influenced the way she was with people. "Yeah. But taking risks is what we do, Devon. I've seen the people your brother spends his time with, he's in danger more than you probably think."

More than she'd faced before her ordeal. Devon wasn't as naïve now as she had once been. Retreating to the bed, she sat down. Hooking her hands under her thighs, she sighed. "I thought he was brought here to keep him safe, and I was the one who made a big deal about bringing him here."

Although Devon knew that Zara was trying to assuage her guilt, she appreciated the effort. "We'd have come round to the same strategy either way. Rig is the only non-Kindred member who we know for sure they want," Zara said as she sauntered over to sit next to her on the bed. "So right now we have three choices."

Could Zara hold the salvation she needed and be able to save Rig from being in danger? "Three?" Devon said, experiencing a flare of hope that made her twist.

But Zara didn't smile and get excited, she remained composed. "Option one is this, we put Rig out there. We start the fight after we know for sure Caine's positioned Grant where we want him. Then when Syn come to take Rig down, we sneak up behind them."

That option was the one she'd been arguing to avoid, and so she was happy to pass on it without giving it much consideration. "Option two?" she asked.

"Option two, we do exactly what they want. Our guys build the tech, we hand it over, we walk away and wait to hear about tragedy on the news."

A tragedy that would be on all of their heads. Zave's guilt would go into overdrive, he'd implode. Because he had been the one who would've built the device that might have caused, or at least facilitated, the destruction of others. It didn't matter that he hadn't been the one to flip any switch or that handing over the tech had been a Kindred decision. That was the way his mind worked. And Devon wasn't sure how committed she could be to guiding him away from his path of self-destruction because she would have to live with her own culpability.

They would only follow option two if she vetoed option one. If there had been an obvious, or preferable, option, someone would have suggested it when she voiced opposition downstairs. But she had to ask, "And option three?"

Zara squeezed her lips around her teeth and lowered her chin to focus on the floor, sending any remaining hope Devon might have had swirling down the drain. Goosebumps cascaded over her forearms. Whatever Zara was about to say, it wasn't anything Devon was going to enjoy hearing. "Option three involves building the devices too. While that was happening we'd have to set up a meet."

"What kind of meet?"

"In Mexico." Tilting her head, Zara made eye contact and must have seen Devon's dread. "Caine isn't the only one who's good at manipulation. Although Syn and the Kindred have a common enemy in the cartels that took you, that can be turned to our advantage. If we can persuade them to our side, we can increase our ranks and try a full-on assault to take Syn down. It's complicated. We would never be able to mobilize and build the trust we need before Syn's deadline. So, we'd have to give them what they want and hope that they don't use it. The second issue, of course, is that we don't know where they are. After the exchange, they could go anywhere in the world. The cartels will only travel so far, depending on how much they want it."

Hardly able to believe it, she felt sick at the prospect. "You want to ally yourselves with the men who took me, the men who took Bronwyn, the men who—"

"No," Zara said, "that's why the option was completely discounted. We know Syn want Rig, and we know they promised Thad they would take down the cartels."

So those were the only two places that the Kindred knew Syn were going to be aiming for. Except Devon couldn't go back to Mexico and face those people. It would mean putting Zave into terrible danger because he was the only face they knew. He would have to be present. So would Brodie, so would Tuck. She would want as much manpower down there as possible, and if they chose that option, Rigor would want to be involved too.

Now she had to decide which she preferred. Her brother in a familiar city with the Kindred controlling the op? Or another mission south of the border in a place that had only ever been hell for her, dealing with volatile characters in the cartel, hoping that they didn't kidnap or torture the Kindred men.

Drawing in a long breath through her nose, she exhaled. "I have to be there. The argument's a good idea because if they believe Rig and I are fighting, they might think no one will notice he's gone."

"Exactly," Zara said, and Devon appreciated that the woman didn't smile because Devon was still terrified and didn't want anyone to think she was happy about doing this.

Resigned, there was nothing left to argue, as Zara had made her point. "Call Caine and get him to start working Grant from his side. I'll get Rig to send his men home, I don't trust any of them." Zara was nodding. "I'll let you do this," Devon said. "But you have to promise me that we will get Grant McCormack. That we will get Game Time back and that Zave won't have to hand over any of his creations to Syn."

Zara took her hand. "If this works," she said, "Syn won't even exist anymore. We're going to neutralize this threat. The Kindred are tenacious, and we'll keep fighting as long as one of us still breathes."

And that was what worried her. For now, they all had air in their lungs. But if there was one hitch, one miscalculation, one delay, someone she cared about could lose their life, and the first person they were talking about putting in the line of fire was her only blood relative.

Devon was apprehensive, but being in the Kindred was no cakewalk, and she'd said she was willing to make sacrifices for the greater good. It was just taking her longer to adjust to this way of life than she'd realized it would.

# SEVENTEEN

"OKAY, I'M GOING," Devon muttered to herself.

She'd just pushed out of the glass-fronted coffee shop and was storming down the street, wearing an expression of ire. Anyone who was watching would've seen, or overheard, her and her brother shouting at each other in the quiet corner shop that was chosen specifically because it was small and out of the way. Their argument hadn't been missed by anyone in, or around, the establishment. Selecting this place made sure it wasn't lost in throngs of people.

It was a whole day after they concluded that this was the course of action they had to take. Zara said that Caine was confident a day would be enough time for him to manipulate Grant into grabbing Rig. He'd already convinced Syn to watch the Kindred building. The man was lazy, but efficient.

Thad would've spoken of the value of surveillance, so he had probably backed Caine up without realizing he was playing into their plan. The Kindred had cameras everywhere. Deliberately placing them not only in US buildings and cities but around the world, watching people and places that they didn't have the manpower to observe at all times.

"Keep going," she whispered, forcing herself to keep her strides long. "That's fine. Walk away from the only family

I have. Leave my brother alone to be attacked."

"Stop talking," Brodie said in her ear.

As this was part of a Kindred op, she was wearing an earpiece. So were Rig, and Zave, and Zara, and Tuck. Everyone was focused on her now because her role was coming to an end; she was about to leave the stage. After she was in the wings, all eyes would fall on Rigor as they waited with bated breath to see when he would be descended upon.

"She's doing great," Zara said to her husband, her voice coming through the same earpiece to Devon. "You can work with voices in your head, beau. It's not easy to walk away from someone you care about."

"Let's not turn this into a domestic," Tuck said.

They'd gone over and over and over the plan. Devon knew she was supposed to turn right, to carry on down the street to the car where her husband was waiting for her. She wished she could hear his voice now, but he wouldn't speak on a public airway, much less reveal anything of his inner thoughts to such a large group. The point was that this had to look realistic.

She and her brother wanted time alone. But Zave, as the new husband, would still be worried about her. So he would insist on taking them to this neutral location, and he would wait for his wife out of concern for her safety.

He'd even gone so far as to put Petri on her tail, and she knew that the man who was becoming her personal bodyguard would be hurrying to keep up with her. Devon was to be protected at all costs, and Syn wouldn't see anything suspicious in her husband waiting for her or putting security on her.

The argument had been so real that for a minute, she'd forgotten it was fake. Rig had bought the drinks and they'd chattered for a few minutes, making the scenario as realistic as possible. In time with her own emotion, as her anxiety rose, she requested that they return to Zave and that was when Rig got angry and he told her to stop looking to her husband to protect her. As her brother, he believed that when he was around, he could do it. He would look after her. Rig didn't want to be second to the man who owned KC and now owned his little sister.

Anyone who knew anything about Rig would know he had an ego. They'd know how much he needed to be in charge. Syn would be blinded by those flaws because the men in their ranks were just the same. They wouldn't appreciate anyone belittling them by deferring to another. And so that was how the argument had started.

*"He's my husband and he loves me. He wants to protect us both."*

Rig had flown to his feet and waved an arm in a much more exaggerated gesture than he would usually adopt. But it helped to emphasize what was going on in case Syn were only looking from the outside. No one inside was a Syn member. But it had been frightening to hear Tuck and Zave talk about technologies that could pick up voices from the width of the street away. So Devon gave it her best shot and wondered how many of Rig's words were for purpose and how many were true.

After he'd tossed a couple of insults Zave's way and she'd got deliberately offended, she told him to go to hell and stormed away. Now she found herself regretting her final words to him. Zave's car was just where it was supposed to be and Phil, the driver, jumped out to open the back door for her.

Security had their own vehicle behind Zave's, and Petri would travel in that car. So when Phil closed the door behind her, she was left alone with her husband. "You did good," he said.

The warmth of the arm he put around her calmed her a little. There were so many things that she wanted to say but had to be sure that they were truly alone, in every sense. "Can we talk?" she asked.

He nodded. "There's tech built into the frame of the car that repels other listening devices. Kindred electronics have a specific signature that allows us to keep listening while others can't." He grazed a fingertip around the shell of her ear. "You can take that out if you want to."

Why would she want to? Her pounding heart was a testament to how terrified she was. The adrenaline of the argument had helped her to fulfill her role, but she wasn't angry about what had been said, she was afraid of what would come next.

"No, no," she said. "I have to keep listening. I want to know what happens."

The privacy screen was up, so Zave had to press a button in order to speak to Phil. "Take us home," Zave said, releasing the button.

The car pulled out of the space and into traffic."

"Wait," she said, clutching his wrists with both hands. "I don't want to leave him there."

Her adrenaline was still going, but Zave was cool as ice. Although, he had no real reason to be upset as it wasn't his brother out there. "That was the whole idea," Zave said. "I know you're worried. I know you are. But if Syn are watching, they need to see us leave. They need to believe that you're so angry that you are abandoning him there. Right now, Grant McCormack is rubbing his hands in glee and they're putting together a plan."

Sitting and waiting wasn't part of the plan, he was right about that, but that didn't mean she had to be out of the loop. "Well, where is Rig?" she asked, touching her ear, wishing she could hear his voice.

"Still in the coffee shop," Zara answered, and it was disconcerting to know that those in her ear could still hear her. "We're gonna be out of range soon. You did good, Devon. We've got it from here."

She didn't want to go out of range and be cut off. But this had been the plan she'd agreed to. They wanted Syn to see this, to see her return to her husband and demand for him to take her home. If anyone was watching the car, they would think Rig was all alone now. They certainly couldn't stay parked only a street away because that would be suspicious and would give Rig an out.

The positioning of the car had been picked specifically because Rig would take his time in the coffee shop, fuming to himself, and when he was ready, when they figured enough time had passed, he would leave and follow the path to where the car had been parked only to find it gone. At that point, his anger would be renewed.

Just a few steps away from that parking spot was a long alleyway that would take him out almost a full block away into a deserted parking lot. If Syn were quick, and they would have to be, that would be where they would take him down.

She didn't notice that she was wringing her hands in her lap until Zave picked one up and uncurled her fingers to kiss her palm. "We'll be ready. Trust the Kindred," he said. "We're watching Rig. Raven and Swift and Swallow, they have nothing else to do but this. Syn will only go for your brother somewhere isolated, and that's all we need. We'll sneak up right behind them. No one will lay their hands on him. If Caine is there, he'll back us up. If it's Leatt, we'll take him down."

And if it was Thad, he would know too well what the Kindred were capable of and wouldn't put up a fight.

Gazing out the window at the city she now called home, Devon understood that her fear was instinctive in the way anyone worries for those they love. But she did trust these people, and she didn't think that they would fail, not really.

There were variables like Caine, who she was still figuring out. He wanted to be Kindred or he wanted to be Syn or maybe he didn't want to be either. If he'd warned Syn of the Kindred plan, it would never work, and they could be led into their own ambush. If Caine switched sides at the last minute, everyone could end up dead.

They needed Grant or Mitchell to be there. If they weren't, the Kindred could kill or kidnap whoever did try to steal Rig, but it wouldn't be as lucrative as holding the eldest McCormack brother. And if they didn't get him, she didn't know what would come next.

Taking support instead of asking for it, she lifted from her seat to move into Zave's lap. Wrapping his arms around her, she closed her eyes and rested her face on his neck. "It will all work out in the end," he said, trying to make her feel better.

Clutching the edge of his jacket, she pulled it closer to her. "It will all work out if we get your cousin. It will all boil down to who blinks first."

"The Kindred know how to hold their nerve. No one's ever won a game of chicken against us."

Someone would shoot first. There were so many threats flying around that the whole scenario was one huge house of cards. All it would take would be one to shift just slightly out of place, and the whole thing would come tumbling down. If the Kindred exposed Syn, Syn would expose them. But if Syn followed through on their threats to put Brodie and Zave in jail, the women would be forced to retaliate.

Zara was strong, they'd follow her lead, and as she'd said, as long as one Kindred member still drew breath, they would fight against Syn.

Tipping her head back, she searched his gaze for answers. "You'll take him back to the island? If you get him, that's where you'll take him?"

Because she'd been so focused on her own role and Rig's safety, she hadn't paid much attention to what would come next. "Yes, Caine will go back to Syn and say he got away while Grant was kidnapped. We'll take Grant back to the island because we can control that environment. We'll see Syn flying in if they try to ambush us."

They had another issue that she hadn't heard addressed in all the strategy building. "But if we go back there, the media will follow."

He didn't let himself get distracted by that. From the way he'd taken everything in stride, she could see he was practiced at keeping his cool and wondered if there would ever come a time that she could be so detached.

"The best way to cope with a Kindred op is one minute at a time. Anything could happen. Any opportunity could present itself, and if it does, we'll seize it. We haven't run out of options yet, shy. It's more secure keeping him in a place we control, in a place that has facilities built to keep people captive."

People like her. She knew what he was talking about because she'd been a prisoner in that suite. The alternative would be keeping Grant in the apartment in the city, and it would be too easy for Syn to mount an offensive in such an urban place. The media could be lurking anywhere, there were a hundred faces on every street corner.

It occurred to her that they were driving away, not only from her family, but from his. He hadn't voiced opposition to playing babysitter, but he was capable of so much more than just looking after her because her nerves were frayed. "Don't you want to be a part of it?" she asked. "A part of the op to go after Grant?"

Apparently, he didn't look at it from the same perspective she did. "I am a part of it and so are you. We all use our skills for the Kindred, and right now we're going back to the apartment so I can pack up the build. I'll work on the schematics until we get word we've got Saint in hand."

Horror made her blink and forget about the action playing out elsewhere. "You're not still going to build it, are you?"

Pragmatic before he was passionate, he kissed her head in a soothing gesture. "I have to assume that plan B, or C, or D may involve giving Syn what they want. I have to be ready for that. If they want Grant back, they'll have to give us Game Time. Who knows what else those negotiations may lead to? If we decide we need to hand over what they've demanded or sabotage it, we'll do it."

But Syn had laid out what would happen if the Kindred tried something like that. "They said they were ready for sabotage, that if Grant or Frank weren't around to prevent—"

"I heard what they said, but things change. Mitchell's going to be angry when he finds out Saint was taken. There's a chance he'll tell us to keep his prized apprentice, and then we're just stuck with Grant McCormack. We're not going to cut him loose, are we?"

Grabbing Grant had been sold to her as the answer to everything, yet now she found out it might not be. "So we'll keep him prisoner forever?" she asked, but he settled her head against his body and ran his fingers through her hair as he turned his own eyes to the window.

This conversation could go on forever because as he'd said, the game was about to change. The Kindred were about to regain the upper hand, and Mitchell would be mad. McCormack would be humiliated. Caine would've proven himself, or not. If they triumphed, they'd be back in the driving seat. If Caine betrayed them and proved that this was sport, Syn would know the Kindred had tried to double cross them, and that would never lead to a positive outcome.

Closing her eyes, she began to worry not only for her brother's well-being, but her husband's too. Syn could arrange to have him snatched from her at any minute. If they got Rig and put Zave behind bars, she'd still be Kindred. Bess would look after her. Zara, Brodie, Tuck, and Kadie would protect her, but she wouldn't have her home, which was right here with this man.

"I love you," she whispered, and it didn't matter if he heard her. Caressing her cheek on his collar, she needed to be this close to him.

Turned out, he did hear her. "I love you too, but don't start thinking that this is going to go to shit. You have to believe we're going to win, and when we do, you'll see that the Kindred are confident for a reason and it's not because we're better, although we are, it's because we're right."

They were. They'd been put in this position by a group of men whose warped ideas could only lead to mayhem and murder. The Kindred were trying to put a stop to it before the mob got out of control. Devon was a part of the machine. Rig was, too, unofficially. And as terrifying as it was to think about that machine falling apart if one of the cogs fell loose, she began to see how, if they achieved their goal and reached their destination, they would have a lot to be proud of.

The daunting mission would bring them all closer together. Closer than any typical family, blood or not, marriage or not. The Kindred priority one was to watch each other's backs. Their foundation had been shaken when Thad betrayed them, but even that had served to solidify their bond. Those who remained were unshakeable.

Devon would prove to her man and to her unit that she believed in them by following their orders, just as she'd done today. She just hoped she was capable enough to see this through to the end.

# EIGHTEEN

DEVON DIDN'T HAVE to be frantic for long. They'd literally just stepped into the apartment when Zave got the call. The Kindred had Grant McCormack.

Grabbing her, Bess, and Kadie, Zave bundled them into a car to transport them to the airfield. She didn't know how Brodie and Tuck got Grant onto the aircraft, but there he was at the back of the plane, out cold.

They might not have their doctor on side anymore, but they'd have learned enough from him to know how to incapacitate a passenger. He was left to roll around at the back of the plane, hog-tied. Although Devon did look twice to register the rise and fall of his chest, confirming that they were transporting a live prisoner, not a dead one.

Zave didn't have a co-pilot anymore, but that didn't slow him down. He went through his checks and got them in the air like this was any normal flight. The journey wouldn't be long, but she felt like she waited a lifetime for somebody to speak.

It was her brother who opened his mouth first. "Landed on your feet, sis," Rig said. "All this shit belong to your man?"

She nodded, half-remembering how impressed she'd

been by the idea of a private jet before she'd experienced it. Still awe-inspiring and grandiose, the plane was immaculate. But she kept thinking about the man at the back of the plane, wondering when he would wake up.

Brodie and Tuck had been hanging into the cockpit, talking for a minute. Now they'd moved into the armchairs that faced each other to talk some more. Kadie unbuckled her seatbelt and went over to whisper something to Tuck.

"It's over there," he said, pointing toward a storage compartment next to the kitchen area.

Kadie went over to retrieve a case, from which she pulled a laptop. Bringing it back to the table, she sat next to Devon again. There were four seats here, two on each side of a table. Bess was opposite Devon with Zara beside her, and they faced aft, while she and Kadie were looking toward the front of the craft. Rigor was seated on a couch that ran along the edge of the plane on the opposite side of the aisle from their table.

Kadie opened up the laptop and turned it on. It booted almost immediately, and Kadie tapped in a password.

"I'm surprised he lets you into that," Rig said on a snicker then called out, "Where'd you keep your porn collection if your girl knows your password, Swift?"

Devon had noticed a change in him since they'd gotten on the plane, and it was more than just being impressed at where they were. She could identify with the feeling of relief that the imminent danger had passed. But she could tell he was being swept along in being included by the Kindred. That had been what she'd wanted, for him to be accepted so that her old family could be a part of her new one.

Except she saw now how that would change his circumstances. Her brother would go from being a low-level wise guy to a full-blown vigilante.

Feeling the weight of responsibility, Devon had brought her brother into this, and throughout their lives, he'd been the one protecting her. She sort of wished she'd spent more time protecting him, because at least in his own world he was oblivious to this level of danger. She loved her brother, but he wasn't as proficient as the Kindred.

"Do you want me to use the headphones?"

Devon had been transfixed by her brother's smug, yet wondrous, expression that was still taking in the features of their environment. It wasn't until Bess nudged her that Devon realized Kadie was talking to her.

Snapping back into the moment, Devon frowned. "Headphones for what?"

"She's going to listen to the op," Zara said. "It's all recorded. You can't see anything, but you'll hear our communications."

"That's our compromise," Kadie said. "I stay out of Swift's way when he's in the field, but I like to catch up after."

"No, I want to hear it," Devon said, kicking herself for not figuring out that the Kindred would have a record. With the amount of time that the men spent whispering with each other, it wouldn't surprise her if they did a post-game study, breaking down each play and figuring out how they could be better, quicker and more efficient the next time.

Kadie was much like her in that they didn't have the experience or skills to be of great use in the field. For Kadie that meant hanging back, letting her man take the risks, but Devon's man tended to stay on the periphery. She had no idea what his future would be if they were successful in their mission to take down Syn because his previous focus, other than KC, had been his missions with Thad. They were now a thing of the past.

She didn't get much time to analyze the possibilities because Zara's voice crackled through the laptop speaker, and silence fell over them all. Listening to every step her brother took, she drew maybe six breaths throughout the duration of the recording.

Zara declared through the tape that Rigor was on the move. Devon waited and waited to hear another sound. Brodie's voice rose to state their target was in sight. Caine was present, too, and despite an exchange of trash talk between the men, the grab seemed to go down exactly as it had been described to her it would.

Rigor took the path down the alley into the parking lot. On over watch, Zara whispered his progress to Brodie and

Tuck as they shadowed his moves from opposite approaches to close in on McCormack in a pincer maneuver.

Zara couldn't shoot for shit apparently, but that was unimportant, as she was good at directing her men. As Grant moved in behind Rig, Caine backed him up. Zara was confident that Caine wouldn't hurt the Kindred.

Grant and Caine got even closer to their target.

Saint's triumphant announcement to Rig that, *"Now's the time to pay for working against Syn"* was a short-lived victory. One second later, he cursed and said his younger brother's name.

From the audio, she'd guess that he was hit. Zara clucked at her lover and told him the punch was unnecessary, confirming Devon's thoughts. *"Give him the shot and let's get moving,"* Zara spoke through the speakers.

Caine asked after Zara, and Brodie replied by telling the sniper to bolt before he took him down too. That was when the trash talk was exchanged for a minute. Caine laughed and seemed to crack his knuckles.

*"Wouldn't be the first time you've taken a swing at me. I'll give you one for free to make it look good."*

A fist hit a face in an abrupt smack. Male laughter followed.

Devon couldn't figure out who was laughing, but it sounded more friendly than perverse. *"If you boys are done playing, pack up the cargo,"* Zara said. *"I'm on my way to you."*

Those were the last words on the recording. Kadie turned it off and everyone exhaled.

It was Rig sitting straighter that drew her attention away from the computer. He was no longer smiling. Clicking his tongue, he rose, and that was enough to get Brodie and Tuck onto their feet, as well.

Scuffling from the back of the plane explained his actions, as Rig must have seen Grant wakening before he'd begun to move.

Brodie strode past all of them into the rear cabin where none of the women could see. Kadie turned off the computer and stowed it in the bag, but when she thought about putting it back, Tuck marched over to snatch it from her and shoved her into her seat.

"Don't move from there," Tuck said to his girl.

Although he was serious, Kadie smiled. "I'll move if I wanna move, Hotshot. But I'm okay with you picking up after me, if you bring me a glass of wine."

Tuck was already putting the laptop back in the storage compartment. "When we get to the island, you can drink as much as you like, Toots. But you keep your sass to yourself here."

Kadie's amusement didn't lessen. She rolled her eyes toward Zara, who was just as relaxed. Devon wished she felt the same.

A body flew forward between the women's table and Rig's couch. Grant McCormack was awake all right. His mouth was covered and his hands were bound at his back, although his feet had been cut free.

Brodie wasn't far behind him. He shoved his brother onto the floor, then bent down to thrust a finger into his face. "You'll stay on your ass if you know what's good for you, Saint."

The tape over his mouth prevented Grant from retorting, although from the sound behind it, it was clear that he tried.

Zara unfastened her seatbelt. "Take off the tape," she said.

Brodie didn't entertain her request. "Not a fucking chance. I'm not listening to his shit."

Leaving her seat, she went to press herself into her husband's side, and she began to stroke his ass. "We have to listen to it because you know what he's like, beau. He has to say his piece before we get to say ours, and he's going to be the key to our negotiating with Mitchell."

Facing the front of the plane, Devon could see each of the trio's faces. Brodie was pissed, as uptight and impatient as he always was. Zara was smiling, not in joy, but in a coy kind of carnal secret that she shared only with her husband through her admiring gaze.

Despite being on his butt beneath the couple, Grant's scowling eyes were fixed on them. If he'd had a relationship with Zara, platonic or not, and hated her brother so much, it was strange to her that he would be so enamored with the couple.

Maybe his fixation was defiance. Like they couldn't make him look away just because they were sharing a private moment.

Tuck sauntered to his seat, which was near where Grant was on the floor. He poked his boot into Grant's shoulder. "I say, we knock him out again."

"Agreed," Brodie grumbled.

But Kadie was on Zara's side. "Let's hear what he has to say," she piped up.

"Yeah, I wanna hear him cry," Rig agreed. "This fucker wanted to hurt me. I say I'm owed. 'Bout time someone kicked the shit out of him."

Everyone had an opinion. Devon didn't voice hers, but she was curious about what Grant would say. Would he apologize? Make threats? There didn't seem to be a point to bringing him forward into the main part of the cabin with the group if they were just going to gawp at him.

"Don't create a crime scene in midair," Zara said. "We don't have the chemicals to clean that shit up, and what would we do with his body?"

Some of this had to be intimidation tactics, but Devon was sure they'd follow through if they had to. "Throw it out the door into the water," Rig said. "Anyway, I didn't say I was gonna kill him, I just want to rough him up a bit."

No one jumped to Grant's defense, and Devon wasn't surprised. "There's gonna be time for that, and the line forms behind me when it comes," Brodie said.

Devon couldn't see his face anymore because he'd turned to glare at his brother, but she could hear how angry he was at the man on the floor. Again, Grant tried to call out.

Bess was the one to break the stalemate. "Oh, for goodness sake, all of you stop posturing," she said. "You have to take the tape off. But Grant, you remember your position here."

Bess was the most senior member of the family, and everyone in the Kindred respected her. Devon didn't know if that extended to Syn or the specifics of Bess' relationship with this nephew. But with the added pressure from his aunt, Brodie bent to snag the corner of the tape to rip it from his mouth. Grant probably didn't want to call out in pain, but he did.

Brodie snickered before pushing the sole of his boot against his older brother's chest, forcing him onto his back. "So, Saint, what have you got to tell us?"

"You're all dead," Grant croaked. "You're all gonna die. Syn are going to—"

"Do we look like we're afraid of Syn?" Brodie asked, maintaining the pressure on Grant's chest. "We took you down, no problem."

Snarling and unafraid, Devon was impressed that he wasn't more snivelly as she might have expected. "Because that snake Caine probably bolted the minute he saw you. We should never have trusted him, he's a coward."

So Caine was at fault for Grant being kidnapped because he didn't stay to back him up? That might be true, except the Kindred knew Caine wasn't loyal to Syn. But it was good to get confirmation that Grant hadn't realized that. Believing him a coward was better than believing him a traitor. "Caine's irrelevant. You believed you were invincible," Zara said. "That was always your biggest flaw, Grant."

Grant's attention pounced to her. "I preferred it when you called me sir."

Putting an arm out to his wife, Brodie requested her hand, and Zara gave it without hesitation. "Those days are gone, brother," Brodie sneered. "We got married."

His disgust was a continuance of the previous revulsion that Devon didn't understand. "I heard," Grant said. "You guys have just made the biggest mistake of your life. What do you think is going to happen now? Mitchell will have sent Jennifer to the cops already."

Brodie stepped off, and Grant managed to wriggle onto his elbows so he could shuffle back to lean against the side of a chair.

If Jennifer went to the cops, then they would come for Zave. It wouldn't take them long to figure out where he was because after they'd checked KC and the city apartment, the next logical place was the island.

Worried about her husband's liberty, she tried to call Grant's bluff to get some kind of assurance that her man was secure. "You won't send them to the island," Devon said. "If they come to the island looking for him, they'll find you."

They'd known there was a chance that Syn weren't bluffing, that they planned to take down Zave and Brodie, although they probably planned to do that anyway, no matter how compliant the Kindred were.

Grant barked a laugh, and his glower touched all of them before he spoke. "Guess you guys don't get the message no matter who delivers it. If they find me, I'll blame you people. You fucking idiots were the ones who faked my death for me. I'll tell the cops I've been kept prisoner so you could get your greedy hands on CI, and all the evidence is in my favor."

Never showing weakness, Brodie responded, "Until we start singing about Mitchell, about Syn, about Caine and Leatt."

"Oh, you think they're going to back you up?" Grant asked to his brother. "Yeah, I'm sure they'll thank you for naming them to the cops. You want more enemies? I've got no problem with you saying their names. Caine and Leatt end up in cells with you? I don't give a fuck. I'm not the one who has to worry about getting my naked ass shanked in the shower.

"What's the worst thing that will happen to me? I'll end up back in my corporate office, making millions, respected. The world will sympathize with my trauma, I'll make a mint just telling my story. While I get famous out here, you'll be rotting in there, listening to the media worshiping me."

"Man," Brodie laughed. "You have some fucking imagination, Saint. You think you can't go wrong? You still think you're golden? You still think you're gonna get out of this alive?"

"I know I am. Because after Jennifer takes her story to the cops and they arrest your fucking cousin, the rest of you will fall apart. You're going to be right there, little brother, for the cops to pick up, too. You don't think Mitchell's already emailing all the evidence we have about what you've done?" Twisting to look Swift up and down, his lip curled. "And they're going to cuff you too. They should arrest you just for being loyal to these fuckers. That should be a crime. You're sure not squeaky clean."

This was it, her breaking point. Devon smacked a hand onto the table as she thrust to her feet. Kadie hurried out of her way to let Devon stride past Rig to come to a stop at Grant's feet between Brodie and Zara.

Unafraid and unintimidated by the pathetic man sitting on the floor, who was boasting about his superiority, Devon snapped, "If you take down the Kindred, you're going down too. I've known you two minutes, and I've learned, all you do is ruin lives. You think that Syn are gonna make the world a better place? That they're gonna be better than the Kindred because they're gonna think bigger? I'll let you in on a secret, Mr. McCormack. You think smaller than every person on the plane because the only thing you're concerned with are the grapes between your thighs."

Rig whooped and Kadie was laughing. "Fuck you," Grant said.

She wasn't done and didn't care about his insult. "All you care about is proving you've got the biggest balls. You think you can be like the Kindred overnight. They don't want respect or notoriety; the idea of telling their story or getting famous repulses them all. You can't be like these guys because you don't have a decent, selfless bone in your body, and the Kindred is all about putting your own needs after what's best for the group."

"That what your husband told you?" Grant asked.

His flippant attitude infuriated her more. "You took Thad from his mother and everybody who cared about him. You didn't need him. Neither did Mitchell. It was all about power, but that stupid boy believes he matters to you, that he's important. You played on his insecurities by promising him that you'd go after the cartels that took the woman he loved. You're playing with a confused, traumatized mind, and you don't even care. If you can't care about your own blood, you can't care about a stranger with any compassion, and you definitely aren't qualified to save the world."

He didn't like being derided. "You don't know anything about me! You don't know what I'm about, you don't know what I care about!"

She knew exactly what he cared about whether he admitted it or not. "Sure, I do. You care about you… and right now, you should, because if you don't do what you're told by us and do it right, we're not gonna play games, set you up or call the cops or involve the media, that's bullshit. You want to know what happens if you fuck with the Kindred?"

Zara looped her arms around her shoulders, and Devon felt the warmth of belonging in her friend's embrace. That acceptance made the heat of her ferocity intensify. Kadie approached her other side, slotting herself into the space between Devon and Brodie. Reaching around Devon, Kadie stroked Zara's hair as she laid her head on Devon's shoulder.

"We'll slit your fucking throat," Zara said.

"Our men don't need theatrics," Kadie murmured, rubbing a hand up and down Devon's back.

Kadie rested a hand on the arm Zara had across Devon's chest. "We don't make idle threats," Devon said.

"You do as you're told," Kadie said.

Zara finished the thought, "Or you die."

Their synergy was enlivening. "You might be given a chance to talk to Mitchell," Devon said, recognizing how important it was to maintain eye contact with Grant even though it was clear he was fuming.

The women held center stage, coiled around each other, but with Brodie at Kadie's back and Tuck not far behind Zara, they had plenty of force nearby to subdue the prisoner if he tried to lash out. Although with his hands tied at his back, they could probably handle any threat alone.

Devon kept going, "If you are, you'll be told what to say, what our terms are, and you better pray Mitchell hasn't sent Jennifer to the cops or forwarded any emails."

Kadie and Zara pulled tighter around her, and Devon hooked an arm around each of their waists. Zara's next words were serious even though they were said through a smile. "Or they'll never find your body."

None of her trio showed weakness; right now they were nothing but strength in stark contrast to Grant's frailty. "Forget Dateline," Kadie said. "The world thinks you're dead. That's an opportunity for us, not you."

Zara showed a similar kind of perverse optimism that Devon had seen in Brodie, but she began to understand its power. " 'Cause we can do whatever the fuck we want with you and nobody is watching."

Sneering, Grant still didn't back down. "You three are fucking crazy," he said. "You're crazier than the bastards you fuck."

Insults weren't going to dent their confidence, and Grant had just shown that he didn't understand the gravity of where he was or what could happen to him. "You better hope not," Devon said.

Zara picked up her thought. "Because we're the only thing standing between you and them."

The empowerment was immense. These women cared about her and stood with her. If their men were taken down, they would remain as the Kindred unit and they had to be formidable. Building that bond was vital to this mission and every mission that would come in the future. Devon wasn't scared. She didn't need to rely on her man to be her liaison to the Kindred. She had support from every angle. They didn't judge her, they embraced her.

Kadie took a deep breath. "All it would take is one word from any of us to any of them, and you won't take another breath."

Zara laughed. "We don't even need to give them a reason."

Devon shrugged and wasn't able to fight her own smile any longer because it was true. Accepting that power was liberating. "We can get rid of you and just come up with a new plan. One that doesn't involve a pathetic prick like you."

Tuck got up and went to the storage locker again. He opened the door and did something inside that none of them could see. But the women were still holding each other, looming over the belittled man on the floor who was furious that these feeble women were more powerful than him here and now.

Tuck came over to crouch at his side, and that forced Grant to look away from them. "What the fuck are you doing?" he demanded, trying to wriggle away.

The women stepped closer in front of him, and Brodie put a foot against his opposite arm, blocking him in from the side, giving Grant no means of escape as Tuck injected him. Grant protested and bucked for another minute but eventually passed out and slumped.

"Well," Tuck said, resting his elbows on his crouched knees. "That about gave me the boner of the century."

Instead of looking at his woman, he looked at Brodie, who bowed to bump fists with the hacker. Each of the women were snatched by their men, and Devon laughed when she saw the fervor in the kisses they were blessed with.

Modesty made her turn away to give them privacy, and her laugh faded when she noticed her own man standing there in the mouth of the kitchen. His attention consumed her, and she didn't need for him to touch her or ask for her. She went to him, and with a single hand, he took her waist, turned her and slammed her back against the storage unit.

He came in so close that his heat made her temperature rise by a full degree or maybe more. His nose grazed her and he rubbed her hips and waist. "A single word," he whispered, touching his lips onto hers. "I'd do anything you told me to. Anything. I'd comply with any command that left those lips."

He was as aroused as the other men were, and she enjoyed coiling her arms around his neck. "I get it now. It's not my family, my brother, my worry; it's ours, it's the Kindred's. Because everything that's mine is theirs."

Picking her up, he pinned her to the compartment at her back, and her new height allowed him to straighten and kiss her deeper. It was so rare that he would touch her like this, be intimate with her when there were other eyes in the room. But she didn't think he even considered them as he tilted his head.

When he put her onto her feet again, her ragged breath ricocheted back to her from his throat, because she couldn't stop. Her mouth was still pressed to him, it was hungry for his neck, his jaw, his skin. Undoing some of his shirt buttons, she intended to kiss his chest, but a voice to her side stopped her dead.

"I don't fucking think so." Zave didn't give her space, but he did turn to her brother who was with them now. "What I just saw, sis. I don't even know where to fucking start."

She didn't know if he meant the kiss or what had happened with Grant. Lowering her arms from Zave's neck, she wrapped them around his waist because it was more comfortable and she didn't want him to leave. Although her brother probably didn't like seeing her enjoying her husband, she wasn't going to let Rig scare Zave away.

"I'm happy here, Rig," she said. That was true of her marriage and of her alliance with the Kindred. "These people care about me and I care about them."

He wasn't sneering. "I guess I'm not the only family you've got now." This time when he looked at Zave, he didn't have any annoyance or confrontation in his gaze. "I'm always gonna be around and I'm always gonna be watching. I don't give a fuck who you're related to, if you hurt her—"

"We'll take him down ourselves," Brodie said, coming up behind Rig to slap a hand between his shoulder blades. "Bess is cooking dinner tonight, she says she's got us a real treat." Brodie looked past her brother to his cousin. "How long we got?"

"Came back to tell you we'll be landing." Zave glanced at his watch. "In less than a minute."

He hooked his finger beneath her jaw to lift her mouth to his for a brief kiss, and this was one situation where she couldn't object to him leaving her. He went back to the cockpit, and Rig took her arm to pull her back down into the cabin. Brodie and Tuck were taking the still unconscious Grant to the back of the plane again, probably to hog-tie him and cover his mouth.

Everyone else was seating themselves and putting their belts on. "The Kindred is about as dangerous as you can get," Rig said, putting her into a seat next to his on the couch. He made sure her seatbelt was fastened before he touched his own. "But it's funny, I don't think you've ever been safer."

The first time she'd spoken to her brother from Zave's island, he'd told her that she was safe with the Kindred. His own confidence in that must have been shaken up after learning about what had gone down since then.

Everyone here was different, but they'd all been brought together because they had love for each other. It may have started as an uncle's love for his nephew or a parent's love for their child. But it was no longer as straightforward as that. There was still a chance that the men would be taken away and the women would be left alone, just as there was a chance that one of them, or all of them, could lose their lives.

But being in danger with the Kindred didn't make her more anxious. It gave her a clearer view of how far these wonderful people would go for each other, and she'd just proved that was a distance that she was willing to travel for them too.

# NINETEEN

THE FOOD WAS gorgeous, but Devon knew that when the meal was over and the somber mood encroached, that business was next on the agenda. This wasn't going to be a typical night on the island. For one thing, Bess didn't have any help when it came to gathering the dirty plates. Piling them up, she was alone in taking them to the kitchen.

The three couples and her brother sat around the dinner table saying nothing. So many developments had occurred that she didn't know where they'd start. Everything had gone to plan so far, but that didn't mean they were out of danger. The Kindred were always in danger.

But she felt better being here because she was safer on the island, in this house that had once been her prison and was now her home. Even in spite of bringing Grant McCormack, an apparently dangerous stranger, here it still felt the same and she was pleased to be back.

After landing and decanting to the house, the men had taken Grant to what would be his new home for the time being. Staying out of the way, she, Bess, Kadie, and Zara went around the bedrooms changing sheets and preparing the rooms.

While they retrieved clean linens and made the beds,

they didn't say much. Devon got the impression that they all were following Bess' lead and using mundane household chores as a distraction from what had gone on. Not because they were scared or even particularly anxious, just because they were tired and needed some time to reflect.

Afterwards, they'd gone down to the kitchen to help Bess cook. Although the matriarch did most of the work, Devon noticed how frequently Bess got a far-off look in her eyes. Two or three times, she had to intercept something Bess was doing, to prevent her from hurting herself or ruining the meal. The drama was taking a toll on the woman who usually tried to stay away from the dirty work. In spite of all that he'd done, Bess was still terrified that her child might be hurt or in danger.

More pissed at Thad than she could express, Devon didn't believe he was ignorant to the trouble he was causing. It just seemed that he didn't care enough to change his ways or apologize.

Back at the dinner table, Kadie cleared her throat, drawing Devon out of her thoughts about the day. "I guess it's safe to say that Syn haven't gone to the police," she said.

Tuck, from her side, lifted her hand from the table to kiss her knuckles. "It's possible that they're investigating," he said. "Although I tend to agree with you, Toots. If Mitchell was gonna do it, I think he would be happy to tell us."

He'd take pleasure in ruining the lives of the men at this table and by extension, the lives of their women. "Is it weird that we haven't heard from them?" Devon asked, because as much as she didn't want Syn following through on their threats, the silence was unnerving.

The rest of the room were calm. "We shouldn't panic yet," Tuck said. "When they wanted to get in touch with us, before they sent Thad to the merger mixer to give us Grant's video. They'll find a way if they have to."

The couples sat next to each other, flanking Zave who sat at the head of the table. Devon sat beside Zara with Rig opposite her, next to Kadie. Bess had been at her side until she departed.

In the modern age, she couldn't believe they had to

be face-to-face just to convey a message. "Thad must know how to contact us here," she said. "He must have your numbers and emails."

Zave shook his head. "We killed those the minute he turned his back on us."

"We've done it so many times, it only takes a few seconds. We keep our devices, but all the numbers change," Tuck explained. "Numbers can be traced, cloned, monitored. It's too much of a risk to leave them the same."

"But don't we want their message?" Kadie asked him. "What if they're trying to make peace?"

Brodie scoffed. "Mitchell won't make peace," he said. "He might negotiate or he might start a war, but he's not going to come to us hat in hand."

Taking Grant was an excellent move. Terrifying as it had been for her at the time, she understood now why it made sense. In retrospect, it was a calculated risk where benefit outweighed cost. But now that they had this advantageous strategic position, they couldn't be complacent and had to remain on the offensive.

An idea had been formulating in her mind since they'd returned. While she completed her chores, she'd been constantly aware of every external sound and paranoid enough that she believed more than once there were boats or planes approaching that could be law enforcement coming to take her man away.

Devon didn't want to hear the pounding on the door and didn't want to cry in this house without him, knowing he was wasting away in a cell. She had Zave at the head of the table and Rig opposite her, and as much as she'd expect her husband and brother to support her, she was a rookie and aware that her idea might be dismissed without consideration.

Except the solidarity of the women on the plane had bolstered her. If these guys disagreed, she'd fight her corner. If she was ultimately overruled, she would go with the group decision, as she'd been told that was how the Kindred worked. They brainstormed, tossed ideas around, sometimes mixing one suggestion with another until they eventually came to a conclusion.

But she would make them hear her first. "I don't want to wait and see," Devon said, maintaining her attention on her husband who slowly lifted his eyes to hers. "I don't want to wait and see if they're going to attack us."

"What do you suggest?" Zara asked, open to the possibilities.

There was no judgment or impatience in her tone. She wasn't overjoyed, but she was certainly receptive. "A preemptive strike," Devon said, trying to figure out how everyone felt about the idea. But they were all so good at shuttering their true thoughts, it was impossible to anticipate their reactions.

Rig was the first to respond, giving the others time to organize their thoughts. "We don't know where they are," her brother said. "How can we hit them—"

"I'm not talking about an assault," she said.

Because if nothing else, it would take too much time to prepare and fly back to the city. Syn had almost a day of advantage over them if they were retrenching or planning their own attack. Syn knew where they were, yet the Kindred were still unaware of Syn's location and it would take time to torture it out of Grant. Besides, a direct assault would cost lives, and Devon couldn't guarantee which side would be victorious. There were different kinds of victory, and one Kindred life lost was too many.

"Then what kind of strike?" Kadie asked.

"Syn's warning shot was the media," Devon said. "So instead of waiting for them to send Jennifer to the cops or for them to go to the next news outlet, I say we tell the truth."

"To the press?" Brodie asked. Just three words, but he managed to convey how ridiculous he thought the suggestion was and how unimpressed he was by it, while keeping his tone level and deep.

Zara patted her hand in a gesture that came off as patronizing. "The Kindred don't advertise."

This was the cusp, the threshold of the moment when they would dismiss her, so she had to speak up. "Not your story, mine," Devon said, and although she knew Zave was still looking at her, she chose to focus on her brother. "I'll go alone, tell them it was random. Everybody wants to know how I met my husband. Well I'll tell them that he rescued me from that hellish place. I'll tell them what happened to me. They'll think that I'm new money on a crusade, but the truth will seep through. Then even if Jennifer does go to the police, she'll just look like she'd jumping on the bandwagon or trying to extort money."

"That's not assured," Kadie said. "The press could just as easily turn on us."

Devon loved how she used the word "us." She and Kadie were probably the two least connected at the table, and yet Kadie accepted Devon's pain as her own.

"No," Zave said in that clipped, monotone. "I will not have my wife paraded on television or our intimacy discussed—"

"I'll go alone," she said again. "I go and I tell them the truth. Then it doesn't matter what Syn do, because we got there first. It will just sound like people trying to make hay out of nothing. Even if the cops try to investigate or try to question you, at least you would have an explanation. If they ask you about Jennifer, we deny that she was here. No one is going to admit having laid eyes on her. You tell the cops how you found me but tell them that Jennifer is a crazy person who heard the story and decided to parrot it."

This time when she stopped talking, nobody jumped up with a contradiction. She gave them time to consider the idea. That was when Bess came back in, approached the table, one careful step at a time and put her hands on the back of the chair next to Rigor's.

"I expected debate," Bess said, "maybe even spirited argument. The Kindred are rarely silent."

"Devon has an idea," Zara said. "She doesn't think we should sit around and wait for Syn to tell tales. She's offering to go to the media, to tell the truth about how she and Zave got together. So Jennifer will look like a crackpot."

Devon expected Bess to keep her opinion to herself, if she had one, because her loyalty had to be stretched. Not that she would ever turn her back on the Kindred. But if anything happened to Syn, her son would be finished.

"I'll go with her," Bess said. Devon was stunned, so much so that she couldn't even begin to think about how the others felt about Bess' vehemence. "If I tell them the truth about what happened with Bronwyn while sitting beside her, they'll understand where it started."

That was excellent and exactly what Devon needed to hear. Not only could she use the moral support, but it would further justify Zave's presence in that place and the cops could investigate all they wanted, all they would ever find was the truth.

"What about Thad?" Zara asked. "He won't be happy if you parade his business on the national news channels."

"Except that's what he's threatening to do with Kindred business, what he allowed to happen when Syn leaked Devon and Zave's marriage. We have to fight fire with fire. We can't just sit and wait to see if Grant is right. Devon and I spoke," Bess said, making eye contact. "What you said in the apartment was right. I can't go to Syn just to be close to Thad, to sit by and watch them destroy everything I love. But I can take a more active role. Maybe if I'd done that, if I'd been more involved, my son wouldn't have run away from me."

Devon hadn't meant to hurt her. "Bess, what he did wasn't your fault."

But the woman was determined when she addressed the lord of the manor. "You can afford the best lawyers, Zave."

"Yes," Kadie said, "you can." Devon was encouraged that they were rallying. Even if she had to do it inch by inch, she was getting Kindred members onside. It was progress. "Your lawyers can talk to Devon and to Bess before they do it. They can even warn, I don't know, the cops or the DA, whoever has to know beforehand. And if Jennifer comes out, even if it's five minutes later, your lawyers will make mincemeat of her. You can hire PR and—"

"We have all that through KC," Zave said.

Devon didn't know if that was acceptance that this was going to happen or simply an observation. "That takes care of Zave's situation, but Brodie will still go to jail," Zara said, taking her husband's hand although he took it straight back.

Brodie wasn't even worried; Devon was impressed by how casual he could be about his freedom. "I told you the first weekend you stayed at my place, if I go to prison, I go to prison," Brodie said.

"Fuck that," Zara said. "You think you're some big, hard man who'd sail through jail time? Oh yeah, you'll be fine showering with a hundred other guys who all want to be your bitch." She poked his shoulder. "I'm your bitch. Not them. You want somebody to suck you off, you call my number. Not theirs."

Brodie slid an arm around the back of her chair. Devon leaned forward to see the slant of a sinister smile focused on his wife. "You're not worried about me living in a concrete cage. You worried there might be competition for space in my bed? You're jealous that all those other eyes will see my cock every day while you're drooling over pictures."

With a stubborn chin, Zara didn't flinch. "Pictures don't satisfy me, beau. I need the real thing."

Passion sparked again between the couple, but it was only a brief kiss Brodie gave to his wife before he curled his fingers around the back of her neck. "To tell the truth, I'm not worried. Art taught me to treat every kill like the first. To be as paranoid as I was when I was a scared kid pulling that trigger for the first time. I make it look easy. But I'm paying attention."

Tuck pointed at the sniper. "That's true. If the cops could put a case together, they would've. Syn can call the cops, and they can question us. Hell, they can even try to gather evidence."

Brodie locked his fingers deeper in the hair he'd trapped at Zara's neck. "If I've left evidence, I deserve to go to prison. That's exactly what Art would tell me."

But Zara was shaking her head. "Don't give me that bullshit. I won't let you go to prison. I don't give a fuck what we have to do. If we have to live in the Andes and shoot elk for a living, we will."

Brodie snickered before he kissed her again. "They

don't got elk in the Andes, sweetheart."

"See, you know shit like that. You can look after me."

Kadie laughed. "You're going to go live in a cave? Get back to your primitive roots?"

She was still laughing while Zara smiled and Tuck stroked the back of her head. "You wouldn't have to go on the run forever," the hacker said. "You can piss off out the country for a year or two. Both the manors are secure enough. Once the heat dies down and they've searched the place, you can come back and split your time between our manor and this one. They'll never pin you down, we've got enough surveillance on both places that we'll see them coming a mile away."

No longer laughing, Kadie's concern grew for her own man. "And you?" she asked her lover. "You always told me that if Brodie went down, you'd be going down too."

He smiled and touched her chin. "There are plenty of caves out there, Toots, you take your pick."

"You'll be like the fucking Flintstones," Rig laughed, slapping a hand onto the table.

Devon laughed, too, but the urge to relax didn't last long. Bess was staring at the table again, wearing that same forlorn expression.

"Devon's idea was great," Zara said, snatching her arm to link it around her own, bringing Devon's focus back to the others. "Except if we're going to be preemptive, we don't have to expose ourselves. How about we expose them?"

This intrigued not only Zara's husband, but Devon's too. "What do you mean?" Zave asked.

"You're all forgetting that the major secret here is that Grant and Frank are alive."

"So we just drop Grant off at CNN and wait for him to tell his stories?" Brodie asked.

He was always quick to shoot down an idea, although Devon was learning it was sense of humor, rather than a desire to ridicule, even though the two sort of went hand in hand.

"Are you forgetting who was closest to Grant for half a decade before he died?" Zara said, going so far as to use air quotes around the final word. "We don't have to drop Grant off anywhere; we can make his name mud. You know I still talk to Julian, one of the CI lawyers, all the time. He knows about Grant's personal and professional finances overlapping. We have all the accounts to prove it. We can publicize what he was doing with Game Time, not what the device is or its schematics, but its capabilities and why he wanted to do it. We can even implicate him in the death of Albert Sutcliffe. There were four people in the room when Sutcliffe went down."

"And two of them are fucking," Tuck said, interested in Zara's plan.

So this was a Kindred strategy meeting, one person's idea led to another person's, and suddenly they had options that left Devon feeling much more optimistic. "Who?" Devon asked.

Tuck took a breath. "Brodie, Zara, Grant, and Sutcliffe were in the bunker," he said. "Sutcliffe never made it out."

He and Zara were fixated on each other, and for the longest time they said nothing. Kadie leaned toward her. "Tuck's in crash mode now trying to figure this out, and Zara's glaring at him like that because this is how she gets into his brain. After this, they'll start agreeing with each other, which basically means Brodie is screwed."

Kadie's smile grew wide and smug as she landed it on the sniper, who was scowling at the hacker's girl. Even if Tuck and Zara agreed, that didn't mean Zave would get onboard. "If we expose them, they expose us," Zave said, and just as she'd thought before about the whole situation being a house of cards, she knew he was right.

While Zara's plan was a good one, Devon still believed in her own because it wasn't attacking Syn directly, giving them an opportunity to lob their own grenade back. It was attacking while protecting themselves.

"We're going to give Grant the night," Zave said. "Let him pace and shout. Mitchell's either already followed through or he's waiting for our next move. Let them drive themselves insane about what might happen while we all get a good night's sleep."

"Regroup at breakfast," Zara said.

Devon wanted to fight for her plan, but it was late, probably too late to start piecing a strategy together, and they would need a precise game plan, not one they rushed to assemble because it was bedtime and everyone wanted to get to sleep.

Even if they chose to follow through with her suggestion, before she uttered a word to the press, she would have to speak to Zave's lawyers. They would have to warn the KC PR department, too, because they may be inundated with questions and requests after any interviews. Needless to say, neither of those things could be done tonight.

Everyone else must have agreed with him, and tiredness had settled over the group anyway. So after the women finished cleaning up from dinner, they retired to bed. Bess went first, then Rig, with Tuck and Kadie not too far behind. Brodie said something to Zara, sending her away, and he stayed to whisper with Zave for another minute before tipping his invisible hat at Devon and leaving the room.

She remained beside the table, looking at her husband, who was facing the night beyond the window. "What are you looking for when you do that?" she asked. "You stare out there like you're expecting some sort of answer to leap out of the waves."

He couldn't see anything, as it was light inside and dark out, so even if something did emerge from the water, it would be invisible to them. "Do you want to sleep alone?" she asked when he didn't respond.

Zave dropped his linked hands from the small of his back, and they swung at his sides as he turned. "You would really go to the media and tell them what you went through?" he asked.

That was an easy question to answer. "Yes."

He didn't understand. "You didn't even want to tell me." He began to approach. "We sat at this table, and you couldn't even get the words out. I told you to speak to a therapist—"

"Are you angry?" she asked, trying to understand his objection. "I understand you don't want the world to know our secrets, and they won't. You have to trust me that I won't talk about our relationship like that. But if you're asking me to do nothing, to just watch the police take you away to punish you for being a good man doing a righteous thing… I can't, lord. I won't."

Stopping a few feet from her, anger hardened his form. "You don't have a fucking choice, shy. Have you forgotten where you are?"

Throwing his weight around or shutting her out, it wouldn't make any difference to her determination. "I'm in my home," she said because she wouldn't be intimidated by him. "My home doesn't frighten me. And yeah, you can lock me up. Except my brother's here and he's not gonna let you throw me in a pit and forget about me."

Scoffing, he looked down his nose. "You think Rigor could take on me, Brodie, and Tuck?"

Playing it coy instead of confronting his anger with hers, she tilted her chin. "Maybe not, so you'll have to take him prisoner," she said, pushing away from the table. "So while you have Grant locked up with me next door and Rig smashing the place up demanding to get out, how long before Bess reminds you how much you love me and tells you that you're being unreasonable? And who's going to feed me?" Bess would, they both knew that. "So when I convince Bess I'm right, she'll convince Zara and Kadie, and then you'll have to lock all three of them up too. Hmm…" she pressed a fingertip to her cheek. "But Brodie's gonna want to get his, Tuck too. They're not used to being celibate. How many people will you lock up before you realize it's okay to let others help you?"

Putting her hands on his chest, she could feel how averse he was to having her this close. But he wasn't angry anymore. "You've come a long way from the girl who blushed when I said the word 'sex'," he said.

Ironically, she smiled and dropped her chin. "It still makes me blush to hear you say it," she whispered.

Cupping her face, he tipped it up to the light. "I know. That's why I do it."

It's amazing. She'd been bare and vulnerable in front of him, she'd slept with him, she'd married him. Devon had confessed her deepest secrets and recounted her worst day to this man, but she still looked into the abyss of his eyes and felt plundered by the intensity of what burned from within him.

He was more than an intellectual genius; he was tortured and pained. She couldn't take that agony away. All he wanted to do was make the world a better place, but he felt every pin prick, every paper cut, every second of pain that was inflicted on those he cared about. It cut him in a place most other humans didn't have. His compassion was an organ or some secret lobe in his brain that overloaded when he couldn't control the happiness and safety of those around him.

"I was thinking about this room," she said when he relaxed and slid his arms around her. "About all the things that have happened here. About how this is the center of the house." It wasn't at the physical center of the house, but it certainly was the heart of it. "The first time I came into this room, I had no idea where I was on the planet." Twisting, she looked at the table, taking his attention to it, as well. "And when you laid me down there, I felt complete."

While he stroked her back, she felt her husband return to her. His mood wasn't as black now that they were holding each other. "I'm sorry that we scared you. When you got here, I know you must have been terrified. If you hadn't gotten all belligerent, we might not be here today. You're timid and tenacious, I don't understand the combination, but it works. You're nothing but contradictions, I never know what you'll say or do, all I know is that I need to keep you."

"You never have to worry about that. We're married."

"But if you go to the media and sell the story, how can I protect you, shy? How can I protect us?"

It had been a major deal for him to sleep with her, and that was private and pleasurable. The only reason he'd returned to work at KC and taken such an active role in the merger was because he believed it was what she wanted. But engaging the media was a step too far. Zave just wasn't capable of entertaining that avenue.

Devon liked how private he was, liked that these intimate moments were concealed from the others. Sure, he'd kissed her on the plane, but he rarely got involved in group conversation. So when he opened up to her like this, speaking and touching her, it reminded her of what she meant to him and how he trusted her more than he trusted the others.

Except if she admitted to him that she didn't really relish the idea of sitting under hot lights in a busy studio, telling the world about her shame, he would lock her up. If he did, she would argue with him, but there would be a part of her that was relieved that she didn't have to go through with it.

So Devon couldn't be honest with him now because that was all the rope he needed to hang her idea with, and she fully intended to follow through. Her own discomfort would be irrelevant if it was decided to be in the best interests of the Kindred.

"You said we should go to bed and talk about it in the morning," she said as she began to unbutton his shirt. "Or is this a private strategy meeting? Because I'd rather discuss more intimate, marital plans than what might happen with your cousin tomorrow."

"We're not getting intimate or marital here," he said.

It would be fun to finish what they'd started on the table all those months ago, but there were too many people in the house, and she didn't want a quick screw that might give him the excuse to send her up to her bed alone after they were done. So, if he was going to take her to his bed, she would save her fantasy of sex on that dinner table for another time, whether it was in a few days or after a life sentence.

Devon would make sure that table wasn't going anywhere. Her luck was in tonight because he took her hand to guide her out of the door at the top of the room into the corridor that led to the staircase, and because she knew it would embarrass him if she didn't, she tried her best to contain her excitement as he took her into the darkened lab and up the stairs into his tower bedroom.

"I've missed this room," she said and stopped undoing his buttons for long enough to let him pull her top up over her head.

After completing her task, she pushed his shirt off his

shoulders when he unhooked her bra and cast it aside to cradle her breasts. "You agreed to move in here," he said.

She was happy that they were returning to the place they'd been in before getting married. "Are we back to stay on the island?" she asked.

But he couldn't answer the question because they were going to bed without a plan. In Zave's wild years, this house had been a den of orgy and decadent depravity. Since those days it hadn't seen as much action within its walls as it would tonight. She would bet that while Zave was stripping her and lying her in his sheets, Brodie was doing the same with Zara and Tuck with Kadie.

They all needed reassurance tonight and to remind themselves of the love they had in their pairs. Because whatever plan the Kindred came up with tomorrow, it could be too late. If Syn got their way, these three couples would be torn apart and this could be their last chance to be intimate.

Zave was kissing her mouth like he'd never kissed her before, and she wanted him to kiss her like this forever. This was more than making a memory or quenching desire; this was the need they couldn't sate, the kind of need that made men and women marry because they knew this connection would last a lifetime.

It didn't seem right to ask questions or say anything when all they needed to do was experience each other. He said so much with his gaze as he slid himself inside of her that her eyes began to water and his need cooled as he brushed the tears from her lashes.

"Shy, did I hurt you?" he murmured, and she coiled her legs tighter around him.

"No."

"Then why are you upset?"

"I'm not upset," she said, stroking his face and kissing his mouth. "I love you so much, sometimes I think it's too much, that I can't make you understand how much I need you and care about you. I know that you're hurting and that breaks my heart."

The motion of him sliding out and back in made her whimper. Her hips writhed beneath the pressure of his dick easing in deep. "I'm not hurting when I'm here," he said. "You've taken it away, shy. Sometimes I want to make it better, and I know I take on too much. It's ego. It's arrogant. It's ridiculous. But finding you has made me think that maybe… maybe I've been punished enough."

A yelp burst out when she opened her mouth. No other words could match the satisfaction those gave her. "You have, geez, baby, you have."

Running her hands through his hair, she touched his skin and welcomed this revelation by moving her pelvis faster. Every weight that burdened him constricted her too. Hearing him forgive himself, even just a little, made her feel like she was doing her job as his wife.

"You make me so happy," she called out, and his pace was increasing.

Zave kissed her, probably trying to end the conversation to focus on their love making. He'd said when he was here he didn't feel the pain and that bonded them, as well as providing her another reason to make sure he wasn't taken from her.

Giving in to the sex initially had made him feel guilty, but now that he had her, now that he'd claimed her, he'd begun to accept that the pleasure was relief for his pain and his guilt and his torture. Devon had told him that it was her job as his wife to ease his burden, and he'd just given her confirmation that she was doing her job well.

He wasn't the only one in need and by the time he gave up the kiss, she was on the precipice of orgasm and wouldn't be able to hold a conversation even if she wanted to. It was his eyes that pushed her over. Something in that gaze reminded her how they belonged to each other, and when all of this Syn shit was over with, she was going to find a way to make this kind of intimacy so normal he took it for granted.

He shouldn't need to question how good he was or if he deserved her love. As far as she was concerned, he deserved the world and she'd been put on this earth to give him it.

# TWENTY

THE WOMEN STAYED in the kitchen with Bess while breakfast was made, and by the time they emerged, the men had made a plan. A loose one, at least. None of what had been said last night had been abandoned. But they were aware that any move they made would be countered by a defensive and desperate Syn, which could lead to the Kindred being vulnerable. So they chose a more direct course of action that might clue them in to how Syn were thinking.

Brodie tried to claim that he could speak to Grant alone. Zara argued against that, knowing how the brothers aggravated each other. So she asserted that she should be present. Tuck wouldn't miss out on the fun and was the best man to act fast if the brothers had to be separated by force. Except, Kadie pointed out he wouldn't be likely to get between them because Grant deserved to get his ass kicked. So it was decided that Zave had to be in the room too.

Zave wanted to observe anyway because this was his house, his suite, his rules. If they had to make a decision on the hoof, the three men could agree or oppose with a single look.

Kadie was actually the only one who ended up being happy to stay out of the room. Devon wanted to hear every word because at the next strategy meeting it would be decided whether or not they were going to come to an agreement with Syn or continue with her plan or Zara's. If she had to fight for her own option, she needed to know what Grant had said, so she could build her argument.

Bess carried a tray of food toward the suite with the Kindred group in her wake. Rig trailed along at the rear. He wanted to be in the room but only because it would be entertaining, and so she'd persuaded him to stay in the hallway, not to act as lookout but backup, in case it turned out they needed an extra pair of hands or someone to run a quick errand.

Using her fingerprint, Bess went into the room and immediately Grant began to protest. "Let me out of here! What is this shit, Bess?"

"Dearie, there's water and fruit—"

"I don't want your food. God knows what's in it!" Grant said. "You better let me the fuck out of here!"

Brodie smacked a hand on the door to throw it wide open, and with Tuck and Zave on each of his wings, he strode inside. Zara looped her arm through Devon's and took her inside then closed the door. It made sense to make sure there was no exit, though with so many people in here, it was unlikely that Grant would succeed in making a break for it. Even if he did, Rig was in the hall with nothing to do but wait for some action.

The prisoner was in front of the frosted window, still dressed, his arms folded. "You need a whole posse to intimidate me?" Grant asked.

The bed looked like it had been made. He probably wanted them to believe he hadn't slept in it, but Devon knew the details of this room, having spent so much time here herself and could see that the bed had been used. "We're gonna give you a chance," Brodie said, still at the head of the group, his stance mirroring his older brother's. "We'll send you back to Syn without a scratch."

Grant's eyes narrowed, and it was right that he should be suspicious. "In exchange for?" he asked.

"The boy... and Game Time," Zara said.

Devon and Zara were still in front of the door and Bess was by the bedside closest to them. They were far away from the men who formed a wall in front of Grant, but Grant leaned to the side to sneer at his former assistant.

"And yet, there was a time you didn't realize how valuable it was. Zara, has it been worth it?" Grant asked. "Everything we've been through in the past two years, are you happier now than you were then when it was just the two of us?"

Devon knew that Zara was a serious woman and that she had a past with Grant McCormack. At one time, she had lived a relatively normal life as an assistant to the CEO of a multibillion-dollar corporation. Devon had never been in such a privileged position, but she understood how life could change overnight.

Her life had changed when she had been taken from the street as Syn's revenge against her brother, Rig. But the true moment her life had transformed had been at the auction when Zave bought her. That was life-changing and the time she chose to remember as pivotal in her journey.

She'd been on a consistent path, long and straight with little hope of excitement or adventure in her future, though she'd never really considered either.

The descent to rock bottom had begun when she was kidnapped by the cartel, and existing with them had affected her personality and her thought process. But it had been this house and this island, this place and these people, who had helped her to find something positive in all the negativity.

If it had been her destiny to die after being bought by an insane sadist who enjoyed torturing and killing, then the Kindred would never have come to her aid, and she wouldn't be a part of their mission. The Kindred had a habit of changing destinies, they'd done it with Zara too, her life had changed the night she met Brodie.

But the relaxed kind of untouchable attitude that had always shimmered around Zara faltered now. Instinct made Devon tighten her elbow around Zara's forearm, giving her physical support. "You were never who I thought you were, Grant," Zara said. "You lied to me for years and tried to make me think I was wrong. I know you hate your brother and I know he despises you. Once upon a time, I wished you two would speak to each other and put all this crap behind you." For once, both brothers acted in unison with a snort of sneering disbelief. "I know that's impossible now. Was I happier? No. Because I was only existing. My whole life was building to the moment I found your brother in my bedroom, waiting for me. This is who I was meant to be."

Grant didn't scoff this time, in fact, he loosened. "Then you understand," he said. "Because this is who I'm supposed to be."

"Mitchell's bitch?" Tuck asked.

Grant's anger returned. "That's a context you can understand, Swift. You run around after Brodie like a puppy. You don't understand how to work as a team. You just do as you're told."

Little did he know, that wasn't the case at all. The Kindred had argued last night, and the men had discussed strategy again this morning. There wasn't a doubt in her mind that each of the women had tried their best to alter their partner's perspective during the course of the night.

This morning, Devon had woken by herself but found her husband in the shower. She'd washed with him, and they'd dressed together. During that time, she'd tried to probe his thoughts to find out what direction his subconscious had taken him while he slept.

He revealed nothing, as he was good at being guarded. But he must have had some ideas because he and Tuck and Brodie had reached their conclusions around the table rather quickly while the women were in the kitchen.

"If you want to live, we want everyone in a room together. Have Mitchell and his little bitches bring Howie and Game Time here," Brodie said.

Shaking his head and wearing a glimpse of a smile, Grant inhaled like he hadn't a care in the world. "We're not coming here. Why the fuck would Mitchell do that?"

"Because he wants his lamb back," Tuck said. "We're not taking you off this island, so if you wanna leave it, you get your fucking unit to pick you up or you start swimming. I hope you paid attention to your father's architectural plans for the houses."

Tuck was ridiculing him and Brodie joined in. "You know how to work out which way's north, right, brother?" he asked.

The hacker's laugh got louder. "That fucker couldn't find his way out of his corporate offices without Siri talking him through the route."

The one thing Grant didn't like to be was belittled, and he began to bluster. "You want to make a deal, you do it on Syn's terms. They come here for me, you hand me over, that's it."

"They bring Game Time and the kid or all of you will be swimming home."

Coming here was a major risk for Syn. It was Kindred territory, there was no denying that. But by refusing, they would be proving that they were afraid of the Kindred and that was the test. The Kindred were established. They could afford to refuse an enemy's terms; they had nothing to prove because they'd survived this long.

Syn were a new tribe. They had to prove that they were fearless because they had no track record, no reputation. If they could say they'd strolled up to their number one enemy's doorstep and walked right in without fear, that would show they were a confident force with balls and faith in their skills.

Turning his attention to Zave, Grant moved away from his brother. "Did you build what we needed?" Zave said nothing. "If you want them to come here, you'll have to give them more than me."

So much for Grant being the most integral part of the team. Maybe this was tactics, his way of getting more for his group than his own selfish release. "If they bring Game Time, you'll get what you asked for," Zave muttered.

"Then take me to a phone."

Their prisoner wasn't a tough negotiator, and for a minute, she was suspicious of exactly what had just been decided because Grant had agreed to give up Game Time so readily that there was a quick discussion in the stairwell about whether or not Syn could've set this up.

Zara still fought for Caine. Rig said next to nothing. She knew her brother, he was bored by the talking part. Bess was quiet enough that when the others took the phone back to Grant, Rig went back to his room, and Devon stayed on the stairs with her.

"What's wrong?" Devon asked.

Taking hold of her hand, Bess guided her down to sit on the top stair. "If all of them come back here, they'll need Thad to fly them," Bess said. "He'll be coming back here to the island."

Her son was probably never far from her mind. "The Kindred will keep their word." Devon reassured her by stroking her arm. "Brodie told you he wouldn't hurt Thad."

"Unless he steps out of line… and I'm not sure that he won't. How can I be sure? He's so angry. I need a chance to talk to him, but how can I possibly do that? What if he says something that upsets Brodie?"

"You trust Brodie."

"Yes, but I feel like it's a no-win situation. If he says something to upset Brodie, sometimes emotions take over and mistakes are made, so… maybe he will be hurt. Except, even if I get a chance to talk to him and we can convince him that what he's done is wrong, then Syn will be here and they could hurt him, and I can't trust them." Tired, to the point of being haggard, Bess exhaled and touched her fingers to her hair while with her other hand, she clutched Devon tighter. "I'm so confused. I'm so angry at Thad for betraying his family. But, as a mother, I'm just terrified that he will get hurt."

Slipping down a stair, Devon looked up with a reassuring smile, trying to encourage Bess to be optimistic while sympathizing with her point of view. "We'll talk to Zave. You know he and Brodie are close. Nothing will happen to Thad if Zave tells Brodie to protect him."

Tears shone in Bess' eyes, and it broke Devon's heart to see the pain. "You should be so angry with him. Zave is angry, I can tell by the look he gets in his eye. I'm worried that things will never go back to the way they were."

That was one promise that Devon couldn't make.

"They won't. I don't know how this will work out or if the Kindred will get what they want. This could drag on for months or years. Whatever happens, you did your best and this wasn't your fault."

"You must spend your life saying that to Zave," Bess said, cupping a hand around Devon's cheek. "You're such a good girl, so patient and accepting. You came to us exactly when we needed you."

Devon had just been thinking about how Zave had found her exactly when *she'd* needed *him*. "Zave told me once that the way to deal with a Kindred op was one minute at a time. I'm kind of like you, I just try to visualize what will happen next and play scenarios forward, but when I did that, when they wanted Rig and me to fight so Syn would go after him, I… I nearly lost my nerve. I questioned if I could be part of the Kindred or even be with Zave if I couldn't take the risks that they take so easily. But when we came out the other side and we were on that plane coming home, everything came together for me.

"There's always a chance that someone will get hurt. But as long as our intentions are good, we have to trust that things will go our way."

"Losing Melinda rocked our whole family," Bess said. "Twelve years later, we lost Philippa, Zave's mother, and it was like reliving the tragedy all over again. My brother Art died, nearly two years ago, and I can't describe the grief that almost consumed all of us." Her words were harrowing, and yet, she smiled. "He taught the boys, he taught me, that everyone is headed for their one day. The one day when we all go on our own mission, and we don't come back. Brodie was always able to accept that, like he accepted every other word my brother said. In fact, he told Zara about 'one day' like it was no big deal, though it shook the girl to her core." Her smile was warm, but resigned, and a tear trickled from the corner of her eye. "I think about my brother every day, and I know Brodie takes him on every mission. Losing him wasn't like losing the others. Although they didn't know it at the time, they died for a purpose, for standing up for something that was right, and I'm proud of all of them for that."

"You should be," Devon said, rocking her knee with their joined hands. "You should be incredibly proud of them. I'm sorry I didn't meet them. I know they've had an impact on you all."

"Art told Brodie, and Zara, and Tuck that they were his legacy. Zara told me everything that my brother said at the end. And when he knew he was finished, the first thing he did was tell Brodie that he was his greatest achievement."

"Brodie is a good man," Devon said, because although he was terrifying and detached, he was braver than anyone she'd ever met.

"When you told me about what Thad had done, I was so ashamed of him. I'm still ashamed of him."

It was impossible to put herself in Bess' position. The warring emotions must be torturous to cope with. "That doesn't mean you don't love him."

"No, it doesn't," Bess said, and the distant look returned to her face. This time, it was glued to the carpet. "I know he's alive. But I think, 'what if I can never hold him in my arms again? What if I can never tell him that I love him?' Thad was my baby and my legacy and my greatest achievement. For most of his life, it was just him and me. We were so close when he grew up. Even after he moved out, he'd call five times a day and visit all the time. It seems like a lifetime since I heard his voice."

If Bess was missing her son this much, she had to assume, or at least hope, that Thad missed her this much in return. But there was no guarantee of that. Thad had made his choice and had made no attempt to get in touch with his mother. Maybe because he knew his mother would judge him, as mothers were supposed to do in disciplining their children for bad behavior.

"Don't give up hope," Devon said, although she wasn't sure what outcome the woman should hope for.

"I can't understand why he did this. If this mission goes ahead and something happens to him, I'll never know why."

The door behind them burst open before a ruckus of people came into the stairwell. The activity forced both women to stand straight. Although as soon as Bess sniffed and the four people saw what was going on, they stopped talking.

"What's wrong? What happened?" Zave asked, but it was Zara who pushed through the men to come over to hug them both.

"Nothing." Devon grinned, and Zara leaned back to swipe tears from her cheeks. Devon hadn't noticed that she was crying. "Must be my time of the month," she said, and her brief exchange with Zara was enough to let the woman know she shouldn't pursue the conversation.

"Well, it's done," Zara said, taking the hint. "Mitchell took some convincing. I guess Grant isn't as influential as he thought. They'll be here tomorrow. That gives us time to prepare."

With an arm around both women, Zara urged them down the stairs. The men's curiosity wasn't satisfied, but it would have to do for now because she couldn't reveal Bess' secrets to the group. Although, she fully intended to talk to her husband at the first opportunity she got.

They hadn't spoken about Thad in a while, but Zave would know how Brodie and Tuck felt. So, as Zara made plans with Bess to tour the island, Devon fixated on her husband.

Kadie was bringing coffee into the dining room when they all got back there. Rig was seated at the table waiting too. Devon told Zara and Kadie about the lagoon and Bess laughed at Zara's declaration that they should skinny-dip, then explained Zave's reaction to Devon's request to do the same.

Rig didn't like the story, but Devon slipped away to creep toward the trio huddled in front of the window. Brodie saw her coming and stopped talking, which was enough to make Zave and Tuck turn to her.

Slipping a hand into Zave's, she tried to ignore the irritation that radiated from them all. Being interrupted was something that never happened when they were holding their private meetings. "Can I speak to you?"

"We're talking," Zave said, glancing back at his colleagues.

"It'll just take a few minutes."

The most understanding of the group, Tuck

supported her, "She wouldn't have come over here if it wasn't important."

"Yeah, hear her out," Brodie agreed, though was more grumbly than the hacker.

With their permission in place, Zave exhaled and pulled her to the door at the top of the room and into the hallway beyond. But he didn't go any further. "What is it?" he snapped.

His attitude pissed her off. "Tuck is right, you know, I wouldn't have come over if it wasn't important. Maybe you should think about that before you get angry… or are you looking for a fight?"

"I'm not looking," he mumbled. "I don't like being interrupted. It embarrasses me."

"I embarrass you, is that what you mean? Because I dared to ask for a minute alone with my husband? You know, if Zara wanted to be alone with Brodie, she would stand up and shout the width of the room at him. Kadie wouldn't even have to open her mouth for Tuck to know what she wanted."

"So I'm not as good a partner as they are?" he asked. "Maybe you're the one looking for a fight."

"You're so used to being alone, so used to being an island, that you forget who the fuck I am. I'm not just your girlfriend, I'm your wife, and I reached out to you because something important happened on those stairs and I wanted to share that with you, to ask for your help and support. Not the Kindred's. My husband's. But you know what?" Stepping backwards, she narrowed her eyes. "Fuck you."

She didn't know any quicker way to get back to her room except to turn around and go back through the dining room. Brodie and Tuck were by the table now, and conversation was much livelier. One of the women was laughing until they noticed her and her intent fury.

A second after she stormed diagonally across the room, the hilarity died. "Devon?" Bess asked, but she ignored the voice and went through the other door to return to her room.

She didn't mind that Zave was distant most of the time. She didn't mind that he was so happy to be alone that he often cut her out of his day. She was way more patient than most women would be.

Her bedroom was familiar, but being here infuriated her, because while on an island she couldn't simply go out for a breath of fresh air, grab a coffee, or take in a movie while she cooled off. The island had been a sanctuary, and the place was still welcoming even when the man couldn't be.

"Fuck me?" he roared when he slammed into her room two seconds later. "Fuck me?"

"Yeah! Because if I need something, I should be able to come to you! So, fuck you if you can't be there for me!"

"Then what?" he asked, marching over to get into her personal space. Pushing on his chest, she tried to get him to back off. "You'll find someone who can?"

She didn't say she was leaving him or that she wanted someone else. "When I tell you I need something, you always get it for me, with everything. Except this?"

"I didn't say I wouldn't get it for you. You tell me what you need, shy, and you'll get it," he snapped without affection.

Did he think that she'd chosen the moment he was convening with his Kindred cohorts to go over and ask for a new paint set? He couldn't think she was that shallow or ridiculous. "Support! Zave, I need support! I need to tell you something personal and sensitive, and I need to know you won't get upset or jump to conclusions. And when you're in this kinda mood—"

"I was in no kinda mood until you gave me your attitude."

"I didn't give you any attitude! I was polite and respectful! I came over to ask for your attention for just a minute, and you won't move until you have the permission of two other men! Am I supposed to be bleeding or waiting for aliens to land, like you said, before I'm allowed to speak to you? Or is it just sex you want? You thought, 'Hey, if I marry her, she has to stay on the island and I'll have my own personal slut!'"

He blinked as his head shook. "Where the fuck did that come from?" he asked. "We've been through this. You're here because I love you and I want to be married to you."

She didn't doubt that; she was just frustrated. "So what the fuck was downstairs all about?" she asked.

They'd argued before but never in such close proximity to so many other people. She hoped that the floors and ceilings were soundproof because the dining room was directly below. Someone had to be sitting on top of Rig, preventing him from coming up to find out what the fuck their domestic was all about.

"I have my cousin locked up in my house. And I have at least four guys planning an assault on this place tomorrow, because don't think for one second they don't plan to bring every weapon in their fucking arsenal to try to take this place. So I'm sorry if I'm a bit on edge at the moment!"

Although he didn't sound on edge, he just sounded angry. "You're not the only one dealing with this," she said. "In fact, I know this is your fucking house and I know you must be worried about losing it, but there's someone who this is more stressful for."

"You think it's more stressful for you?" he asked. "You're going to be nowhere near the fucking meet. I don't care if I have to lock you in our bedroom upstairs, you're going to be safe and far away from every one of those fuckers—"

"I'm gonna be there," she said. "And I'm gonna look in every one of their faces to let them know that they don't fuck with the Kindred. Maybe Kadie and I don't count, like Caine said, but the Kindred's demand was that every party be present and that includes me."

Kadie might choose not to be there, as she and Tuck had arrangements about when she did and didn't take part. But Devon had made no such promises to her husband. Rig wouldn't sit this one out. The Kindred would need all the manpower they could muster. So Devon wasn't going to let her husband and her brother walk into that fraught situation without as much back up as she could offer.

"This is fucked up enough without the woman I love standing there."

They had to deal with one argument at a time, and

this one hadn't started over tomorrow's meet. "This isn't what we're fighting about," she said, opening her arms at her sides. "Whether or not I'm there tomorrow isn't up for debate. I will be there. With you. With Brodie. With Zara. With Tuck. Kadie, if she wants to be there. And with Bess."

"Bess won't be there, either," he said.

Could he really be this naïve? One of the smartest men in the business world and he didn't see who this situation was most stressful for. "Bess hasn't seen her son since before you and I were married," she said, and some of his anger seeped away as clarity took over. "She's terrified that he's going to get hurt. She's terrified that even if the Kindred promise not to harm him, Syn will if he shows any hesitation in hurting the Kindred or doing what Mitchell asks. She still believes that he can be redeemed."

"Redeemed?" he asked, reversing a fraction of an inch. "It would take a helluva lot for him to be accepted back into the Kindred. She can't really think that we're going to—"

"All she cares about is that he lives. I mean, she wants him to be back with you and with Brodie, and I think she wants things the way they were, but all she cares about, really, deep down, is that he lives and he stays the hell away from Syn."

His eyes closed so slowly that she could almost hear his internal groan. Turning on the spot to put his back to her, Zave gave her a chance to take her own cleansing breath to let the stress of the argument dwindle. She guessed they weren't really arguing with each other; they were just stressed and worried.

Her theory was reinforced when she rested a hand on his back and slid it down to the groove of his spine. He didn't back away or argue with her. He stayed silent for another minute and then bent his arm around to take her wrist so he could hold her hand as he returned to face her.

"I'll talk to Brodie."

She knew he would and that was all she wanted, reassurance that Bess' feelings would be taken into consideration. This wasn't about saving Thad or even about forgiving him. Bess was still Kindred, even if Thad wasn't.

"You won't hurt him?" she asked, and he shook his head. "How will you stop him from leaving with Syn?"

His brow slunk downwards and he peered into her. "Syn won't be leaving this island, shy."

A chill tickled her shoulders. "What do you mean?"

"I mean, Leatt's irrelevant, Caine's an asset, Thad is family…"

"And Mitchell?" she asked when he said nothing about Syn's leader.

Brushing the back of his fingers down her cheek, he bowed to kiss her. "He has an appointment with Maverick we intend to ensure he keeps."

# TWENTY-ONE

LESS THAN TWENTY-FOUR hours later, the stage was set. Devon had never been so terrified, she'd become accustomed to the flavor of adrenaline in her throat. After Zave had left her alone in her bedroom, she'd pondered what he said but wasn't horrified by it. The more she thought about it, the more it made sense. There could be no other outcome.

She didn't know if Zara knew or if Kadie did or who of the men had broached the subject in the first place. It didn't matter.

No more talk of plans or strategy joined them at the dinner table last night, but when the women said they were retiring to one of the dens for wine and conversation, the men didn't object or join them.

That must have been when they came up with the details of how to approach this day because the next morning, Devon awoke to her husband's attention.

He didn't usually initiate morning sex, maybe it was a tradition he wanted to start that they should make love before Kindred missions. But she doubted it. It was more likely that he was worried that Syn would bring law enforcement or the media as back up and that they may not have many more chances to be intimate. She hoped that was his thought. The alternative was he considered the chance that someone wouldn't make it out alive.

The Kindred were strong together. They stood in the entryway, listening to the helicopter rotors closing in. They couldn't just shoot the men as they stepped off the aircraft. They had to ensure that Syn had brought Game Time because they weren't devices that could be left out in the open for anyone to discover.

Grant was still a prisoner and technically, Caine was on their side, but there was no guarantee Caine knew the true location of the devices. He'd even admitted to Zara that he wasn't sure Mitchell had been honest about the whereabouts of the tech.

The four men, Brodie, Tuck, Zave, and Rig, were at the bottom of the stairs, with Zara standing at the top of the stairs that faced the door, on the mid-landing before the stairs took a quarter turn to the mezzanine. Devon, Kadie, and Bess had elected to stay on the mezzanine in front of where Devon's bedroom was. They would come down when everyone was settled. Kadie wanted to be present to reassure Howie, and Bess was eager to talk to her son. She still wanted a chance to try to break through to him, and Devon had spoken to her again last night during their wine conversation.

Once she'd retired with Zave for the night, she'd pled Bess' case. The mother wanted a chance to talk to her son alone if the opportunity presented itself. There was a question mark over whether it would.

Right now, all Devon was worried about was that everyone in the Kindred made it out alive. She couldn't think about the relationships between Kindred and Syn members. Everyone was watching the same black door at the front of the property.

The Kindred had locked the manor up tight, ensuring that they would funnel Syn to exactly where they wanted them to be. The only way inside was through that door.

Although there was no clock in this space, Devon was sure she could hear ticking, each thumping second echoing faster, matching the pace of her heart. The swing of the imaginary pendulum whooshed like the blood in her ears. The nothingness was driving her crazy.

The rotors slowed and the sound died. Syn had landed. It could be that they were looking for another way in or they were planning to blow the whole building to smithereens, anything was possible.

Movement in her peripheral vision made her turn. Tuck was wearing a watch that displayed video feed from the new cameras the Kindred had mounted on the outside of the manor so they could watch Syn's progress and ensure they didn't get up to anything sinister out there.

"Leatt, Mitchell, Caine," Tuck said. "They're pulling a black chest out the back of the chopper, looks heavy… Oh, and there's Thad."

Maybe the doctor was spared manual labor as he'd have flown them here. "Are they bringing it in?" Brodie asked.

Tuck shook his head. "They're just leaving it there… idiot, fucking rookies," he murmured. "Either bring the product inside or leave it in the getaway vehicle. Now if they want to make a break for it, they'll have to load it again."

Hazarding a guess, Brodie muttered, "Could be explosives."

"Nah," Tuck said. "They're leaving it right there, by the chopper. They try to detonate and they'll be blowing up their only way out."

Zave had deliberately put his plane in its hanger and moved the chopper that was on the island to the airstrip. Thad might tell Syn that he could take any craft Zave had, but that would be difficult if the vehicle was the whole length of the island away. Listening to the men converse gave her something to focus on beyond the tingling anxiety crawling beneath her skin.

Kadie was as alert as she was, though she had more reason to be anxious than Devon did, and she was reminded of this when Kadie asked, "Howie? Can you see him?"

Lifting his gaze to the upper floor where the trio of women were gathered, Tuck soothed his woman with a gentle tone. "Not yet, Toots. Doesn't mean he's not there. We'll get him back."

Devon could appreciate the comfort of the exchange

between this veteran couple. Even when they weren't on the same floor, they managed to consider each other's feelings. Her understanding of how that worked grew when she noticed that Zave was looking at her, and she was hit by her own dose of love. It didn't matter that he wasn't as tender as Tuck. Just seeing his determination was encouraging enough to make her frantic heart began to calm.

Knowing that he wouldn't want her to say it aloud, Devon mouthed, "I love you." The twitch at the corner of his mouth was enough to remind her that he felt the same.

In these last moments of guaranteed safety, they weren't the only couple who wanted to express their feelings. "Beau," Zara said, shattering the intimacy of their moment of peace. "If you get yourself hurt today, I'll beat the crap out of you, and don't think you'll be getting laid for a year."

"Yeah, yeah," he grumbled like she was a nagging wife. "You put yourself in harm's way again and I'll build a damn dungeon for you."

That couple didn't look at each other. Tuck was smiling and Rig laughed. The humorous exchange calmed them all and just in time because half a second later, the front door opened.

Caine came in first, probably full of gumption, or as Mitchell's human shield, because with his hands up, he moved forward and Mitchell entered behind.

Mitchell didn't close the door, but no one else came inside. He didn't put his hands up either, not that it would've made a difference if Brodie had chosen to shoot before asking questions. "We said everyone," Brodie said, foregoing pleasantries. "That means Thad and Leatt, too, you fuckers."

Wandering forward, Caine was as loose as ever. "Thad is doing some chopper stuff," Caine said. "Mitch here left Leatt watching the door... Don't know what the fuck for, this place is at the end of the Earth. There's no cunt sneaking up on this joint."

Caine's advice made no difference to Brodie's position. "Then we wait," Brodie said.

As usual, Caine resorted to teasing. "Miss your little cousin?" he asked.

Devon would never understand this guy. Here he was in the middle of two factions who hated each other and he'd played both sides, yet he was still cocky enough to pop jibes into every exchange he had.

"Thad is older than him, you prick," Zara said. "Keep your shitty comments to yourself."

Up until now, Mitchell had been admiring the space, but now he chose to lay his focus on the woman on the mid-landing above the men. "Zara Bandini, you are more beautiful than I remember."

Proving that he intended to rebel against Zara's order, Caine maintained his mood. "That's the just-fucked look," Caine declared. Zara trusted this guy, and Devon had to believe their attitude toward each other was part of a show rather than something more sinister. "Were you two going at it before we came in? If you wanna carry on, we'll wait… don't forget to pass her on when you're through, Raven. I heard this place was orgy heaven few years back."

"You wish," Zara snarled.

Caine surveyed the room, taking his time to examine every woman, even the ones on the mezzanine, letting them know that they'd been spotted. "I say we've got plenty to share, boys… you've got them trained to do what they're told, right?"

Thad came in, without half as much confidence as the other two had displayed, and when Bess gasped, he paused. "Thaddeus!" Bess called out. Her whimpering tone was as angry as it was upset.

"Aww, it's your mommy," Caine said, sauntering over to grab Thad so he could throw him forward toward the stairs. "Go give her a kiss."

Maybe he was working for the Kindred, after all. Separating Syn from each other and getting Thad out of harm's way was just what the Kindred wanted. Unfortunately, Mitchell was too impatient and controlling to let it happen.

"Nobody's moving," Mitchell said. "We're not here to play games. Where's Grant?"

Kadie began to stride away from Devon and Bess, which wasn't part of the plan as she knew it. "Where's

Howie?" Kadie asked, and the pent-up anger in her voice made Devon think she was being motivated by emotion, instead of the agreed strategy. The hacker's girl kept on going and only paused when she got to Zara's side on the mid-landing. "You don't get Grant before we lay eyes on Howie. You know we have him."

Devon had to give kudos to Kadie for her gumption. "We don't know he's alive," Mitchell said. "You bring him out here."

"Not a chance," Tuck said, backing up his girl. "You show us the kid… You talked to Grant yesterday, and you know he's our chip, we wouldn't kill him. Show us Howie."

Mitchell didn't want to be the one who budged first, but somebody had to. They'd come all this way and yes, this was technically Kindred property, but there was something hungry in the way Mitchell had been looking around the place since he came in. If he had been a part of Grant McCormack Senior's life and that man had been close to his brother-in-law, Owen Knight, then there was every chance that Frank Mitchell had been here before.

She hadn't considered how this place was absolutely perfect for Syn until what Zave said in her room yesterday. Coming here may be a rookie mistake or it may be part of their game plan. They couldn't have intended for Grant to be kidnapped, but they were adaptable, which was a strength, and they could turn this situation to their advantage if they could pick off, or overpower, the Kindred.

Devon was no combat veteran and sometimes the things she was told to do didn't make sense to her, or she didn't understand their significance. But now she got why the women had been positioned where they were because it was the women who Syn wanted to use against the Kindred men. All of them would give up this island to Syn to protect any one of the women, and by putting them behind the barrier of men, up the stairs, nearer escape, they were being offered protection.

The houses may have been modeled differently, but their structures were the same. Zara and Kadie knew this house because they knew their own. Bess practically lived here, and Devon did, too. The confusing layout was their secret weapon. But they didn't want to scramble because splitting up made them weak.

Motion sensors would allow the men to find, not only where their women were, but where the enemy was too. There had to be forty feet between the bottom of the stairs and the front door. Watching the men size each other up from such a distance apart, she recognized that this was a good old-fashioned showdown.

Someone had to break first, and it wasn't the Kindred. "Caine tell Leatt to get the kid," Mitchell said.

From above, she couldn't quite tell which of the Kindred men were in his focus. Brodie slapped a hand onto Rig's back and shoved him forward a step. "Go with him."

This would be the test. Caine didn't want to miss the action any more than Rig did. Brodie was asking Rig to step outside, to keep an eye on a man no one was sure they could trust. Tension crackled in the air, and it made her nervous.

She had to trust the Kindred, she couldn't let irrational, juvenile fears about her brother's safety make her cause a scene. The Circle had been right the last time she'd been worried, they had to be right this time too.

Zara trusted Caine, so Brodie trusted him, and that had to filter through to the others or they'd never be as efficient as they were. But her heart began to speed up again as Rig strode forward without showing an ounce of fear. She was proud of him because he had to be apprehensive, but he didn't let it show.

Caine lumbered backwards in four slow paces, waiting for Rig to catch up. That interlude gave Caine a chance to scrutinize Zara with an air of mistrust that was either an act for Mitchell to prove he wasn't on the Kindred side or was a positive sign that he was just as worried about Rig doing something to take him down.

All they had to do was go to Leatt and get Howie and that was what Brodie was really asking her brother to do: to go and rescue the kid who meant so much to Kadie. Those men slipped out, and silence echoed for a moment.

"This house is just as I remember it," Mitchell said.

"It's amazing, isn't it? A wonder of architecture that two houses so far apart can share so much in common."

Mitchell must have a problem with silence, or he had a need to be holding court, because he always had to be saying something. It wasn't a need anyone in the Kindred shared. "We don't need a history lesson," Brodie said without patience. "And we don't need to listen to your monologue. You think you're better, you underestimate us. We're pathetic at what we do, and you plan to do it better, blah, blah, blah."

"Brodie, you've grown into your arrogance," Mitchell said. "I liked you better when you were a brooding teenager with nothing to say. Xavier, you were always the one who liked to be heard. You were always so determined to make your point and be the center of attention. But my boy tells me that all that changed after you lost your parents. Such a tragedy."

Mitchell held an arm out toward Thad, who was still a few feet behind him. Scurrying forward, Thad let his father put a hand to his shoulder. But when pride warmed the elder man's expression, Devon didn't believe it was for his offspring because it was focused on the Kindred men.

"You tried to make your cousin believe you pulled yourself out of that depression for him when he lost his beautiful girl because of your carelessness." Mitchell was going to talk about Bronwyn, and it seemed insensitive to do that in such a public forum when the woman had been so important to Thad. "I don't have to tell you that we're better. We'll prove it when we take down the bastards who hurt her."

"You don't know who hurt her," Brodie said. "Zave and Thad spent years trying to figure out what happened. No one knows what went down."

"Zave told me he didn't know when she left the island," Thad said with bitter resentment rippling through him, vibrating in his words. "That was a lie, cousin, wasn't it? You know exactly when she left."

Bronwyn hadn't been discussed during strategy as far as Devon knew. This was emotional warfare orchestrated by Mitchell; he was far more cunning than she'd thought. "I don't," Zave said. "But you're right that I know more than I told you."

"See!" Mitchell exclaimed, slapping his hand on his son's back. "He's a liar! Just like I told you!"

With his father's support nearby, Thad wasn't afraid of confrontation. "What do you know?" he barked, pouncing forward. In his eagerness to know, though his anger didn't lessen, he edged away from the shelter of his father.

"She made a move on me," Zave said and he wasn't recounting the story to be hurtful. Maybe telling her the truth had been cathartic because since then she'd seen him progress. He wanted to be better, for himself, for his family, for his company, for the Kindred. And she hoped he'd learned that bottling up those emotions didn't make him better. Getting them out freed him.

"You're lying," Thad spat. "She called me from the city. She said that you went to her bed, that you slept together."

Zave was so calm, but Devon was stunned by the lie. "We didn't have sex."

"Oh, God," Bess whispered at her side.

Devon was shocked that Thad had been holding this secret of his own while Bronwyn had been spreading lies about Zave. She wanted to slap the woman for being dishonest, to shake her and tell her she was signing her own death warrant by pitting the men against each other.

"She lied to you," Zave said.

"And that was what I told her," Thad said. "We fought. I told her I didn't believe her. I told her you wouldn't do it. She got pissed off and said she didn't love me anyway. She said our family was fucked up."

"Why didn't you tell us this?" Bess asked, but when she tried to leave Devon's side, Devon caught her hand and held her in place.

Thad kept his eyes on Zave. "Because at the time I didn't believe it, I thought she was a liar. I thought she was a bitch, trying to drive a wedge between me and my cousin. When she lashed out at me, I assumed I was right, she broke up with me and I thought that was it. I was pissed off and upset and I didn't tell anyone... I called her the next day, she told me she was in a bar, getting drunk, and she was going to find herself a real man. I didn't care. I told her to go to hell, I thought she was a crazy, game-playing bitch... When everyone started to panic that she was no longer at the manor, I couldn't bear to tell you all the truth, I thought we'd find her with another guy and that would be it."

"But she wasn't at her apartment," Bess muttered, and Devon didn't know if it was meant for the group or just herself. "She wasn't going to work. Her friends hadn't heard anything. She was missing."

Thad carried on without acknowledging his mother's mutterings, whether he heard them or not. "I was terrified because I believed that she was fine and that she wasn't answering my calls because she was punishing me for making her tell the truth. When we found out what happened…"

"You felt guilty," Kadie said. "And you lied because you didn't want to admit that you knew she was in trouble."

"I didn't know she was in trouble," Thad said. "Last I spoke to her, she was in a bar, getting drunk, hitting on guys. How do I know what happened next? Maybe it wasn't that night she was taken, maybe it was, who knows? I didn't want to admit we broke up, didn't want to admit that I'd fallen in love with a slut… But when I found out she was dead, it seemed like such a stupid argument. She just wanted my attention. The love was still there; it was just a lover's tiff and I wanted to hurt the people who hurt her and our quest made sense."

Which didn't explain how they ended up here like this. "Then why betray us?"

"He didn't betray you," Mitchell declared. "You all betrayed him, stringing him along, using him, and sidelining his needs, his mission. If any of your women had been taken, you'd have torn the world apart to find the culprit, but you didn't care about him or his pain."

"That's bullshit!" Devon cried out. The words overwhelmed her and burst out without thought for whether it was smart to antagonize their enemy.

"Watch your tongue!" Mitchell barked. "Don't forget what I did to the last Mrs. Knight."

# TWENTY-TWO

DEVON WASN'T AFRAID, though she felt the tension rise in the men at the foot of the stairs. "This is my house, you will listen to what I have to say," she said. "The Kindred care, and Zave put his life and his reputation on the line to go down there and hold these men to account. There are a dozen cartels with a hundred men in their ranks, maybe a thousand. Figuring out which one hurt Bronwyn is impossible. They don't keep records; they don't care about names and descriptions."

"He didn't fight harder," Zara said, showing the same kind of passion that Devon felt. "He didn't ask Raven to take down one man at a time. Didn't ask us to kidnap and torture the bastards. He was happy coasting along because he didn't have the stomach for revenge. He was happy chipping away, making a difference in the best way we knew how."

Blaming everyone else was the coward's way out as far as she was concerned. "It wasn't enough," Thad said. "I needed to do more. I felt she'd died and nobody gave a fuck. Nobody cared. I thought about that night I spoke to her, and I couldn't talk to any of you about it. I was holding onto the secret that I'd spoken to her and then I wondered, what had happened? Was she trying to get my attention by lying about spending the night with my cousin... or was it true? I never asked you what happened in this house when I wasn't here, Zave. All through those years I think I was worried I might find out she was telling the truth."

"She wasn't," Zave said. "You know it. I didn't give a fuck about women then. If I had, do you think I'd have chosen yours?"

Through Thad's melancholy, his anger remained steady. "It's not like you don't have a history of taking women away from their men."

"When I was a kid," Zave said. "Yeah, I was a bastard back then, and I deserved every bit of shit I got for it. But I never touched any woman who belonged to my kin. It didn't mean fuck all when she tried it on with me, she was drunk, and I was there... she thought you were screwing around on her. She never saw you, said you spent all your time at the hospital. I told her I wasn't interested. She tried again. I shoved her away, and that was it."

"So why the fuck didn't you tell me?" Thad asked. "If there was nothing to it, why didn't you—"

"Because I didn't want this. Because when she went missing, I saw how devastated you were, and I didn't want to shatter your illusion of her. I didn't want to take away that love."

"I don't believe you," Thad said.

Grief could become resentment, but she wouldn't let her husband be slandered. "It's true," Devon said in her husband's defense. "He told me."

"Oh, yeah, and what reason did he have to lie to you? He was trying to get into your panties for months," Thad sneered.

"Stop it!" Bess exclaimed. "I didn't raise you to be spiteful like this. If Zave wanted your woman, he'd have had her and he'd have told you. Zave's done a lot of shit in his life, but he's never been a liar. And there isn't any reason for him to lie now. If anything, after what you did to his wife, he should want to hurt you. He could tell you anything, he could tell you that they were having an affair that lasted for years and that Bronwyn never loved you."

"Yeah, if we were vicious pricks like you," Tuck said. "We'd tell you we all had her."

Thad took another leap forward. "You don't say shit about her!"

"It's all right to be angry," Zave said. "I understand how guilt does that to a man, how it twists your guts, how it makes you fear your reflection, how you can be so disgusted with yourself that you think about all the things you've ever done wrong and take on the burdens of the world. If you want to believe I slept with Bronwyn, believe it. If you want to believe her story, or mine, it doesn't matter. What matters is, she's gone. And we didn't forget her, not for a single day. Because whether it was enough or not, we saved lives for her. In her name. Slut or not. Liar or not. No woman deserves to go through that.

"You are Kindred, and you know we've all fucked up. We've failed missions. We've achieved goals. We've taken lives and saved them. And you were a part of that until you took your resentment and gave it to the fucker standing behind you."

"Looks like the history lesson was needed after all," Mitchell said, interrupting probably because he was concerned that the conversation may lead to a conclusion he didn't like. "But it means shit."

"Then let's get back to business," Brodie said. "Your guys are taking too long."

Mitchell wasn't interested in Brodie's concerns. "There are too many people in this room. Before I bring the kid in, before you see your damned devices, I want to see mine. You," he said, pointing a finger up at Kadie. "You take the old woman and you go, get me what I need."

Old woman was a bit harsh, as Bess was Mitchell's contemporary, and they'd shared a bed. "Go get the tech, Toots," Tuck said and wouldn't mind getting Kadie and Bess out of the firing line.

"I'm going, too," Thad said. "I don't trust them."

His father nodded once, and Kadie began to ascend the stairs as Bess walked away from Devon and Thad followed them. The products that Syn had requested weren't on the lower floor.

"Zara, I don't like you up there," Mitchell said. "Come down the stairs... switch places with your husband, let's even the odds a bit and see what you're made of."

"She stays there," Brodie said.

A man used to power didn't take kindly to being questioned, and Mitchell's anger returned, "What makes you think you get to call all the shots? We can still get in our chopper and fly away with your precious Game Time."

Brodie sneered. "Without your golden boy? I don't think so. You're not going anywhere without Grant. You need him, and you sure don't need him to be an enemy, which he will be if you walk away without him."

Mitchell wasn't dissuaded, he took on a satisfied glow. "One of the perks of having a former Kindred member with us. Your doctor can take us to exactly where he is."

"Our doctor?" Tuck asked. "I thought you'd claimed him as your own."

Without addressing the slip-up, Mitchell issued his ultimatum. "If Zara stays put, then Devon comes down. One of the women needs to be down here. So far, you've got everything you want, so if you want my goodwill, you better do as I say. We might not have all the fancy tech you guys do, but we can still do plenty of damage with the old-fashioned stuff." He took a phone from his pocket to hold it up. "One call and the cops will be here in a flash. I've got Jennifer on speed-dial, and she's right outside the station."

The one promise Devon had made herself was that she wouldn't let her husband go to jail, so she began to move down the hall. But Zara held up a hand. "Stay put, Finch." Zara was already running down the stairs, and she broke between Brodie and Tuck. "I'm here."

Brodie gritted his teeth and growled, "What did I tell you about harm's way, Swallow?"

Zara dug her elbow back into his ribs. "Go up. Up, now, beau."

Brodie slunk up the stairs to take his place above the others.

Mitchell clapped once. "Now, I think we need to get

Grant here, don't you? Best way to do an exchange of prisoners is to have everyone in the same space. What do you say? Xavier, Tucker, go and get him." They looked at Brodie. "All we're doing is waiting here, boys. Send your women if you want."

Devon wouldn't be able to subdue Grant McCormack on her own. She hoped that Kadie and Bess were talking to Thad, keeping him busy, because the thinner Syn were spread, the easier they would be to take down.

"We'll go get him as soon as we see Howie," Tucker said, and as if right on cue, Caine came in with Rig dragging a hooded Howie between them. As soon as they stepped over the threshold, they dropped him onto the floor.

Caine rubbed his hands together. "The fucker's built like a beanpole, but he weighs a ton."

He strode forward, past Mitchell as Rig crouched to untie Howie's hands. When he pulled the hood off his face, they saw that he was unconscious. "He's alive, don't panic," Rig said. "We checked."

Thad was used to transporting unconscious people, so his skills were useful to Syn after all.

Caine kept on moving toward Zara. "What did I miss?" he asked.

"Xavier and Tucker are about to go and get Grant," Mitchell said. "Wasn't that the deal? Go on then."

They began to move to the opposite side of the entryway from where Devon stood. "Did you bring Game Time?" Zara asked, because the Kindred couldn't act until they knew for sure.

"It's in the chopper. They plan to use it as soon as they leave here," Caine said. "They packed up everything 'cause they're not planning to go back to that last place we were staying at. They're fucking nomads."

"They?" Mitchell asked in the same way Tuck had about Thad.

Caine was halfway between Mitchell and Zara when he turned. "You didn't tell me what the fuck we're doing with it. Just that after we take this place, we've got another mission."

Just as Zave had suspected, they intended to steal this house. "You're not taking this place," Zara said, her anger was a good diversion from Mitchell's suspicion.

Devon saw Brodie begin to lower. Mitchell's arm darted behind him and before she could scream, he pulled a weapon from his waistband and fired off a round toward Zara.

Caine moved faster than anyone else, and his body blocked Zara's. The bullet hit him in the upper chest, sending him backwards a couple of steps. One gunshot followed the other, and when she screamed again, it was because of the gun in Brodie's hand aimed at Mitchell, who was on the floor with a lethal hole in his head.

Zara shrieked and leaped forward, grabbing the staggering Caine, who tried to push her away. "Get away from me!"

"No! You fucking idiot, what did you do that for!" she screamed.

The blood soaked his tee shirt, and when his back hit the newel post, he slid downward against it. Zara crouched and ripped open his shirt to press her hand over the wound.

"Knew you couldn't wait to get me naked," Caine muttered, his eyes and lips heavy. "You see that, Rave, your bitch is mine."

"Oh, shut up, just stop it for one second," Zara begged him. "Look what happened! You idiot!"

Snatching her hand, he locked them together palm to palm. "There's one thing I promised myself I'd say to you before I died," he said, hauling her closer.

Devon covered her mouth and darted down the corridor to rush down the stairs. Zave met her on the lower case, capturing her in his arms. Nestling into him, she watched the heartbreaking scene unfold. Tears escaped, though hers were nothing to the volume seeping out of Zara.

"What?" Zara sobbed.

Pulling her even closer, Devon thought he might kiss her, except he turned his head to speak into her ear, though he didn't whisper because they all heard what he said. "You're a fucking bitch, and I can't stand the sight of you."

Smacking his chest, Zara leaned away, but their hands

stayed together. "You're not going to die," Zara said.

Kadie, Bess, and Thad appeared at the top of the stairs. They must have heard the shots. Tuck took the stairs two at a time to snatch Kadie on the landing beside where Brodie still was. Bess and Thad remained at the top on the mezzanine, and Zara began trying to seek out the doctor.

Caine touched her cheek. "I got your pretty face to take me to the other side… blowjob would make it easier on me though," he said, and Zara put her head on his shoulder for a second before rising higher to look at Thad.

"Why aren't you helping him?" she screeched.

"They're not gonna help me, honey," Caine said and coughed, blood trickled from his mouth, but Zara put her head on his shoulder again.

Brodie descended, one step at a time. Devon was sure he was going to pull his wife away when he got to the bottom, but he didn't. "Yeah, they are," Brodie said and fixated on Thad. "Get your fucking ass over here and do your job. You might not be Kindred anymore… but he is."

Zara wasn't half as surprised as Caine was by that statement if their expressions told any story. Zara leaped up into her husband's arms and forced an open-mouthed kiss onto him. "I get the bullet and he gets the babe," Caine said.

Zave kissed Devon's head and then left her alone to retrieve the nearby medical kit that had been placed just in case of injuries today.

The men gathered around as Zara dropped onto her knees beside Caine to offer reassurance. "You're going to be okay," she murmured.

"Get him onto his back," Thad said. Zara helped to lie him down, and Thad began to examine the wound.

Zara stroked her fingers into Caine's hair. "You're an idiot," she murmured.

"Just your type," Caine said and groaned when Thad gestured Tuck over to apply pressure to the wound as he pulled supplies from the pack Zave had brought to him.

"Give him some room," Thad said, trying to push Zara away, but Caine clutched her hand.

"You back off, quack," he snarled. "We're

negotiating a price."

Zara laughed and put a finger on his lip as she flashed a look up at her looming husband. "I'm not giving you oral. He has a long memory, you know, don't push your luck."

Caine's eyes closed and he began to pale. "I'll blame the drugs."

Kadie was laughing when she got to Devon's side with Bess not far behind. "He hasn't given you any drugs," she said.

"He should," Caine mumbled. "I want all the drugs. The good ones."

Devon was impressed that he was still joking while all the women's eyes were wet. "Blood loss might work," Tuck said, standing shoulder to shoulder between Brodie and Zave.

"Let's remember that when it's your gal he's hitting on," Brodie mumbled.

Tuck slapped his back. "Blondes aren't his thing," the hacker said, peering around Brodie to Zave. "Your woman will be next on the menu."

"Fuck that," Rig said, climbing the stairs to join the women. "My sister isn't into sick fucks like him."

"Ha," Caine exclaimed, wincing through his gritted teeth. "Do your research, scumbag. Knight is the kinkiest fuck you'll ever meet. Means your sister is all kinds of nasty. Just my type."

Zave bristled. "Changed my mind. Let him die."

Thad paused to see if he was serious. Tuck laughed. "We've got enough bodies to bury tonight... I guess you took care of Leatt out front?" Caine nodded. "Snapped his neck... it was fun to see the smug bastard go down. Those goody-goody dimples gave me migraines."

"If we're digging tonight anyway, what's one more?" Zave asked.

Zave was kidding, and Thad still knew him well enough to know that. Bess whispered in her ear after Thad returned to work. "We have a medical bay and a gurney," Bess said. "Rig, dearie, will you bring that down while we prepare the room?"

Like her, Rig had never had a mother figure, so the

gentle words and soft demeanor startled him still for a minute and then he nodded.

The room, almost exactly like a typical hospital room, wasn't far away from the custom suite, which made sense because the medical supply store was in this wing too. She, Kadie, and Bess worked to prepare the room while Rig took the gurney as Bess had requested.

"What will happen now?" Kadie asked, helping Devon with the sheets as Bess dealt with the medical equipment, being the only one experienced enough to set it up.

"What do you mean?" Bess asked. "Syn have been eliminated, and now the Kindred must take time to heal."

# TWENTY-THREE

CAINE WAS SETTLED in his own private room and given plenty of time to recuperate. Thad had access to all of the medical supplies, and when he wasn't treating Caine, he was kept under lock and key.

The whole situation was a mess. Grant was still a prisoner and didn't know what had happened. Brodie liked keeping him in the dark. Thad was technically a prisoner, although no one could decide what to do with him, but Bess had returned to being her cheery self and no longer got that distant look because, although her child had betrayed everyone and he was unhappy, a dialogue opened in the family and an honesty was burgeoning in a sort of group therapy session way as they all confessed secrets.

As brusque as ever, Caine was not a good patient. But the women enjoyed sitting with him, and he liked to make a big deal of his nursemaids, requesting sponge baths five or six times a day, although he'd yet to receive one.

One week passed and then two, until they had all been in this house for a month. Zave had left the island once to return Rig and Howie to the city. Dempsey picked up Howie, and it turned out that Kadie's cousin was happy to remain in the dark about the specifics. He just wanted to get back to work.

After that, Zave returned to KC business, via conference call from the island. He hadn't gone into the office while the Kindred were staying.

It had been a month since Mitchell was killed, and everyone was starting to get on each other's nerves in these close quarters. With the mission complete and the Syn threat eradicated, there was no need for them to stay cloistered. Game Time had been dismantled and crated, it was safe in the basement and no one had any intention of removing it any time soon.

Brodie, Zara, Tuck, and Kadie had another mission in their future. One that Caine was going to assist with. So they'd gathered in the entryway to say their goodbyes.

"Come back soon," Bess said, hugging the women for what had to be the tenth time. "We miss you."

"We're gonna miss your cooking and you looking after us," Kadie said. "And don't forget our video call next week."

"Definitely not," Bess said and pulled Devon into her embrace with Zara and Kadie.

The four women were hugging, and as usual the men were huddled, talking in whispers by the door. When Bess eventually let the women go, she hurried over to hug the men. "You take care of these women, and thank you, boys."

"We can take the bastards with us if you want," Brodie said. "We've got plenty of room at my place."

"But not a full-time babysitter," Zave said. "Don't worry about it. They won't get off the island. We have experience of keeping people penned in."

Usually it was women. Thad had been given some freedom, enough to be a doctor when they needed him. Maybe there was hope for him and Zave to rekindle their former relationship, maybe not. But Bess certainly liked having her son on-site.

"And Caine, you be good," Bess said, waving a finger at him. "Don't go upsetting Brodie. Zara is off-limits."

"That's why I want her so bad, Mrs. P. I make no promises," he drawled, winking and touching her chin like she was a nineteen-year-old in his sights.

But Bess was having none of it. "If you want to be Kindred, you look after them all, not just the pretty ones."

Caine shrugged. "We'll see," he said and opened the door. "Are we getting this show on the road, or what?"

Caine would need to take it easy for a while, and he would need to rebuild his strength. She'd been told there were ample facilities at Brodie's manor that would allow him to do that. Tuck hugged her, threw an arm around Kadie and followed Caine outside.

Brodie grabbed the back of Zara's neck and pulled her, but she resisted for a second. "Devon, you can come and stay with us soon, right?"

Devon nodded. "I'm desperate to see where you live."

"The house is beautiful," Zara grinned.

"I can't wait to see it," Devon replied.

The inside joke was that they all knew the houses were the same. Zara left her husband to come over to kiss her cheek, then hugged her. "Thank you for fixing Zave. He was broken for so long... I don't know how you did it, you're amazing."

With two long strides, Brodie seized his wife's neck and hauled her off. "Fuck sake, baby, we need to move. Zave has to get back here before it's fucking night out." He landed a scowl on Bess and Devon. "Neither of you go near those rooms. You leave Saint and Wren exactly where they fucking are, you hear me?"

Both women nodded. Bess hurried forward to pull Brodie down to kiss him. "You do us proud, chief. You do Art proud."

The compliment was more than he could handle, so he simply nodded once and took his wife out.

Bess kissed Zave and then melted away, leaving Devon alone with her husband. "You'll be back tonight?" she asked.

"I'll be as quick as I can. I'm not any happier with you being here with Saint and Wren than Brodie is. You're going to hear a chopper overhead in about ten minutes, it's Petri and a bunch of other guys. They'll stay outside, but if you need them…"

Typical that he was adamant to look after her. "We won't," she said, and he took her into his arms.

"Please do as I tell you, shy. I'll worry the whole way there and back."

Before he went to the first auction after they were together, she'd said the same thing to him. "I command you not to," she said with a smile, and he kissed her again.

"I made you a new toy," he said. "I want to play with you when I come home."

Tempted and tantalized, she would fight the urge to go hunting for it while he was away. "I'll never say no to that… What happens now? Can we just be normal?"

"Normal?" he asked, contemplating this until a smile curled his lips. "As normal as a couple who live on a remote island, with two full-time prisoners in residence, and two corporations under their command."

Yeah, okay, so maybe they weren't exactly textbook normal. "As normal as we can be for a couple who are also part-time members of a secret crime-fighting group."

"I don't think we'll be fighting crime for a while," he said. "Something's been missing this last couple of months.

When he lowered his gaze to her torso, she shook her head and laughed. "I can't hide anything from you."

"I don't know why you would try," he said. "As soon as the others are gone, we'll get you the best obstetrician in the city."

"We have a doctor on-site," she said. "I think I'd like to give birth here, in this house."

"I have never said no to you before, anything you want, you get, Mrs. Knight."

"I was worried that you would be against it."

"Against it?" he asked. "You told me you wanted children, and Bess loves having people to look after. It won't be easy keeping the kids away from our secret prisoners. But, in a year or two, Grant will realize he has nothing to go back to. He's a dead man with no future, no identity."

"And Thad?" she asked.

"I don't know. Either we disown him and cut him loose in the city or we get over it. We'll figure it out in time, we're family. He's fucked us over and I'm pissed at him, but we're Kindred."

"Yes," she said, taking his hand to put it on her belly. "Generation after generation, we'll be proud to teach them, and one day, they'll pick up the mantle."

"You'd let them?" he asked. "Do something so dangerous?"

"Dangerous?" she asked, narrowing one eye. "What the Kindred do is right. As long as we stick to priority one and watch each other's backs, our love will keep us safe. There's nothing that can get in the way of that… Because there's nothing stronger than Kindred love."

## Thank you for reading this tale!
If you can, please take the time to review.

~

Ask your local library for more Scarlett Finn novels!

~

For all things Scarlett Finn
check out:

*www.scarlettfinn.com*

The Kindred characters appear later in the 'To Die for...' series.

All books are available now!

The adventure begins in...

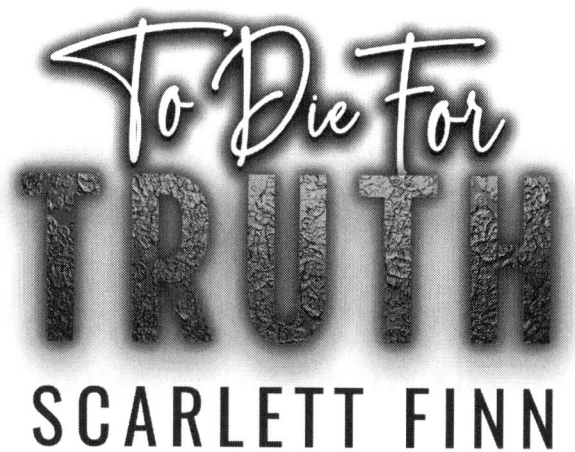

# TO DIE FOR TRUTH

## SCARLETT FINN

Made in the USA
Columbia, SC
01 June 2025